For Jim and Franny

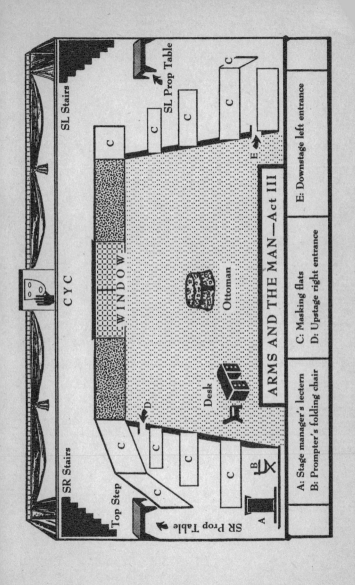

ARMS AND THE MAN—Act III

A: Stage manager's lectern
B: Prompter's folding chair

C: Masking flats
D: Upstage right entrance

E: Downstage left entrance

SL Stairs

SR Stairs

CYC

Top Step

SR Prop Table

SL Prop Table

WINDOW

Desk

Ottoman

☆ 1 ☆

I GOT A PART!

Please excuse the exclamation point. I know I'm not the first actor in the world who ever got a part. But, you see, it's been a long time. A real long time. It's been so long I don't even think of myself as a failed actor anymore. That was in another country and the wench is dead. I hardly even think of myself as a failed writer anymore, though that career's more recent. No, much as I hate to admit it, lately I've come to think of myself as a successful private detective. Successful in that I make a living at it. Which is something I never did with my acting or writing careers. But I've been a private eye long enough now to call it a profession, which is ironic, since it was originally a job-job, something to do to tide me over between the acting and writing.

One might ask, if I'm a writer and a private eye, why don't I write about it? I would, except I don't carry a gun or have fistfights or car chases or anything like that: in short, anything that sells. What I do is investigate accident cases for the law firm of Rosenberg and Stone. While Richard Rosenberg is one of New York City's top negligence lawyers, working for him consists largely of interviewing people with broken arms and legs and taking pictures of

1

cracks in the sidewalk. I can just imagine the look of joy on a publisher's face if I brought in a manuscript about that.

At any rate, as I was saying, I felt my acting career was behind me. Way behind me. Like about twenty years. But at one time it had been my passion. I'd studied acting at Goddard, and when I graduated, a bunch of us theater majors actually got together and opened a summer theater. It was Mickey Rooney time. We got an old barn and we ripped out the stalls and we built a proscenium arch and a thrust stage and a bank of risers and we filled it up with seats on the theory that, if you build it, they will come.

They did, but not in sufficient numbers to keep us going. We lasted one season and lost our shirts. But it was great. Really great. We did Molière and Chekhov and Shaw and Shakespeare and Harold Pinter. And we got good reviews in the local papers and support from the community and encouragement from the college in the tangible form of the loan of lighting equipment, and nonetheless, the whole thing went down the tubes.

Which was the way it had to be. Because a summer theater of that type simply cannot survive. I worked it out after the season, after it all went bust, and figured out that even if we sold out every seat for every performance—which we certainly didn't—it still would have left us with a deficit of three thousand dollars. Our actual deficit was closer to ten. Twenty years ago that was money. And so, the grand and glorious Vermont Theater Company declared bankruptcy, that magical I-was-only-kidding-let's-pretend-it-never-happened sort of thing that I don't quite comprehend, but that failed companies are somehow able to do, and all us actors faded away and vanished in the mist.

As I say, that was in another lifetime, and I had not acted in years and years. Still, I had had a taste. And deep down inside me was the dream, the dream every actor who has ever acted has, the dream of that magical moment, the dream of that Hollywood–Horatio Alger–Cinderella–rags-to-riches story. And through it all, somehow, some way, a part of me knew that, despite everything, someday lightning would strike. I would be summoned, told the star of the show was sick and I, and only I, could step in and save the play. I fully expected that to happen.

So you can't imagine how surprised I was when it did.

It was early in the morning and I had just stopped by my office to pick up the mail and check the answering machine when the phone rang. I figured it was Wendy or Janet, one of Richard Rosenberg's secretaries, calling to give me a case. Either that or my wife because, aside from them, who would call? So I was surprised to hear a man's voice.

"Stanley Hastings?"

"Yes."

"This is Herbert Drake."

I blinked. My mind raced and I felt a rush of panic.

I must explain. I have a very poor memory for names and faces. Not the best trait for a private detective, but there you are. And working for Rosenberg and Stone, I've handled literally hundreds of cases. In the course of which I've worked with other lawyers, investigators and even police officers. Which of them would be calling me in my office for god knows what reason I could not fathom. And I really hate embarrassing myself and other people by my inexplicable and inexcusable inability to remember just who the hell they are.

Herbert Drake? The name was familiar. Alarmingly familiar. Clearly someone I *should* remember.

As I thought all that the pause lengthened.

Then the person on the other end of the line chuckled. A high-pitched half giggle, half chuckle.

With a rush, I got it. "Herbie Drake?" I said, incredulously.

The chuckle deepened. "The one and only."

"From Goddard?"

"I said the one and only. You know any other Herbie Drakes?"

"Good lord," I said, my mind reeling. "How did you find me?"

He found me through the alumni newsletter, which all Goddard graduates of course received, and which a few years back had reported I was a private eye working in New York City. Don't get me wrong—*I* had not sent that tidbit in to be published. On the one hand, I'm not the type to brag. On the other hand, I'm not that proud of what I do. But some other college grad had reported the fact, the newsletter had published it, and Herbie Drake had called Manhattan information and damned if I wasn't the only Stanley Hastings listed. He'd called me at home this morning, just missed me; my wife Alice had given him the number of the office and he'd called me there.

What he had to say took my head off. Because, unlike me, Herbie Drake was still in the business. He'd stuck it out, lo these many years, first as an actor, then as a director, now as a producer. And damned if he didn't have a part he wanted me to step into.

No, it wasn't Broadway. Or even off-Broadway, or regional theater, either. No, it was only summer stock, at a small playhouse in Connecticut, and not for the whole season, either, only for a week. But it was an actual, legitimate part.

The play was *Arms and the Man*. The part was Captain Bluntschli, the chocolate cream soldier, who is the lead, in fact the title character, the "Man" in *Arms and the Man*. It was a part I knew well. A part I'd played in that old barn in Vermont twenty-odd years ago.

It was the classic situation. There they were, just days away from opening, and the actor playing Captain Bluntschli had taken ill. There was no chance of him recovering, either. The poor man had had a heart attack and dropped dead. Very sad indeed for his family and relatives, but a tragedy and a half for struggling producer Herbie Drake.

And I was the salvation, the savior, the answer. And, boy, did that make me feel good. Never mind the fact that I'm not being chosen for my talent, I'm being chosen for the fact that I've done the part before, I'm a quick study and there is no time. That didn't matter one bit. All that mattered was that I'd been asked.

I said yes. I didn't say I had to talk it over with my wife. I didn't say I had to think about it and get back to you. I didn't even say how much does it pay? I just said yes.

You have to understand, under any other circumstances I would have said all those other things. But not this time. This time there was nothing to think about. Much as I need it, the money didn't matter. And, much as I respect Alice's opinion and consult her about all things that affect the family, I knew there was absolutely nothing she could say that could change my mind.

I had gotten The Call.

☆ 2 ☆

HERBERT DRAKE MET ME AT THE BUS STOP AT FIVE-THIRTY that afternoon. It was an hour and a half bus ride from New York, and I put the time to good use going over my part. Which was quite an emotional experience. Just learning lines again would have been enough of a kick. But as it happened, when I pawed through the bookshelves, which in our apartment are wide enough and crowded enough to be stacked two-deep with paperbacks, the copy of *Arms and the Man* I eventually found turned out to be the actual script I had used for the Vermont Theater Company production some twenty years ago. I could tell by the faded but still quite legible stage directions I had penciled in for the production—*Enter SR* for stage right, and *X-DL* for cross down left—and the flood of memories those ancient pencil marks released were somewhat overwhelming.

Maybe that's what made the lines so hard to learn.

I wanted to get a jump on the part, and it had occurred to me, wouldn't Herbie be impressed if I had the whole first act memorized by the time I got there? But it wasn't happening. I had an index card, and I was sliding it down the page, reading the cue but covering up the next line, a technique I'd always used for memorizing scripts, but the lines would not come. Or when they did, they'd come out twisted. I'd either trip over my own tongue and have to stop, or get the line out, then slide the card and see I'd paraphrased and done it wrong.

This bothered me at first. It bothered me a lot. That's what got me thinking it must be all the emotional baggage that was fucking things up, that was messing with my head and garbling the lines.

It *couldn't* just be that I was getting old.

Be that as it may, I stuck with the script for the better part of an hour, and while I couldn't say the lines became chiseled indelibly in my brain, they at least became familiar. Which, I realized, wasn't that big an accomplishment, being familiar from the start.

It was somewhere in there I began to get a bad case of the jitters. Jesus Christ, who the hell did Herbie think I was, and where the hell did he get the nerve to ask me to step into a part on two days' notice, for god's sake? A major part, and the lead to boot. Sure I'd done it before, but twenty years is twenty years, and I bet there isn't a person alive with a memory like that. I mean, why me? Why couldn't he get someone else?

It occurred to me that Herbie Drake had been in our original production. I hadn't remembered before, which shows how self-centered I am—up till then I'd only been thinking about me. But Herbie had done the play too. He hadn't played Captain Bluntschli, of course, but he'd played Major Sergius Saranoff, which is another leading role. So he was quite familiar with the play. And he'd directed this production as well as produced it, so he was *recently* familiar with it and probably knew all the lines already. So why didn't *he* step in and play Captain Bluntschli, for Christ's sake?

That question answered itself when Herbie met the bus. As Major Sergius Saranoff, the dashing young cavalry officer and suitor for the lovely Raina Petkoff's hand, Herbie Drake had cut quite the figure of a handsome young man.

That was twenty years ago.

Now, I'm sure our perceptions of time vary. I'm sure I
don't see myself as old as others see me. Still, I would have
to count myself as relatively young-looking for my age. My
hair, though gray, is still abundant. When I overindulge on
ice cream I tend toward a pot belly, but my overall body
type is still slender.

The years had not been as kind to Herbie Drake.

I was looking out the window for Herb as the bus pulled
up in front of the depot, which wasn't really a depot at all,
just a bus stop in front of the local drugstore. There were
only two people in the bus stop, a woman so thin she could
have passed for Olive Oyl in the "Popeye" comic strip, and a
bald, paunchy, double-chinned businessman with horn-
rimmed glasses.

Great, I thought. He isn't even here.

He was, of course. The bald, paunchy, double-chinned
businessman was him.

Fortunately, Herbie rushed up and grabbed my hand,
which spared me the embarrassment of walking right by
him. I tried to hide my dismay, but I couldn't help thinking,
good lord, do I look as bad to him as he does to me?

My second thought, totally irrelevant and out of the blue,
and probably a result of my mind having been blown, was,
good lord, why would a man so fat marry a woman so thin?

That question answered itself immediately as Herbert
introduced the woman as Amanda Feinstein. He did so with
some ceremony and emphasis, as if I should know who that
was. I didn't, of course, but I smiled as if I did and took the
proffered hand, which I wasn't sure if I should shake or kiss.
Instead I held it and tried not to stare.

Which was hard. The woman was even thinner than I'd
thought and in a flash reminded me of the X-rays, the high-
society women of *Bonfire of the Vanities*, who starve
themselves until they're almost transparent. This was a
perception which, unlike most of mine, turned out not to be
that far off.

"Mr. Hastings," Amanda Feinstein said. "I can't thank
you enough for saving our show."

She punctuated the statement with a smile. It was not a warm smile, however. It was at best mechanical, at worst condescending.

Herbie's smile was broader. He clapped me on the back, said, "We're both very grateful, Stanley. I should explain. Ms. Feinstein and I are co-producers."

I'm often accused of being a sexist pig, and, I must concede, sometimes rightfully so. Well, if you're keeping count, chalk up another one.

I resented the *Ms.* I resented it because I'm a social cripple, terrified of introductions and shy about asking questions, and I need all the help I can get, particularly in dealing with a high-powered type like Amanda Feinstein. And, sexist or not, it would have been a kindness to me to be told without asking whether I was dealing with a *Miss* or a *Mrs.* Not that I cared one way or the other, you understand. I just didn't want to make a faux pas, or breach some rule of etiquette, the existence of which I was not even aware, by making the wrong presumption. If you can't understand that, you're either not as neurotic as I am or you're the macho type that eats high-society women for breakfast.

Or you're a woman. In which case, confess, you're secretly gloating at the sexist pig's discomfiture, aren't you?

All this happened within seconds, you understand, and while Herbie and Amanda were guiding me to the car. With the Ms. Amanda Feinstein–high society–co-producer bit, I had half expected a Mercedes, if not a limo. But the car turned out to be a Ford station wagon. Herbie threw my suitcase in the back, said, "Get in."

I held the front door for Amanda, but she said, "You ride up front, Herbie needs to talk to you," and climbed into the back. I revised my estimate of her. A practical, no-nonsense, high-society co-producer.

I got in the front seat next to Herbie and he pulled out.

"Not like it's a long ride," Herbie said, picking up off Amanda's previous comment.

"Oh?" I said. "Where's the playhouse?"

"About a quarter of a mile."

"Is that in town or out?"

He shrugged. "Take your pick. There's no stores around it, just houses. But it's zoned commercial. That's all that matters."

"Was that a problem?" I asked.

"What?"

"Getting it zoned commercial?"

"No, no," Herbie said. "It's an old theater. Over sixty years."

"How long have you had it?"

"It's our second season."

"How's it going? Aside from this, I mean."

"We're turning things around. Right, Amanda?"

I wasn't sure if he meant her to answer, but I half turned in my seat in case she did.

"I wouldn't go that far," Amanda said. "But we're making progress."

"Real progress, considering what we had to work with. A few years ago the thing went belly up—Chapter Eleven. We came in, had to start from scratch. Which wasn't easy with a lot of local people with bills that weren't going to get paid."

"How'd you deal with it?"

"Cash. C.O.D. Pay as you go. Pain in the ass, but there you are. Want programs printed, we sent out the order with a check."

"Right," Amanda said. "And then they wait till the check clears before they do the job."

"That was only once," Herbert said.

"That's with the printer," Amanda said. "What about the *Rivals* costumes?"

"Oh, you did *The Rivals*?" I said.

"Right, right," Herbert said. "You were in that, weren't you? What'd you play, O'Trigger?"

"Acres."

"Right. Well, I'm close. They had all their scenes together."

"And you were Faulkland."

Herbert laughed and smiled. "That I was." Then, perhaps

at the thought of playing the young lover Faulkland, or perhaps jerked back to reality by the left-hand turn he was making, repeated more soberly, "That I was."

We had turned into the driveway in front of a large, wood-frame building with a sign on the front proudly proclaiming it The Millbrook Playhouse. We were nowhere near Millbrook, Connecticut, so I figured there must be a mill or brook somewhere that wasn't readily apparent, perhaps in the four or five acres the playhouse seemed to have out back for a parking lot.

Whether we were in the town or the country was indeed a moot point—if the area was zoned commercial no one cared, because the houses around the playhouse were all residential, mostly two-story, wood-framed affairs on half-acre lots. The playhouse was nestled in among them like the queen bee of the wood frames, a huge, sprawling affair, high enough for a grid over the stage at one end and a balcony over the audience at the other.

Herbie followed the driveway around to the side and pulled in at the space marked No Parking—Staff Only. I figured as co-producers they qualified. At any rate, no one rushed out to stop us. We got out, and Herbie led us around the building and up the front steps. We went in the front doors and found ourselves in a small lobby with a box office at one end.

A young woman in the box-office window glanced up from her magazine when we came in. She offered no greeting, however, just noted the fact we weren't customers and went back to her reading.

To the left of the window, under a sign Now Playing, was a poster for *Zoo Story* and *White Whore and the Bit Player*. To the right of the window, under a sign Next Week, was a poster for *Arms and the Man*. I blinked slightly at that, and I couldn't help taking a closer look. It was stupid what I was thinking after all, I'd only gotten the phone call that morning—but I couldn't help thinking maybe it would be there. But no, there were no actors listed for either production.

"Stanley," Herbie said. He was holding the door open to the auditorium.

"Right," I said. I tore myself guiltily away from the poster and said, "So, curtain's eight o'clock," as if that was what I'd been checking.

"Right," Herbert said. He stole a glance at his watch. "It's a little after six. Everyone's at dinner now. They'll be back at seven-thirty. Half hour, right?"

"Right," I said. I gestured to Amanda Feinstein to precede me, which she did, and followed her into the auditorium.

It was, as I'd expected, your basic proscenium stage. The curtain was up, and onstage I could see a set consisting of a single park bench.

I jerked my thumb at it. "*Zoo Story*?"

"Right," Herbie said.

I frowned. "I wasn't in that, were you?"

"No. Me neither."

"What did we do that week?"

"*The Dumbwaiter*."

"Oh, right. Pinter," I said. I turned, looked out over the audience. "Well, this is pretty nice. How many seats?"

"Five hundred fifty."

"Really?" I looked around, nodded approvingly. "Not bad at all. You sell it out?"

That was one of those statements, you want to catch the words the minute they're out of your mouth. Jesus Christ, that's all I need to ask the guy in front of his partner.

"Weekends, yes," he said. "Weekdays are tough."

"Particularly with *our* schedule," Amanda said.

I could see a pained look on Herbie's face. "It's always tough," he said.

"Figures don't lie," Amanda said.

Good lord, what had I started off?

Herbie laughed, tried to cover. "Hey, Stanley's got enough troubles. He doesn't have to hear this."

"He's in the show," Amanda said. "Do you really think he's not going to notice it's opening Friday night?"

I looked back and forth from one to the other. Blinked.

Put up my hand. Babbled. "Hey, guys, don't mind me. I'm just an actor. God, I love saying that. It's been so long."

"It's all right, Stanley," Herbie said. "What Amanda is pointing out is the fact we open the show Friday."

I looked at him. "Yeah? So?"

He smiled. "It *has* been a long time, hasn't it? In summer stock most shows open Tuesday. Remember? You're dark Monday. You open Tuesday, run through the weekend. Sunday night you strike the set, work all night putting up the next one. Monday, when you're dark, you have your tech and your dress rehearsal. You work out the final bugs Tuesday afternoon and open Tuesday night."

I frowned. "Hey, that's right."

"Sure sounds smooth, doesn't it?" Amanda said dryly. "Except we don't do that here. Herbie has this theory."

"It's working," Herbie said.

It seemed there was no escaping the argument, so I frowned and said, "What theory?"

"More people go to the theater on the weekends than during the week," Herbie said. "That's a given. Weekends are great, weekdays are dead. Okay. You open a show Tuesday, no one comes. Tuesday, Wednesday, Thursday. They start coming Friday, Saturday, Sunday. Sunday night you sell out and close the show. The people who saw it on the weekend may like it and tell their friends, but so what? It's over. You waste the word of mouth.

"So you open the show Friday. Friday, Saturday and Sunday are good. You got good word of mouth and the show's still running. Monday, Tuesday, Wednesday people can go."

"That's fine in theory," Amanda said. "On paper?" she held up her hand, waggled it back and forth.

"It's a building thing," Herbie said. "People aren't used to going to the theater on Monday. We're training them. On Tuesday and Wednesday we're running ahead because of the word of mouth."

"And Monday we're getting creamed."

"Like I said, it's a growing thing."

I jerked my thumb at the set. "It's Wednesday. So tonight's the last night?"

"Of course," Herbie said.

"Can I see the show?"

"Afraid not. You'll be working. After all, dress rehearsal's tomorrow night."

"Good god."

"Well, when did you think it was? We open Friday."

"Yeah. I know it, I just don't *know* it. Hasn't sunk in yet."

"Wait till we start rehearsing," Herbie said grimly.

He led us over to the stage. There were no stairs from the auditorium, so he had to climb up. It was only four feet or so, but still an undertaking for a man of his bulk. He managed it, and extended his hand for Amanda. She glided up like a paper airplane. I hopped up after her and looked around.

The work lights were on, so I could see into the wings. Downstage right was a lectern with a small light clipped to it and a three-ring notebook on top.

I pointed. "Stage manager?"

"Right," Herbie said.

"What about crossovers?" I asked, referring to how the actors got from the wings on one side of the stage to the other.

"Good question," Herbie said. "As it happens, there aren't any. Act Two's the garden, we're open all the way to the cyc. Acts One and Three are interiors, but there's windows, so you can't cross behind the set either. You gotta go downstairs on one side and upstairs to the other." He frowned. "I don't think it affects you though. Act One you come in through the window. Act Two you enter once and never exit. And Act Three you only go on and off from stage right." He cocked his head, looked at me. "You remember any of this?"

"Frankly, not as much as I should. It'll come back to me, though."

Herbie smiled. "Of course it will," he said. "Don't worry. Everything's going to be just fine."

As he said that a Leko whizzed by my head and shattered on the stage at my feet.

★ **3** ★

"RIDLEY'S A LOUSY ELECTRICIAN," HERBIE SAID.

I barely heard him. I was sitting in the front row of the auditorium and trying to recover from the shock of almost having been hit on the head by a Leko.

If you're not familiar with the theater, there are basically two kinds of stage lights, Lekos and Fresnels. A Fresnel is a small lamp, capable of throwing a beam of light a short distance, consisting of a single lens with a bulb behind it, which can be slid up and back, causing the light to spot or flood. A Leko is a large, double-lensed instrument, capable of throwing a beam of light a great distance. It also has four built-in shutters which allow you to frame the beam of light from the top, bottom, left or right.

But such technical descriptions are rather academic. The point is, a falling Fresnel gives you a bump on the back of the head. A Leko mashes you into the stage.

"Ridley?" I said.

"Our electrician," Amanda said, returning with a glass of water. "Here. Drink this."

I accepted the water and took a sip. "I'm all right," I said. "It was just a bit of a shock."

16

"I'll say," Herbie said. "That light should have had a safety chain."

"Oh, stop," Amanda said. "Now you're going to spring for that?"

"We could have been killed."

"We can get killed crossing the street. How many lights are there, forty, fifty? I'm not buying fifty safety chains."

"Well, if another light falls—"

"Lights don't fall," Amanda said. "Did you ever see a summer theater where they used safety chains? Of course not. There's no need. These lights are bolted on. They *can't* fall."

"Yeah, right," Herbie said, with a glance at the smashed Leko in the middle of the stage. He turned, bellowed toward the back of the house. "Hey, Rita!"

Moments later the woman I'd seen in the box office appeared in the back door. "Yeah?"

"You know where Ridley went?"

"Out to dinner."

"I know that. I mean where?"

"The diner."

"They got a phone?"

"Why?"

"I need him. Call up, tell him to get back here. One of his lights fell."

"Huh?"

Herbie pointed. "A light fell. He's gotta clean it up and hang another."

"He's not gonna like that."

"He's lucky he's not fired. The damn thing almost hit us. Just call him, will you?"

She shrugged and flounced out the door.

"If Ridley's so bad, how come you hired him?" I asked.

"You don't understand," Herbie said. "Ridley's an apprentice. He's sixteen years old."

"Oh, right," I said. "But even so."

"I know," Herbie said. "He drops a light on someone,

they'll sue our ass off. I'm not sure if we're even insured for it."

"And it's such a nuisance replacing the actors," I put in dryly.

"I know, it's terrible," Herbie said. "But you have a business, you can't help thinking dollars and cents. I got a free apprentice doing lights, which saves a salary. I can't help thinking, is it cost effective, or am I losing money in the long run?"

"You got a sixteen-year-old kid designing lights?"

"No, no. Just running them. The tech director designs. Who is, of course, a professional. Same way with all the other jobs. We got apprentices in what would be salaried positions. All accountable to some other professional in charge."

We were just talking to calm down. I needed to calm down, so I found myself much more interested in the apprentice program than I otherwise would have been. "Oh yeah?" I said. "Like who else?"

"Okay," he said. "There's no lighting designer and no set designer, per se. The technical director does all that. Name's Joe Warden. Big guy with a crewcut, looks like a football coach. Good guy. He designs the lights, Ridley hangs 'em. He designs the sets and builds 'em too. Not himself, of course. He's got a bunch of apprentices for carpenters. They build the sets, paint 'em. He supervises the whole thing.

"Then you got Mary Anne, the costume designer."

"Mary Anne who?"

He chuckled. "Everyone says that. Mary Anne nothing. Just Mary Anne. Mary's the first name, Anne's the last. Everyone trips on that. Anyway, she designs the costumes and the apprentice girls sew. "Then there's the stage manager. Goobie Wheatly."

I grinned. "Goobie?"

"Don't let the name fool you. He's a regular tiger. Rules the set with an iron hand. The apprentices are scared to death of him. He's an old geezer, got a way of looking at you. People tiptoe around him."

"Even you?"

"Especially me. Producer don't cut no ice with him. As far as he's concerned, producers are nonessential personnel who only get in the way and who should certainly be kept off the set and if possible out of the theater."

"Herbie," Amanda said. She gestured backstage. "It would be just your luck if he was right there."

Herbie waved it away. "Relax. Everyone's at dinner. Anyway, the prop man's an apprentice responsible to him. And the assistant stage manager. And the prompter. Who may or may not be the same person."

"What?"

"The assistant stage manager and the prompter. Usually they're the same person."

"Right," I said. "Listen, I think I'm okay."

"You sure?"

I stood up. "Yeah. Yeah, I'm fine. Look, here I am, a real person, standing up. I mean, it's not like the damn thing hit me."

"I know. But still—"

I smiled. "Hey, you got enough problems without lights falling. If that hadn't happened, what was next?"

"I was gonna take you down and show you the greenroom and the dressing rooms."

"Then let's go."

We climbed back up onstage, detoured around the fallen light and went down the stage-right stairs. We came out in the basement, with cement floor and Sheetrock walls.

A door to the left led to a darkened room. Herbie jerked his thumb. "Costume room," he said.

We walked by it into a long, rectangular room running the length of the theater. There were a few chairs from various periods, a couple of coat racks with costumes hanging and several doors down one long wall that I presumed led to dressing rooms.

"Greenroom?" I said.

"That's right."

It wasn't green. It was unpainted Sheetrock, like the rest

of the basement. *Greenroom* is just a theatrical term to refer to the lounge or common room where actors hang out when they're not onstage.

"And the dressing rooms, of course," Herbie said, pointing to the doors. He walked down the rooms to the last one. "This one's yours. You're sharing it with Nellie Knight."

I looked at him. "Nellie Knight?"

He put up his hand. "Look, I'm sorry you gotta share a dressing room. It's the least of our worries right now. You can do me a big favor by not making a fuss."

"I'm not about to make a fuss," I said. "I just wondered why?"

"Because Walter was going in there, that's why."

"Walter?"

"Yeah. Walter Penbridge. Your predecessor." He frowned. "Poor choice of words."

"Oh," I said.

"Yeah. I had him in with Nellie, and if you don't object, there's no reason to move everyone around."

"Were they an item?" I said.

He frowned, shook his head. "No, no. Not at all. It's just the way the dressing rooms worked out. If it's a problem . . ."

"Hey, it's no problem," I said. "I'm sure this will be fine."

I walked in the door, groped on the wall, flipped the light switch.

It was your typical stark summer-theater dressing room. The lights that came on were a row of bare bulbs affixed to the wall over a long mirror over a long makeup counter. Aside from that, two folding chairs and a coat rack were the only furniture.

I turned back to Herbie. "This will do fine," I said.

I switched off the light and came out the door.

"Good, thanks," Herbie said. He looked at his watch. "We'd better go. We're meeting Margie at seven."

"Margie?" I said.

"Yeah. Margie Miller." He looked at me, smiled. "Raina."

He pronounced it correctly—*Rah-eena*, with the stress on the *ee*.

"Oh," I said.

"We can get out this way," Herbie said.

We turned the corner at the end of the greenroom, just beyond my dressing room, and walked down a short hall to a closed door and another hall running off to the left, presumably in back of the dressing rooms. I looked down it and spotted the doors to the men's and women's rooms, a useful tidbit to file away, since the dressing rooms were not so equipped. Just beyond them was another door on which I thought I saw a star. There was no time to speculate on that, however, for Herbie had just jerked the door open, and we stepped through and found ourselves facing another pair of rest rooms, which proved to be for the paying customers, because when we climbed the stairs next to them, we found ourselves in the lobby.

The sulky Rita, as I dubbed the box-office apprentice, was back in the ticket window with her head in a book. She didn't look up, but as he was ushering us out the front door, Herbie called to her, "You reach Ridley?"

She jerked her thumb. "Just came in. He's in there now. Oh, and you got a call."

"Oh? Who?"

"I don't know. Said it was important, though. I got it here."

Herbie frowned. "If it was important, why didn't you tell me?"

She looked at him as if he were a moron. "You weren't here."

He rolled his eyes. I knew just what he was thinking— apprentices—you don't pay 'em anything, so you can't fire 'em.

"Who was it?" he said in exasperation.

"I don't know. A Mr. Calendar or Colander or something."

"Cadwallender!" Amanda said. "You'd better call."

"Shit, I'd better," Herbie said and headed for the box office.

"What's the problem?" I said.

"This is a major fund raiser," Amanda said. "*The* major fund raiser. Personally contributes and brings in all his friends. You wanna run a theater, you return the man's phone calls."

"I see."

She lowered her voice again. "In fact, I'm not sure I should let Herbie handle it. Excuse me, I'm going to get on the extension."

And she turned and hurried to the box office.

Left alone, I stood there looking around the lobby. It looked pretty much as it had the last time.

The doors to the auditorium were shut. I walked over, pulled one open, stepped inside.

The house lights were still off and the work lights were still on. I let the door close behind me, stood in the darkness of the auditorium under the shadow of the balcony and looked at the stage.

Sitting in the middle of it was a young boy, presumably Ridley. He had two lights in front of him, two Lekos. The remains of the one that had smashed on the floor and another one, quite old, but in slightly better repair. Ridley had apparently cleaned up the debris and was now in the process of working on the two lights. As I watched, he removed the plug from the cord of the smashed light and began screwing it onto the cord of the other one. He obviously had no working Leko to use as a replacement and was attempting to repair an old one by using the smashed one for parts.

He had not looked up when I came in and seemed totally unaware of my presence, so I stood there in the dark and watched.

It was the first time I had really had a moment to reflect since the whole thing happened. Not the light falling, I mean being given the part. On the bus ride up I'd been too concerned with my lines. But now, in the darkened theater with the respite of the phone call, I had a chance to sort things out and put them in perspective.

Like what I was doing here. It was not, I realized, just that I had gotten The Call. Basically, I needed a vacation. Alice had even said that much when I'd come home and told her. She hadn't been angry that I'd said yes without asking her, she knew it was the right thing to do.

You see, it wasn't that long ago that I was shot by a drug dealer. It wasn't serious and I'm fully recovered now, but still. A thing like that does things to your head. It makes you reevaluate a lot of things. Like your entire life.

I'm saying this badly. It's not like it changed me or anything. It did, but nothing dramatic, you know what I mean? It's not like, hey, I'm going to leave my wife and kid and go out and live life to the fullest because tomorrow I die, or anything like that. But still, I kind of needed a vacation.

A vacation I never got. Because after I got shot, things got complicated, and straightening them out was no picnic, believe me. And by the time I did, I'd lost some work and was behind on the rent, and the whole vicious cycle. And of course I'd been busting my ass for months trying to catch up. Without making appreciable progress.

So this acting thing was like a godsend. Kind of like a paid vacation from my detective job.

I thought all that as I watched Ridley working on the stage. He had finished the plug, and now he was working on the lenses. Apparently the ones from the light that fell weren't cracked too badly, because he had popped the lenses out of both lights and was now holding them up, comparing them.

Which gave me a good look at his face. It was round, almost moon shaped, with a fringe of short, sandy hair.

But what got me was the expression.

Granted, I was way in the back of the theater and seeing him in poor light from a long distance away, but I swear the kid looked like he should have been playing "Dueling Banjos" in *Deliverance*. It flashed on me that his skill in electronics had to be the same sort of moronic genius. Dueling Lekos.

I shook my head. It's hard to feel anything about a kid like that, particularly a kid you never met.

But, as I said, I'd been shot. Shot in the chest by a dope dealer. Whose every intention was to kill me, to exterminate me, to wipe me off the face of the earth.

It was a sobering thought that young Ridley up there onstage had come a lot closer than him.

☆ 4 ☆

SHE WAS GORGEOUS.

Margie Miller came bounding out of the restaurant, hopped in the back seat of the car, leaned forward, tapped me on the shoulder, flashed me a dazzling smile and said, "Captain Bluntschli, I presume?"

I wanted to reply in kind, but attractive women fluster me, and for a moment I blanked out and couldn't recall the name of her character. To cover I said, "At your service, ma'am. And who might you be?"

Her eyebrows went up in mock surprise. "My dear sir, you mean you never heard of me? *I* am a Petkoff."

"A pet what?" I said.

Those two lines, straight out of Act One, broke the ice. We both laughed and Herbie said, "See, Margie, I told you, it's going to work out."

"Of course it is," she said. "Herbie tells me you've done the role before."

"That was a while back, but yes I have."

"Well, don't worry about it. What you don't remember, I do. I know Bluntschli's blocking, and if there's a problem I can help you out."

"Thanks."

25

She shrugged. "Hey, I'm not in the one-acts, so we got time. We'll just work until we get it. Where we workin', Herbie?"

"My house."

Margie made a face. "Couldn't we use the rehearsal hall?"

"It's strike night. They're working tech in there."

"Oh, right."

"We'll have to approximate the set."

"Your living room's not that big."

"The lines are more important anyway," Herbie said. "We can firm up the blocking in the tech."

"Yeah, I suppose," Margie said. But she didn't seem happy.

"These are difficult times," Amanda said. "We're doing the best we can."

"Of course," Margie said.

I gathered there was no love lost between the two women. Amanda's remark had been tinged in acid, and Margie had replied without looking at her. But before I had time to speculate on that, we arrived at Herbie's house.

It was your basic split-level suburban home, with garage, yard, fence and the whole bit. Herbie stopped in the driveway and we got out.

Margie and I found ourselves standing side by side and I noticed what I hadn't before. She was short, not much over five feet. I'm five-eleven, which made for a considerable difference.

I smiled down at her. "Well, Miss Petkoff. Is the height difference going to be a bar to our relationship?"

She waved it away. "No, don't worry about it. Walter was six-two."

"Oh, really?"

She put her hand on my arm and smiled. "Trust me. Everything will be fine."

Herbie unlocked the front door, called, "Honey, we're here."

Herbie had told me he had a wife and kids. I believe two kids, and I think a boy and a girl. If he'd mentioned their names, I couldn't remember them, and I couldn't even be sure if he had. I'm poor at such things anyway, and finding out I'd just gotten a part blew whatever chance of retaining the information I ever had.

At any rate, as we entered the house, a plump woman emerged from what was apparently the kitchen and was introduced to me as "my wife Martha." Martha, though quite large, appeared determined to emulate the movements of a hummingbird. She flitted from place to place emitting tidbits of information, such as, *she'd gotten the living room ready, she'd try to keep the kids out of our hair,* and *she'd have sandwiches ready when we wanted them.* Finally she fluttered back into the kitchen and we went in the living room and got to work.

As we did, all kidding was momentarily put aside as the enormity of the task engulfed us. Dress rehearsal was twenty-four hours away. We opened the show in forty-eight.

Holy shit.

At first it went slow. Real slow. There was all the blocking to be learned. Or relearned. Or, in some cases, unlearned. Because, of course, the new blocking wasn't the same as in the old production. I'm sure I wouldn't even have remembered after all these years, except for the fact I'd found my old script, and in studying my lines on the bus ride up, I'd subconsciously relearned all those old stage directions I'd penciled in. Which wasn't all that helpful, since the set was somewhat different, rendering most of the directions moot. Fortunately, Margie had a near-photographic memory and was quick to point out things, such as, "No, on that line, Walter crossed down left," or, "Walter sat first, then said the line." This was good, because Herbie seemed somewhat distracted and didn't always catch these points.

I'd never worked with Herbie as a director before. He hadn't been a director way back when, just an actor, so I had no basis with which to compare. Plus the circumstances of the situation were far from the best. Still, if I had to evaluate

Herbie's directorial talents based on this evening's rehearsal, I would be hard pressed to label them anything but meager.

Not that I was in great shape to observe. I had my hands full with my part and was somewhat preoccupied by the task. Still, even an unobservant person such as I couldn't help noticing that Herbie seemed exhausted, drained, overwhelmed, yet at the same time distracted and on edge.

Funny what thoughts flit through your mind. But I am not particularly proud of my ten-bucks-an-hour and thirty-cents-a-mile ambulance-chasing detective work, and on the bus ride up I had entertained a pang of envy for producer/director Herbert Drake, still working happily within the system.

Amazing how quickly that disappeared.

Anyway, as far as blocking Act One went, Herbie proved a real washout, but with Margie's help I got through it.

If you're not familiar with *Arms and the Man*, Act One takes place at night in the bedchamber of Raina Petkoff, a young Bulgarian woman. In the first scene, as Raina is preparing for bed, her mother Catherine comes in to relate that she has just received news that Raina's fiancée, Major Sergius Saranoff, has led a cavalry charge, routing the Serbian army, and that she should lock her window, as the retreating Serbs may be fleeing through the town. This paves the way for the entrance of yours truly, who during the retreat climbs through Raina's window in an effort to escape. Raina takes pity on him and hides him while the soldiers search the house. The rest of the act is just the two of them, until close to the end when Raina goes to inform her mother that he is here, and Bluntschli, overcome with exhaustion from two days of battle, falls asleep in her bed.

It's a hell of a long act. Well, not really, but it sure seemed so. From climbing in the window until climbing into bed, there seemed like a million other things that had to get done. And it was up to me to remember them all. As well as remember my lines. Which, as you'll recall, weren't coming as quickly as planned.

I'd forgotten another thing about theater—funny how quickly you forget—but you learn the lines much easier with the blocking than off the printed page. Because you associate the line with the movement. The one complements the other, it goes together, and bingo, you're there.

So the lines came. Slowly, at first, then better and better. Until I was able to put the script away and try it off the book. An added burden for Herbie, who had to prompt, Amanda having left long ago, after the first read-through. But as I say, he wasn't really into it, and it was often Margie who was giving me the prompt. Which I was needing less and less. And as that happened, the scene began to flow.

More than flow. It began to move. There began to be some real chemistry onstage. The two characters were really playing off each other.

And Margie wasn't bad. My first impression of her had been that she was too young for the part. I guess that was partly being so small and partly having short brown hair and a turned-up nose, which gave her a schoolgirl look. But as the evening progressed, and as I saw her perform, it occurred to me she was just right. In the play, Raina is twenty-three, but Bluntschli mistakes her for seventeen. Which he could easily do. At the end of the play, when he finds out she's twenty-three, he's astounded, and realizes this is a possible match. In the play, he's thirty-four, which is somewhat younger than me but certainly in my acting range. So there was no reason theatrically this shouldn't work. The chemistry was right.

Realizing this gave me an added lift, made me throw myself into the part. Margie responded in kind, the last run-through was pretty darn good and I finished it on quite a high.

Rude awakening.

It was now twelve-thirty in the morning, and we had only completed Act One.

That brought me back to earth and reminded me in short order how little time was left, how much we had to do and how long it had been since I'd visited a bathroom.

I asked directions from Herbie and excused myself to find it, which I'm sure would have been easy if Herbie's wife hadn't already gone to bed after carefully turning out all the lights. Anyway, I maneuvered down the hall, took the short stairs a half level and found myself in another hall where an open door did indeed prove to be the bathroom. I was sure glad it was, cause I couldn't see a thing till I flicked on the light, and I had a paranoid flash as I did, that I had stumbled into the wrong room by mistake and the light would illuminate a mountain of Martha coiled up on the bed. But it was the bathroom as promised, with every accoutrement I could have wished. I availed myself of it, switched off the light and headed back.

You know how it's hard to see in the dark when you've just turned off a light? Well trust me on it, now I couldn't focus at *all*.

Which is my only excuse for what happened next.

Because I didn't find the short stairs. At least, not the ones I'd come down. I went through a door and found myself groping through another room, and when I did find the stairs they weren't the ones I thought they were. Of course, I didn't know that. I went up them like a fool and wondered why I couldn't see the light from the living room at the end of the long hall.

But I couldn't see anything. It was pitch black, and I hadn't any idea where I was. I groped my way slowly and gingerly along, and my hand encountered something which proved to be the spout of a sink, and I realized I was in the kitchen. That was good—Martha had emerged from the kitchen, so I knew it was right by the living room. I groped my way a little farther and out the kitchen door.

They were standing not ten feet from me.

Oh boy.

There are some things you wish you never saw. This was one of them.

Herbie was holding Margie in his arms. They made quite a picture—her so small and him so fat. Her head was on his chest and he was stroking her hair.

A million thoughts flashed through my mind. First was denial, inventing reasons why it couldn't be so—it's a long rehearsal, she's exhausted, he's the producer, she's losing heart and he's trying to encourage her, keep her from giving up. But explanations of that kind just weren't going to fly. There's encouragement and encouragement. This was something else.

My second thought was, sure it all fits, what she said in the car, not wanting to rehearse here. It wasn't a lack of space. She didn't want to see his wife.

My third thought was show biz—my god, did she sleep with him to get the part?

But all those thoughts were secondary to the big overriding thought, which wasn't so much a thought as an act of instinct, which was to shrink back into the shadows so I wouldn't be seen.

Which I sure as hell did. Boy, oh boy, I wanted none of this.

It occurred to me that this was the absolute worst thing I could have found out by taking a wrong turn in the dark.

Wrong again.

At that moment Margie raised her head from Herbie's chest, fixed him with her eyes and said with quiet intensity, "Herbie, I can't work with that old *fart!*"

☆ 5 ☆

AMAZING HOW ONE'S PERCEPTIONS CHANGE.

I have to tell you, I sure had a different impression of Margie during the rehearsal of Acts Two and Three than I had during the rehearsal of Act One. Her every action seemed to grate. She only had to open her mouth and say, "Walter used to do it this way," to get my back up. I had to stifle a strong impulse to say, "Oh yeah? Well, he happens to be dead."

I realized something else too. One of the *reasons* Act One took so long to block was her insistence that I do everything exactly the way Walter did. When, in point of fact, there was no reason why I should. In fact, I realized, attempting to mimic the actions of another actor could only result in a stiff, stilted, wooden, mechanical performance. Large, general blocking, yes. But the nuances of every line? Fuck you, bitch, I'll do it my own way.

That was not, of course, how I phrased it. I was actually perfectly polite. I merely pointed out that, due to the time constraints, we had better concentrate on the broad brush strokes and leave any subtleties alone. Margie wasn't happy with that, but she eventually went along, largely due to the lateness of the hour.

And you know what? When she did, it went better.

I take no credit for Act Two. My character only comes in at the very end, has no blocking and only a couple of lines. But in Act Three he's on most of the time, including one long scene with Raina, in which it turns out she's made a bit of a fool of herself over him, sending him her picture inscribed "Raina, to her Chocolate Cream Soldier." When this comes out she's embarrassed and he kids her about it. She is thoroughly exasperated with him, but he is blithely unruffled and continues to have great fun at her expense.

I can't begin to tell you how well *that* scene went.

At any rate, by the time we finished up it was only three in the morning. If one can use the word *only* to refer to such a time. Act Three had taken two and a half hours. That may seem like a lot, but it was a breeze compared to the five hours we put in on Act One.

And for my money, it was in a lot better shape. Not that I knew the lines—I was doing the whole thing on the book, which was one reason it flowed so well. But that didn't really bother me. Now that I knew the lines would come with the blocking, they were the least of my worries. The hell with the lines, all I wanted to do was play the scene the best I could.

I assure you I did.

At any rate, by three o'clock we were all ready to hang it up, pack it in and who could blame us?

Herbie had to drive me home. The house where I was staying was only a couple of blocks away and I could have walked it if I'd known where it was, but Herbie hadn't shown me my room yet. It occurred to me at that late hour that this was just another example of Herbie doing everything ass-backwards. Any other person would have gotten me squared away first, instead of dragging me straight off to rehearsal. But no, as we climbed into Herbie's station wagon I noticed my suitcase still sitting in plain view in the back. In New York City, that suitcase would not have lasted a half hour, and I wondered if even here in Connecticut, leaving a suitcase in plain view in an unlocked car—for so the station wagon proved to be—was entirely kosher. I do know if that suitcase had been gone I'd have been ripshit.

As it was, I was none too pleased. Herbie's little fling with Margie had put him way at the top of my shit list. It wasn't just that he was stepping out on his wife and kids and making a fool of himself over a hopelessly younger woman—though that was certainly part of it. It was also that his passivity during rehearsal, which I had put down to incompetence, was no longer necessarily an indication of his being a bad director, but now had all the earmarks of his letting a pushy young actress wrap him around her finger and walk all over him. And all at my expense. So I would have to say, at that moment, Herbie and Margie were far from my favorite fun couple.

He had to drive her home too, of course. I wondered how he planned to get me out of the car and keep her in it, which I was sure was his intention. But that was no problem. It turned out we were staying at different houses, and he simply dropped me off first. He left her in the car, grabbed my suitcase and ushered me into a relatively large, wood-framed building. At least relatively large was my impression—though at that time in the morning my usually razor-sharp powers of observation were not that keen. It was larger than his house and smaller than the theater, and that's as far as I'd care to go. We went inside, up some stairs, down a hallway and into a room on the left.

A room that had all the comfort and cheer of my dressing room. A bed, a table, a lamp, a dresser and that's it.

Herbie plopped down the suitcase, straightened up and gave me an almost guilty look. I wondered if he suspected I was onto his little game with Margie-poo in the car outside. But it appeared he was only concerned with the accommodations, because he said, "I know it's not much, but it was such short notice, and then you won't be here that often. If it's a problem . . ."

"It's no problem, Herbie. No problem at all."

He seemed genuinely relieved. "Thanks, Stanley. Thanks a lot," he said. Then he turned and hurried out the door.

I stood, looked around. The room looked just as bad as it had before. Worse, in that I couldn't see the door of a closet. All right, no big deal, I don't need a—

Shit.

No closet door meant no bathroom door either. Which meant sharing a bathroom down the hall.

Wonderful.

The room did have a window. I went to it, looked out, and saw Herbie's station wagon pulling out the driveway and heading down the road. Great, Herbie. Run off to your paramour's bungalow. I sure hope *she* has running water.

I was really steamed. By now I was feeling uncharitable enough about Herbie to suspect that his abrupt exit, which I had originally attributed to a desire to get back to Margie, was actually motivated by his haste to get away before I noticed I didn't have a bathroom.

You never need something so much as when you don't have it. It occurred to me right then it had been a long rehearsal and I really could have used a bathroom. It also occurred to me that that made twice running that looking for a bathroom had really pissed me off.

No pun intended.

I went out in the hall to find it. There were a number of doors, but it figured to be the one facing me at the end. I sure hoped it was. If it turned out to be on another floor, I was going to be *really* ripshit.

Some of the rooms I passed had the doors open and the lights on, but no one appeared to be in evidence. That puzzled me at first. Then I remembered. These guys were much younger than me. When I was their age and doing summer theater, I stayed out all night carousing too. It was a depressing note that I'd become such an old fogy that such an explanation hadn't immediately occurred to me.

I went down the hall and located the bathroom, which consisted of a toilet, a sink and a stall shower, which I realized I was going to have to fight for, there being so many rooms on this floor.

I finished in the bathroom and went back to my luxurious accommodations. I had a big day ahead of me. Time for some well-earned rest.

Only I wasn't the least bit tired. I was in fact all keyed up from rehearsal, and all bummed out from not having a bathroom, and all pissed off at dear old Herbie, and much as I knew I *ought* to be tired, the fact is I was wide awake.

Plus it was kind of spooky being alone at three in the morning in a big, empty house.

I went outside and looked around. There was no moon, and aside from the lights from the house there was only a faint glow off to the left. I figured that could be only one thing, and set off for it. I figured right. After a block and a half I could see the playhouse, glowing like a beacon in the night.

There's nothing quite like a summer theater on strike night. The town around it is dark and dead, and yet here in the midst of it is this incredible beehive of activity.

A quiet beehive. As I walked up to the theater, I couldn't see a soul. The doors were all open and the lights were all on, but there was no one in sight. Which could mean only one thing. The set was already inside.

I walked around the side of the theater. Sure enough, there on the side wall was a loading dock some six feet high and, above it, wide-open double doors leading to the stage. Light was pouring out the double doors, and I walked closer and tried to get a peek in, but it was too high. All I could see was a patch of blue in the very back, which I assumed was the cyc.

I heard the sound of footsteps on gravel and looked around to see two figures approaching from out of the darkness. They were marching with their hands over their heads, which gave them a surreal appearance, made them look like two soldiers surrendering to no one in particular. As they came into the light, they proved to be two apprentice boys carrying a black masking flat. They took no notice of me, just plodded right by with the listless tread of those who had been working all night. They heaved the flat up onto the loading dock, then clomped off into the darkness again, obviously back to the scene shop in search of another flat.

I watched them go, then went back to the front of the building and up the steps to the lobby. Naturally, the box office was closed and there was no one there. The doors to the auditorium were closed also. I pulled one open, slipped inside.

I found myself in total darkness. What the hell? There were lights on all over the place.

Then I heard a voice from the stage bellow, "Six A, damn it."

From above, an adolescent voice said, "Sorry, sorry, gotta get to the booth."

There came a clomping up above, then a crash and a small cry followed by the adolescent voice again, "Just a minute, just a minute, I can't see. Hold on."

More clomping, and suddenly a light went on, a Leko, which seemed to be aimed down around the fourth or fifth row of the audience. In the glow behind it I could see the silhouette of a man standing on the stage.

"Damn it, Ridley," the man said. "Where the hell's Tom?"

"He took a break."

"We're never gonna get finished if you have to keep running back and forth. I need someone in the booth."

"It's all right. That was an accident. The circuit just blew."

"That's not six A?"

"It will be. I just replugged it to aim it."

I heard footsteps overhead during this exchange, lighter and less clumpy, since Ridley wasn't moving in the dark, and now the spotlight on the fourth row of the audience jumped, swiveled and then tilted up to illuminate the figure on the stage. He was a burly man in sneakers, shorts and a T-shirt, who only needed a whistle around his neck to pass

as a football coach. Obviously the tech director, whose name
for the life of me I couldn't remember—I'm terrible with
names.

"Okay, hit me with the hot spot," he said. "Up a little. A
little bit stage right. Hold it there. Fine. Lock it off, shutter it
off the proscenium."

There was a pause, then the sound of metal on metal,
which would be Ridley locking off the light with a wrench.
That stirred unpleasant memories—he hadn't locked off the
other one very well—and I instinctively looked up appre-
hensively, even though I was under the overhanging balcony,
out of harm's way.

I looked back up at the stage. What I'd seen through the
loading doors was indeed the blue of the cyc. The set the tech
director was standing in front of was an exterior, the garden
set for Act Two. That made it the one that least concerned
me, since I only come in at the end. Still, I was curious
enough that I would have liked to have taken a closer look,
if it hadn't been for Ridley hanging Lekos overhead. I knew
that was stupid—lightning doesn't strike twice in the same
place, and the odds of me getting hit by a second Leko the
same night had to be astronomical—still, there was no way I
was walking under where Ridley was working.

I went back in the lobby and downstairs to the dressing
rooms. The greenroom was full of apprentices. At one end,
two boys and a girl were assembling set pieces—tables,
desks, bookcases, what have you, to use in the show. Two
girls were sitting on the floor sewing a curtain. And a few
apprentices were simply sitting on chairs and appeared to be
sneaking a break.

None of them gave me a second look. I knew how they
felt. I'd been an apprentice myself, way back when. So these
kids had my sincerest sympathy.

I walked around and looked down the hallway I'd seen
before, the one with the two bathrooms and the door beyond
them where I thought I'd seen a star. Yeah, there was a star
all right. The door was shut, but I turned the knob and
pushed it open. I groped on the wall and turned on the light.

Well, you son of a bitch.

This dressing room was slightly different. It had plush furniture, including a comfortable chair, a mini-refrigerator and a TV. It also had its own bathroom complete with shower. Compared to the other dressing rooms it was the Ritz.

Was I pissed? Well, under any other circumstances I would not have been. But, as I said, my character Bluntschli is the star of the show. The Man of *Arms and the Man*. By rights the star dressing room goes to the actor playing Bluntschli. Not to the actress playing Raina.

Unless she's sleeping with the director.

As it was, I was ripshit. I don't know if I was going to *do* anything about it, being a basically easygoing type, but by that point I was just *programmed* to be ripshit.

I stomped out of the star's dressing room and discovered a screen door right across the hall. Not the kind you immediately think of, but a wire-mesh chicken-wire–type screen door. It had a hasp and padlock which was unlocked now, so I could have opened the door if I'd wanted to, but there was no need. The light inside was on and I could see right through the chicken wire.

It was the prop room. Inside was a wide metal-shelf unit with the shelves labeled for the various shows. There was one labeled *Zoo Story*, one labeled *White Whore*, and others labeled Act One, Act Two, and Act Three, which held the props we would be using for *Arms and the Man*. On the Act One shelf I saw the pistol I would climb through the balcony window with and aim at Margie-poo.

Considering the dressing-room situation, she was lucky it wouldn't be loaded.

Stupid me. For a moment I'd wondered why Herbie hadn't shown me the prop room. But if he had, I'd have seen the star's dressing room.

Oh well. I had enough to worry about without such petty considerations. I turned, walked on down the hall.

And into the costume shop. Where three more zombie

apprentice girls sat sewing costumes in the company of a rather pleasant-looking, middle-aged woman.

The woman squinted up over the bifocals she wore down over her nose and around her neck on a chain. "Can I help you?" she said.

"Not really," I said. "I didn't mean to intrude. I'm Stanley Hastings. I'm filling in in the show."

Her eyes lit up. "You're Captain Bluntschli?"

"That's right."

She got out of her chair and actually grabbed me by the arm. "Come in, come in," she said. "This is fortunate. I'm so glad you came by." She led me over to a rack in the corner, talking a mile a minute. "They gave me your measurements, but they're not always accurate, are they?" She looked at me slyly. "An extra piece of pie and that thirty-six waist just doesn't make it anymore. And two full costumes you need time to alter."

She grabbed a costume off the rack. A soldier's uniform, ratty and torn. "Here we are. Act One." She handed it to me. "Try it on."

"Oh. Should I take it to my dressing room?"

She waved her hand. "Please. You're wearing underpants, aren't you? We're all family here."

She included the teenage girls in her wave. I looked at them, thinking they might giggle at that. But no, they sat sewing blindly.

"Fine," I said.

I kicked off my sneakers, pulled off my pants and pulled on the trousers from the costume. I tried to button them. They were snug.

She batted my hands away from the button, took hold of it herself, nodded her head up and down. "You see?" she said. "It's like I told you. You could suck your stomach in and get this done, and maybe it holds and maybe it doesn't. Maybe it pops some night onstage when you sit down. That's why I give you another inch. Here, take 'em off."

"You want me to try on the other pair?"

She shook her head. "It's the same fit, I'll give you another inch."

"How about the jacket and the shirt?"

She shrugged. "Sleeve lengths don't change and you don't have a double chin. You're not so fat the shirt won't fit, so they're fine. Slip the coat on if you want. It doesn't button, so no big deal."

I put the coat on. It fit fine. I suddenly realized I was standing there in an army coat and my underwear. In a summer theater that didn't seem particularly strange. I took the coat off, handed it back to her, pulled on my pants.

"Glad you came by," she said. "Now I'll have it ready for the dress. What did you say your name was?"

"Stanley Hastings." I smiled. "And you're the woman with no last name."

She looked at me. "Who told you that? I have a last name. Anne. Mary Anne."

Okay. Served me right. So much for joking with a woman you just met at three-thirty in the morning. I excused myself, found my way out the door and continued on my secret mission, which was to sneak a peek at the set without Ridley dropping a light on my head.

I went up the side stairs to the stage. The work lights were out, so it was dark in the wings. The only light was coming from a spot onstage. I crept between two masking flats and peered out.

The tech director was standing in the light, shouting to Ridley as before. "Up a little. To the right. To the right. *Stage* right, Ridley. Not *your* right, *my* right. That's it. Right there. Now down a hair."

A hand clamped down on my shoulder.

I jumped a mile and almost peed in my pants. After all, it was the middle of the night, I was strung out beyond endurance and this was the very stage where I almost got bopped on the head. I came down, whirled around and gawked.

Staring at me from the shadow of the wings was an apparition, a ghostlike figure obviously sent by some vengeful god to rid me of whatever was left of my rapidly depleting faculties. What I saw was gleaming eyes in sunken sockets, a thin protruding nose stuck twixt pale, emaciated cheeks, framed by a fright wig of snow-white hair. Clearly a demon straight from hell.

"Just what do you think you're doing here?" the demon demanded.

The voice was cultured, clipped and British. Coming from that face it was positively chilling.

I blinked, found myself momentarily incapable of speech.

"Come, come, are you deaf? Who are you and why are you here?"

At that moment my brain clicked over and I realized this must be Goobie Wheatly. Associating that name with that face was too much for me. I smiled. "You're the stage manager," I said.

He looked at me as if I were an idiot. "I know who *I* am," he said. "Who are *you?*"

"Oh," I said. "I'm Stanley Hastings. I'm taking over the part of Captain Bluntschli."

That statement did not press Goobie Wheatly's cordial button.

"I thought so," he said. "Why are you here?"

I was unprepared for such rudeness. I blinked. "I wanted to see the set."

"Well, you'll see it tomorrow in the dress and the tech. Right now we have work to do."

"I understand," I said. "It's just that I'm taking over the part on very short notice—"

"Exactly," he said. "And if you expect to be any good tomorrow, you should either be sleeping or learning your lines."

He still had hold of my shoulder. Now he yanked me out on the stage. "Joe," he said to the tech director. "If you could just hold up a minute, I'd like you to meet someone. Now, I know you got three sets to light and sixteen apprentices who aren't going to get any sleep until you're done, but I got an actor here who'd like to see the stage."

That was too much for me. I said, "I didn't mean to interrupt anyone. I was just taking a peek from the wings."

The tech director laughed, held up his hand. "Hey, don't mind Goobie. He's a nasty bastard, but he's got a heart of gold." He came over and shook my hand. "Joe Warden. I'm the tech director. I heard about you. You're fillin' in on one day's notice, of course you want to see the set." He turned and gestured. "Now, this here's Act Two. You in Act Two?"

"Not really," I said. "I come in at the very end, I don't really do much. I'm mostly in Acts One and Three."

He frowned. "Aha. Well, I can't really put those in now. Not till I finish lighting this. It'll take a little time. Plus I sent my crew up to the shop for more masking flats. I could call up there and bring 'em back, but—"

I held up my hand. "Hey, I'll see 'em tomorrow. That's soon enough."

"Exactly."

It was Goobie Wheatly who said that. I turned to find him, head cocked, looking at me with a superior smirk. In the stage light he looked a little less scary, but still an imposing figure of a man. Remarkable, when you considered how old he actually was.

I looked from him back to the tech director. What a contrast, both in physical type and in attitude. But it occurred to me, for all the difference between Goobie Wheatly's smirk and Joe Warden's affable smile, both men sincerely wished me gone.

By that point I was ready to oblige. I nodded to them, walked down to the front of the stage, hopped down into the audience and with barely a thought to Ridley overhead, walked up the aisle and out.

When I got outside, fatigue really hit me. That and the paranoid flash that I really hadn't paid that much attention to where the house I was staying was. It took me a moment or two to get my bearings before I started off in the most likely direction from which I'd come.

Which turned out to be right. Praise the lord. Just as I had visions of being picked up by a cruising patrol car for stumbling around a residential neighborhood at four in the morning, I reached a house that looked promising. I couldn't swear it was my own, but it was close enough to give it a try. I have to tell you, by that time I was so spaced out it wasn't until I got upstairs and found my suitcase that I was really sure.

I heaved a sigh of relief and proceeded to get ready for bed. Which isn't that big a deal in my case, since I sleep in a T-shirt and my underwear. Anyway, I took off my shoes, socks and pants, only to remember I had no place to hang them, since I hadn't a closet, and found my toothbrush and toothpaste, only to remember I didn't have a bathroom.

I didn't have a bathrobe, either, since I hadn't expected to be using a bathroom down the hall. And, as I said, I was just in my underpants and T-shirt. But after all, this was summer stock and four in the morning, and what the hell? I pushed the door open and padded down the hall.

The lights in the rooms were still on. At four in the morning that seemed excessive, even by actors' standards. And where the hell were they? From what I'd seen, the town was totally dead. It was none of my business, of course. I had my own problems.

I went to the bathroom and brushed my teeth. It was on my way back to my room that something caught my eye.

It was a view through one of the open doors. Before, I hadn't really noticed anything other than the fact the rooms were empty and the lights were on. No reason why I should. But this particular sight caught me in mid-stride.

It was a plastic bag. Not altogether unfamiliar to a child of the sixties. Plus I used to sell plastic bags in one of my job-jobs.

But I sold 'em empty.

This plastic bag had something in it, and something lying next to it.

Now my eyesight may not be quite as good as it was when I was twenty, but it's still pretty sharp, and I had a pretty good idea what this was. I pushed the door open to take a better look.

Sure enough, sitting on the end table by the rumpled bed was an ounce of marijuana with a pack of rolling papers.

Okay, call me nosy if you like, but I was under real pressure on this job, and if I had to work with a bunch of stoned-out actors I wanted to know it now. Which is why I invaded that pothead's privacy and entered the room.

It was stark like mine, and I have to admit I was glad to note it. I'm only human, and if the other actors were being given better accommodations it would piss me off. But no, their digs were just as drab as mine.

Except for a poster on the wall, which on inspection proved to be for the rock group New Kids on the Block.

I looked at it and blinked. Good Christ. I could understand the actor wanting to brighten the room up, but New Kids on the Block? It occurred to me the acting troop must be even younger than I thought.

There seemed to be nothing else of note, so I gave it up and started out.

That's when I spotted the Walkman by the bed. The blanket was hanging down partly covering it, which was why I'd missed it before. I bent down, pushed the blanket aside and picked it up. Not that I expected to find anything. Except, perhaps, the latest New Kids on the Block cassette. But no, there was a piece of adhesive tape stuck on the back. Doubtless the owner had labeled the Walkman with his name.

I turned it over, looked at the adhesive tape.

It was indeed a name tag.

I blinked, and I have to admit it was a few moments before it hit me. No wonder the lights were on and there was no one here.

The tag said Ridley.

I was in the apprentice house.

✫ 6 ✫

"BLUNTSCHLI IS A VERY GOOD PART."

That remark alone, though said with a smile and offered in the spirit of benevolent encouragement, was quite sufficient for me to form an unfavorable opinion of Avery Allington.

I guess you have to understand the context.

It was the next morning. Or the same morning, if you're keeping score, actually only a few hours later, around 10:00 A.M. The cast was assembled in the greenroom, waiting for the tech crew to clear the stage so we could go up there and finish blocking Act Three. So far I'd only worked with Margie-poo, but in Act Three I had to interact with most of the other actors.

These included Major Petkoff, Raina's father, portrayed in this production by a man way too young for the part, an actor who couldn't have been more than thirty, tops, and whose only qualifications for playing older men seemed to be the fact that he was roly-poly fat and wouldn't have done for juvenile leads. I was told his name but missed it, as is my fashion. Indeed, I was introduced to all the actors and actresses, and out of all of them the only name that stuck was Avery Allington.

Naturally.

But I'm getting ahead of myself. I started out describing the other actors and only got through one before I got back to Allington. That ought to tell you something.

Anyway, for the rest there was Catherine, Raina's mother, played by an actress old enough to *be* Raina's mother. Which made for an odd couple when teamed up with Raina's father, whom she also looked old enough to be the mother of. She was not plump, by the way, but a rather handsome figure of an older woman. Her name, of course, I could not tell you.

Nor could I recall the name of the other woman in the piece, the one I'd been told I was sharing a dressing room with. Whatever her name was, she was playing the part of Louka, the Petkoffs' maid. She was a perky young thing, so young in fact she made Margie-poo seem positively mature. She wore shorts and a T-shirt that only needed a letter on it to make her look like a high-school cheerleader. Indeed, she was so young it occurred to me she might actually be an apprentice.

The other servant, Nicola, was played by a rather bland-looking man who looked as if he'd stumbled into the rehearsal by mistake.

Is that all of them? Can I get back to Avery now?

Avery Allington was around thirty. He had carefully groomed hair and sideburns. In fact, he looked as if he'd just stepped out of a barbershop. The hair was brown and wavy. It framed a solid, square-jawed face, with clean-cut features and a striking profile, which I got to see a lot, since Avery always seemed to be posing. He also always seemed to be acting, and everything he said was as if he were delivering a line. Delivering it center stage with everyone's attention naturally on him.

Avery was, of course, Major Sergius Saranoff, my rival in the play for Raina's hand.

Which brings us to the line, "Captain Bluntschli is a very good part."

What was I supposed to say—"Yes, it is, Avery, it happens to be the lead in the fucking play, you twit"? Does that sound overly hostile? I guess it does. You still can't see the context. The pretensions and the implications. Let me give you the rest of the scene. Not the scene in the play, I mean the scene in the greenroom.

As I said, we were waiting for the tech crew to finish, and every now and then we could hear a crash overhead to tell us that the loyal, dedicated and fumble-fingered pothead Ridley was still on the job and we would have to wait a little longer. It was while this was going on, and Herbie was introducing me to the other actors in the greenroom, feeding me a host of names that even if I'd had any sleep I wouldn't have been able to remember, that the following conversation ensued.

Avery began it.

Naturally.

After all the introductions, he said, "So, you've played Bluntschli before?"

"It was a while back, but yes, I have."

"Have you ever played Sergius?"

"No. That was the only production of the play I've ever been in."

"Well, don't fret. You might still get a crack at it."

"What?"

"You don't really look your age, you know."

I blinked. "I beg your pardon."

"Well, Bluntschli you can get away with. But Sergius is a much younger man."

"Oh. Well, I suppose he is."

"Of course he is. And I can understand you wanting to do it if you could pass. After all, it's a much showier part."

As I say, I'd not had much sleep and I was obsessed with trying to do my part and a lot of this was going right over my head, but even to a dense fool like me, this was too blatant to be missed.

Not that I could fathom any response. "What?" I said.

Avery smiled. "Of course it is. When Brando did the play on Broadway, he naturally played Sergius."

"Brando?"

"Marlon Brando. He played Sergius of course. It's a showier role. It allows you to posture, clown, play the bravado, the swagger, the dashing romantic fool. I quite understand your wanting to play it."

I wasn't about to protest that I'd never said *anything* about wanting to play Sergius, but I felt some response was called for. "I'm quite happy playing Bluntschli," I said.

Avery cocked his head so he could favor me with his profile while giving me a condescending smile, and delivered the line. "Bluntschli's a very good part."

See what I mean? A wholly gratuitous and egocentric diatribe for the sole purpose of defining our relative positions in the show.

I wondered why it mattered to him so much. Why he would take such pains to attempt to impress his importance on a stranger, who was not on equal footing to begin with, who was only there making an effort—and if I may say so, a heroic effort—to save the show and allow it to go on. It was the circumstances more than anything else that made his posturing a little much. Not that it wouldn't have seemed excessive under the best of circumstances. Even near brain-dead, with no sleep and line-and-blocking overload, I could tell that the man was way off base.

But no one else seemed to. As I looked around, none of the other actors looked at Avery as if to say, "Get a load of this." From what I could see, they all appeared to be taking his statements at face value. Either that, or he was a known quantity to which they no longer paid attention. But that couldn't really fly with a stranger in their midst. I mean, how were they going to relate to me?

It was at that moment that Herbie jumped in and suggested we run lines while we were waiting.

That didn't really suit me. You will recall, I'd done Act Three on the book, intending to learn the lines with the blocking, and I wasn't really up on the lines. There was no point running the lines with me on the book, so my only recourse was to take a stab at it. Which I didn't really want to do, knowing so few lines to begin with. I mean, this was the actors' first impression of me, and I didn't want it to be so bad. Which was not really vanity as much as insecurity. I mean, here I was with my first real part in twenty years, and all those people would be watching me, wondering if I could do it. Counting on me to do it. Because if I stunk, the show would go right in the toilet. And them with it. So I would have liked their first impression of me to be learning the blocking, script in hand, saying the correct lines, not sputtering my way painfully through a line rehearsal.

But what was I to do, say, "No, I don't think I'd like to do that"? What a great first impression that would be: Prima donna refuses to run lines at special rehearsal called for his benefit; actors and actresses, giving up morning off in order to help replacement actor learn part, gawk in amazement as boorish clod spurns aid and sulks in greenroom while waiting for tech crew to finish.

So I didn't reject Herbie's suggestion. I just said, "That would be fine, but I have to tell you, I don't really know Act Three yet."

"I'll get a prompter," Herbie said. He looked up, spotted Goobie Wheatly with an apprentice boy just coming down the stairs. "Goobie," he said, "could I borrow Jack a moment?"

The stage manager put his arm around the boy's shoulder almost protectively. "Jack's doing props," he said. "What do you need?"

"We're doing a line-through of Act Three, I need a prompter for Stanley."

Goobie gave me a look that spoke volumes—*of course, I should have known, the trouble-making intruder from last night strikes again.*

He turned back to Herbie. "That would be Kirk. Jack's on props. Kirk is the prompter. I'll send him down."

"Is he here?" Herbie said. "Because we're going to start right away."

"Excuse me," Goobie said witheringly. "I certainly

wouldn't want to hold anybody up. Jack, start without me. I'll be right with you."

"But I don't know what to do," Jack protested.

"I know that, but there are priorities. Right now I have to summon Captain Kirk." Goobie waved his hand. "Go, go."

Jack walked off in the direction of the prop room.

"Is Kirk here?" Herbie asked.

Goobie, who had turned to go, reacted as if stung by a bee. "Yes, he's here. He's in the audience, and I believe he's asleep. I will rouse him and send him down."

I knew Goobie was only doing his best to make us feel bad, but in my case it was working. I didn't want some teenaged boy who'd been up all night working woken from a sound sleep just to prompt me on my lines. But before I could protest, Goobie had turned and, with amazing dexterity for a man his age, tripped lightly up the stairs.

He was back minutes later, ushering a short, chubby, bespectacled boy, who gave every indication of having indeed been woken from a sound sleep. He kept inserting his fingers under his glasses and rubbing his eyes. The fingers were chubby, the lenses were thick, and the action kept raising the glasses off the nose to forehead height, and once knocked them off the head. They fell to the floor, did not break, and the lad retrieved them and put them back on.

"Gentlemen," Goobie said, clapping him on the shoulder. "May I present Captain Kirk of the *Starship Enterprise*, your commander and prompter. If you wouldn't mind briefing him on this mission, I have other work to do."

With a curt nod of his head, Goobie stalked off after Jack and we began the line-through.

Which was terrible.

Just terrible.

As I said, I didn't know the lines. Which in itself wouldn't have been so bad, if Captain Kirk of the *Starship Enterprise* had had any idea how to prompt.

If you're not in the theater, you may not realize that while prompting may seem simple, it's not, it's a real art. I know, because I did it myself when I was an apprentice in summer stock, many, many years ago. It's a delicate thing and it takes getting used to. It's not just giving the actor the line. It's knowing when he needs it and feeding it to him at just the right moment.

There are two absolute no-nos in prompting—prompting too late or prompting too soon. For one thing, an actor should never have to say "line." If an actor says "line," it means the prompter fell asleep and didn't do his job. The prompter should be able to tell when an actor's in trouble and give him the line before he has to ask for it.

But you gotta be careful, because an even greater sin is prompting too soon. Because there's nothing that trips an actor up quite so badly as knowing the line and having the prompter throw it at him anyway during a dramatic pause. So, in prompting, timing is the key.

Still another art in prompting is giving just enough. If an actor is in trouble, the prompter doesn't have to read the whole line. Because in theory the actor *knows* the line, and all he needs is a reminder, not the line itself. For instance, if an actor has forgotten "Four score and seven years ago," the prompter need not intone "Four score and seven years ago," to put him on track. A good prompter will hiss the words "four score," and the actor, reminded, will instantly jump into the speech.

These are the key qualities of a good prompter.

Captain Kirk of the *Starship Enterprise* had none of them. He was every actor's dread: a dull tool, thrust into the job, probably because he was incapable of performing anywhere else. When prompting, Kirk droned the lines in a loud, nasal monotone. Far from throwing key words, he began at the very first word of the line, or sometimes even before it, for Captain Kirk seemed to draw no distinction whatsoever between dialogue and stage directions, even though the latter offered a hint as to what they were by virtue of coming in both italics and parentheses. This cut no ice with Kirk. He read everything after the character name Bluntschli. In fact, sometimes he even *read* the character name Bluntschli, just in case I had forgotten what character it was I was playing and he was prompting.

As if this weren't bad enough, Kirk did this only when asked. In other words, he suffered from the other malady of incompetent prompters, of never knowing when a prompt was needed. He was capable of sitting there in dead silence, with the eyes of everyone in the cast on him, and never suspecting anything might be needed from him until I said "line." Indeed, often *that* was not enough. In most cases, I had to first get his attention by saying "Kirk," before I said "line." I can't begin to tell you what this did for the pace of the line rehearsal.

Or for my performance. I'd been afraid I would look bad. Well, I not only looked bad, I looked *glaringly* bad.

Now, a certain part of it was indeed my fault, and I would be the first one to admit it. But, as it happened, for the most part I was being *made* to look bad by the glaring incompetence of the hopelessly inadequate Captain Kirk.

I tried to be calm, I tried to be rational, and most of all I tried to be kind. I really tried. But I'm only human. I do not have the patience of a saint. And I have to tell you, even Gandhi would have strangled Captain Kirk.

Anyway, as the line rehearsal wore on, slower, duller and more deadly and more ominous, my patience became somewhat frayed and I'm afraid my irritation showed.

And as I stood there, impotently seething in helpless frustration, while I waited for the moron who had lost track to find the right *page* for Christ's sake, what absolutely killed me was the sudden realization that in all of this I had not one person's sympathy. To the other actors, the fault did not lie in Kirk for not prompting the lines, but in me for not knowing them. And my impatience with his incompetence was not seen as the just ire of a sane person attempting an extraordinary feat against insurmountable odds while being thwarted by a blundering dolt, but was seen instead as the peevishness of an arrogant actor blaming his own mistakes on a poor teenaged boy who was doing

the best he could considering he'd been up all night and had
had no sleep.

Even that I could have borne. But what made it in-
tolerable was catching a sight out of the corner of my eye of
the smug smile of Avery Allington, obviously enjoying my
plight immensely.

★ **7** ★

BY THE TIME RIDLEY GOT THROUGH PUTZING AROUND WITH the lights, we just barely had time to block Act Three before the tech. And when I say just barely, I mean just barely. We had time to block it but not run it, which ordinarily go hand in hand. You block the scene, learning and writing down the moves, then run it to make sure you got them right. The blocking part is of course a slow, laborious process, stopping to go over each new move. So though I had the book and didn't have to depend on Captain Kirk for my lines, I still couldn't demonstrate my acting ability (if any) because the stop-and-go blocking rehearsal naturally had no pace. The run-through would have, but, as I said, we never got to it. By the time we finished the blocking—working right through lunch with sandwiches brought in, and I could tell the other actors just loved me for that—it was one-thirty, the tech rehearsal was scheduled for two, and the actors had to be dismissed to get into costume and makeup.

Including me.

Especially me.

It had been a long time, and I was never any great shakes at makeup anyway. Of course the makeup for the part of Bluntschli was not complicated, just straight makeup. A little pancake base, a little eyebrow pencil and perhaps just a trace of rouge to make up for the fact the guy's a little younger than I am. No big deal.

But by now I was flustered enough after my encounter with Captain Kirk to believe that, in this production, Murphy's Law was not only in effect but working overtime, and that anything that could go wrong would become an absolute disaster within seconds. So the minute the blocking rehearsal ended I went straight back to my dressing room, sat down at the makeup counter and got to work.

Or at least tried to. It had been a while, but when I examined the pancake makeup I still remembered enough to know that all the shades of base makeup on the counter were for women, were too light for me and simply would not do.

That figured.

I went out and applied at the dressing room next door, which turned out to be occupied by the roly-poly actor playing Major Petkoff and the bland chap playing the servant Nicola. If I'd won their hearts during the line and blocking rehearsals you wouldn't have known it. While they weren't hostile, they weren't eager to part with their pancake makeup. On the other hand, that might have had nothing to do with me, because men's pancake makeup seemed to be at a premium. Of the eight containers of base makeup on their counter, six were light, women's shades like mine, and there were only two they actually used. After a bit of grumbling they grudgingly parted with one, but only after I had promised to bring it back.

The makeup situation must have been screwed up all over the place, because as I came out of their dressing room I saw Margie-poo heading into a dressing room I'd already noted as belonging to the older actress playing the part of Catherine. She had her hair up in curlers, was wearing a makeup smock and was obviously in quest of *her* particular shade.

It occurred to me I probably had three or four containers of it myself, and why the right makeup couldn't have been put in the right dressing rooms was beyond me. Though it occurred to me Captain Kirk's sister was probably in charge of it.

I went back to my dressing room, pulled off my T-shirt and got to work. I took the top off the precious, borrowed pancake makeup and filled it up with water.

Oops.

Right. No water. Just like my room in the apprentice house. I still hadn't mentioned that to Herbie—either the lack of a bathroom or the fact that it was the apprentice house—but I was gradually working myself into a mood where these things were bound to come up.

Anyway, I hopped around the corner to the men's room. I got there just in time to see the door with the star on it close, obviously Margie-poo returning triumphantly to put on *her* makeup. At least *she* had running water. Not to mention a chair, a refrigerator and a TV.

Right, Herbie. It's on the list.

I filled the top from the pancake makeup with water, went back to my dressing room, sat down at the makeup counter and went to work. I took a small sponge, dipped it in the water, then rubbed it over the pancake base, transferring the makeup to the sponge. I looked in the mirror, raised the sponge and wiped a streak of base onto my cheek.

I was thrilled.

I have to admit it. I mean, I've been bitching and moaning about everything that happened to me since I got here. In spite of all that, in spite of Captain Kirk, Margie-poo, Avery, Herbie and everything else, in that one moment, in that first touch of makeup in such a long time, I felt just like a kid again, a star-struck kid, thrilled at the prospect of going onstage.

I grinned at myself in the mirror.

And while I was sitting there smiling at myself like a moron, the perky young cheerleader playing the part of Louka the maid came in, pulled off her shirt and sat down at the makeup counter next to me.

She was not wearing a bra. Her breasts were not large, but they were firm, pert, perky or whatever the hell words writers use to refer to young women's breasts. The nipples were dark pink and half erect, perhaps because it was cool in the dressing room.

She was positively gorgeous.

With barely a glance at me she picked up the pancake makeup, unscrewed the lid, filled it with water from a plastic squeeze bottle I hadn't noticed among the other makeup items, grabbed a sponge and calmly began putting on her base.

Let me say, this was not that unusual or unexpected. It caught me off guard, but it shouldn't have. After all, I had worked in the theater before, and as I observed last night in the costume shop trying on my uniform, there is a certain casual attitude among actors and actresses when it comes to inhibitions concerning stages of undress. So this was not a particularly unusual and startling occurrence, and twenty years ago I wouldn't have given it a second thought.

Of course twenty years ago I wasn't a middle-aged man with a wife and kid.

Big difference.

To a man in my station of life, a pair of nubile bare breasts doesn't come along every day. Or even every other day. And commonplace as it might be in the theater, it is for a man like me indeed a noteworthy occurrence.

I didn't know where to look. No, don't get me wrong. I knew where to look. I just didn't want to be caught staring.

All right, so I'm a pig. Guilty as charged. I must admit, while I support feminism, women's rights and equality, and oppose sexual discrimination and sexual harassment—in short, take every politically correct stand—for all that, I will love looking at women's breasts till my dying day, and if that's what makes a sexist pig, I'm a pork roast.

Anyway, I'd already expected to have trouble putting on my makeup. Now I was lucky I didn't poke my eyes out with the eyeliner.

The perky young actress whose name I couldn't remember—but realized I'd better learn fast before I came up with some inappropriate nickname—put the finishing touches on her makeup, then pulled on the white blouse she was wearing as the servant girl Louka. She turned around, looked at herself in the mirror, then looked at me.

She smiled. "It's been a while, hasn't it?"

Exactly what I'd been thinking. I'd covered my face with Tan No. 2 pancake makeup, but underneath it I was sure I was blushing furiously. "Huh?" I said.

She pointed. "Putting on makeup. You started before me, and you're not even finished."

I realized I wasn't. I knew why that was. I didn't want to point out that I'd been somewhat distracted.

"Right," I said. "I'm afraid I'm a little preoccupied with the part."

"Yeah, well don't let Avery get to you," she said.

I looked at her in genuine surprise. "What? You noticed that?"

She smiled. "Don't be silly. It's not just you. He does it to everyone. Did you know he's done a TV series?"

"No, I didn't."

"Really? He usually manages to slip it into every conversation."

"No, I didn't know. What show is that?"

She shrugged. "Some CBS pilot. Got picked up as a series, shot six episodes before the ratings bottomed out and it got cancelled. I never saw it, but I heard it stunk. And he wasn't the star or anything, just one of the supporting actors, but to hear him tell it, it's a wonder he didn't get an Emmy."

"Thanks," I said. "That explains a lot."

"Hey," she said. "It's not like we're not rooting for you. I know we don't really have any scenes together, but for what it's worth, give 'em hell."

"Thanks," I said. "Thanks a lot."

"And now," she said, "since we don't happen to be in the star's dressing room, I have to go to the ladies."

She smiled and bounced out.

I must say, I felt considerably better. No, that's not a sexist remark. I mean, to find I had her support. No, that's not a sexist remark either. Oh, I give up, they're *all* sexist

remarks. What I mean is, it was really nice to find out I
wasn't alone in finding Avery Allington an arrogant, boorish
clod.

I finished up my makeup and then put on my costume for
Act One, the tattered soldier's uniform in which I would
climb through the balcony window of Raina's bedroom. I
hadn't *seen* the balcony window of Raina's bedroom yet, I'd
be seeing it for the first time in the tech, and I sincerely
hoped it was an easy climb. Somehow, in this production, I
expected it to be booby-trapped.

I finished up my costume, walked out the door of the
dressing room and bumped straight into Herbie.

"Hey," he said. "Hey, let me see you. Oh, you look fine."
He stepped back, surveyed me critically. "Perhaps a little
heavy on the eyeliner. If you don't mind my saying so."

"Why should I mind? You're the director."

"Yeah, well it does look a bit thick."

"Yeah, I think I may have lined them twice."

He frowned. "Why would you do that?"

"I was a bit distracted. My dressing-room partner was
putting on her makeup topless."

"Who, Nellie? Yeah, she does that, doesn't she?" He
grinned. "I guess you've been out of the theater for a while,
haven't you?"

"My thoughts exactly." I paused. Then, "Herbie, I'm in
the apprentice house."

Herbie put up his hands. "I know. I know."

"I know you know, Herbie. I didn't know."

"It was such short notice and I didn't know what to do."

"Why is that?"

"I didn't have a room. I mean, ordinarily you'd have the
other actor's room. But Walter didn't leave, he died. His
stuff's still there. In his room, I mean. See, it turns out his
only living relative's some sister in Oregon, and of course
she hasn't come to get his stuff, and I don't know what
arrangements are being made, and along with everything
else no one got around to cleaning out his room and—well,
there you are."

"Right. There I am. In the apprentice house with no bathroom."

"I know. It's a terrible imposition. It's just there was no time. If it's a problem . . ."

"Herbie, it's no problem. I just wondered why. I thought it was better than not knowing and getting pissed off to just ask. Clear the matter up. Now I know, and what you say makes perfect sense."

"If it's a problem . . ."

"Herbie, it's not a problem. Learning my lines and getting through this tech rehearsal is a problem. Where I'm staying may be an inconvenience, but it's no problem."

"Are you sure?"

"Believe me, I'm sure. Now if you'll excuse me, I have to go to the bathroom."

I hadn't meant anything, but Herbie reacted to that as if it were another dig. "I know. I'm sorry about the dressing room," he said.

"Hey, Herbie. Am I complaining?" I said. "You couldn't have assigned me a better dressing-room partner. Let's just worry about the things that matter."

I slapped him on the arm and walked off to the men's room.

I felt much better about the apprentice house, having brought it up and talked about it. You always do feel better. Get it off your chest. No, not you, Nellie, me. Thanks, Herbie, for the name. Now I don't have to face the feminists' wrath for making one up. Just for cheap-shot remarks like that last one.

Anyway, I felt a lot better about the whole thing. I couldn't even begrudge Herbie giving Margie-poo the star's dressing room anymore. And it wasn't just that I had bare breasts in mine, though that probably had a lot to do with it. It was just that after hearing his explanation I was able to see it from his point of view. My viewpoint was naturally limited to coming in, learning the lines and doing the show. But fitting me in was only one of Herbie's responsibilities. He also had directing a show, running a playhouse and dealing with a dead actor on his hands. So I could sympathize somewhat with his plight.

I finished in the men's room and came out the door just in time to see Avery Allington dressed only in his jacket and underpants go into the star's dressing room and close the door.

Son of a bitch. I wondered if Herbie was aware Avery was hitting on his Margie-poo.

Instead of heading back to my dressing room I walked down the hallway, paused and listened at the door.

I heard her voice, high, hysterical, "I think he knows about us!" Then his, "Shh! Quiet, he doesn't suspect a thing." Then a long pause when they must have been kissing. Then her voice again, "Oh, Kevin!"

Kevin?

Then suddenly I realized. It was a soap opera. The TV was on.

That made me feel foolish enough to move on before anyone caught me listening. I walked on down to the end of the hall, turned left by the steps up to the stage-left wings and walked past the costume shop.

Mary Anne saw me and said, "Oh, you look good," or something to that effect. It came out, "Uh, gu lu gud," because she had a mouthful of pins. She was working on the skirt of a young woman who, when she turned around, turned out to be my dressing-room partner, Nellie. I hadn't recognized her from the back, but then in the dressing room I hadn't seen that much of her face.

Yet another sexist remark.

"That's fine," I said, and left Mary Anne to her pinning, so she didn't have to try to make any more conversation with her mouth full.

I walked around past the stairs up to stage right and into the greenroom. I needed only to walk to the end of it to have come full circle and back to my dressing room.

The first door on my left was the dressing room of the older woman playing Catherine, the room where I'd seen Margie-poo borrowing makeup earlier. As I walked by I glanced in the door, not necessarily looking for yet another pair of bare breasts, though I could not swear to it if being interrogated for a post on the Supreme Court. But at any rate, I glanced in and saw two women sitting at the makeup counter. I took two more steps and did a double take.

No, that wasn't it. They were completely clothed. No, what got me was there were *two*.

There are only three women in *Arms and the Man*: Raina, Louka and Catherine. Louka was in the costume shop getting her dress hemmed. Raina was in her star's dressing room watching soap operas and getting hit on by Avery Allington. So who was this fourth woman putting on makeup with Catherine?

I backtracked, looked in the door.

One woman sitting at the makeup counter was indeed the older woman whose name I didn't know, the woman playing Catherine.

The other was Margie-poo.

I'm a slow take, and I have to admit it was a few seconds before it hit me.

Margie-poo was sharing a dressing room with the woman playing Catherine.

Avery Allington had the star's dressing room.

☆ 8 ☆

IT'S HARD TO EXPLAIN.

Maybe it was just that I'd been on an emotional roller coaster ever since I hit this place, being tugged in one direction after another, and it seemed like every time I came around a curve and righted myself, the damn thing looped on me again.

Avery Allington in the star's dressing room? I mean, I'd just gotten to a point where I could forgive Herbie for putting Margie-poo in the star's dressing room. She *was* the lead actress in the show. And he *was* having an affair with her. Now there's convoluted logic. I *blamed* him for that, but at the same time it would have justified the decision, if you know what I mean.

But *Avery Allington?*

What made it worse was the fact I'd been so dense not to realize it before. I mean, I'd seen Margie-poo going into another dressing room. And I'd seen Avery going into *that* dressing room. And to make it even worse, that was right after Nellie Cheerleader-Tits—damn, I did it anyway, you must forgive me, I'm upset—told me about him being in a TV series and how arrogant he was. And I'd *seen* how arrogant he was. The lengths he'd gone to, to impress upon

64

me the fact that my role wasn't that important, that *he* was the star.

Which now made perfect sense. A TV actor was doing summer stock. It was something that happened all the time, but when it did, it was the TV actor who got the recognition. Of course, being a late arrival, I had not seen any of the publicity for the show, but I was sure every press release given out was along the lines of Avery Allington starring in *Arms and the Man*.

Unless the dear, departed Walter what's-his-name was a TV actor too. But no, then *he'd* have been in the star's dressing room. Unless he was a lesser light than Avery, but how could he have been any less than appearing in six episodes of a cancelled show? Unless Avery had been in another show before that that Nellie hadn't told me about. Or didn't know about. Or didn't care about.

Why did I care?

It suddenly flashed on me. Stanislavski. Method acting. Memory of emotion.

I'd just realized that last thought—*Why did I care?*—was a perfect model for one of Bluntschli's lines at the end of Act One. Raina has agreed to grant him sanctuary at her house and is going to tell her mother that he is here. Because he has had no sleep for two days and is utterly exhausted, she is afraid if he sits down for even a moment he will fall asleep, so she makes him promise to stand up until she returns. Left alone, he stumbles around her bedroom, talking to himself, trying to keep himself awake, telling himself he mustn't sleep because of danger. This monologue, of course, only becomes more and more confused until he suddenly stops in the middle of the room and says, "What am I looking for?"

Which is the line that *Why did I care*? was the perfect model for. After all, I'd had no sleep, was on the point of exhaustion and was desperately trying to make sense of things that on the surface didn't make any. And it was the realization that my obsession with Avery Allington having the star's dressing room was stupid and pointless, and didn't really amount to a hill of beans in the greater scheme of things, that really blew my mind. Why did I care?

Because I *did* care. That was what *really* blew my mind. For all the rationalization—for all the realization that Avery got the star's dressing room because he'd been on TV, that always happens, what's the big deal?—I still couldn't let go of it.

Maybe it was just the way he treated me at the line rehearsal. Or maybe it was just that I saw it as so blatantly unfair—not that he had the dressing room, just that he could get away with treating me and everyone else the way he did. I mean, Jesus Christ, there had to be a more noble reason for the simple, petty jealousy that seemed to be what was overwhelming me now. I mean, it wasn't *just* petty jealousy, was it?

Why did I care?

Anyway, as if I didn't have enough problems just getting through the part, I had all that emotional baggage rattling around during the tech.

Which might explain what happened.

Because, you see, I did something in the tech rehearsal of which I am not particularly proud.

I'm leading up to it.

Trying to pave the way first.

If you're not in the theater, a tech rehearsal is exactly that: a rehearsal of the technical elements of the show, when all the various departments—costumes, props, lighting, and so forth—make sure that everything is set. It is not a rehearsal for the actors. They are there, of course, in costume and makeup to be checked out under the lights, but the rehearsal is not really for them. What's being rehearsed are the set changes, lighting cues and sound effects. The actors are onstage, of course, and play whatever part of the scene the technical cue requires. But the standard procedure is to start a few lines before the technical cue (whatever it might be—usually lighting), run the scene through the cue, then cut and skip to just a few lines before the next cue. So in a tech rehearsal very little of the play itself is actually rehearsed.

Except for this one. Because, what with me being shoe-horned into the show, Herbie insisted as part of the tech rehearsal that we run every scene I was in. As I've said, that's most of Acts One and Three. Which in itself would have been a colossal strain on everyone. Because by the time a tech rehearsal begins, most of the tech crew has been up for a day and a half straight, they're all falling on their collective face, and all they want to do is get through it as quickly as possible so they can sack out for a couple of hours before the dress. Having to watch me stumble through my part as well had to be a major kick in the ass.

As if that weren't bad enough, having me doing my part created a jurisdictional dispute between Herbie and Goobie Wheatly. See, normally the director doesn't run a tech rehearsal, the stage manager does. Since the stage manager is in charge of all the technical cues during the show, he naturally has to be the one to rehearse 'em during the tech. Unless the director spots something wrong, something he wants changed, he's really supposed to keep out of it. If he does change something, once he *does* change it, it is the stage manager who will run it. But with me on stage running my part, Herbie was of course in charge of things.

Which I could tell was pissing Goobie Wheatly off. Not that hard to tell, actually—*everything* seemed to piss Goobie Wheatly off. But this in particular seemed to get under his skin.

There was no reason for me to take this personally, but I did. Because he *made* it personal. It was as if the man didn't like me. Maybe he didn't. If you asked me, I'd *say* he didn't. Because he certainly gave that impression. Ever since our first meeting, when I'd foolishly but innocently invaded his space, I'd somehow become the number-one persona non grata in that theater. And Goobie Wheatly didn't seem at all inclined to let me off the hook.

Yeah, I'm leading up to the incident. All this is important because it's what *created* the incident. At least, I'd like to think it was.

But anyway, here's what happened.

In the beginning, Herbie and Goobie set the ground rules
for the rehearsal, which consisted largely of Herbie being
apologetic and Goobie being sarcastic. But in the end they
ironed them out and the tech rehearsal began.

Goobie took his place at the lectern in the downstage-
right wing next to the curtain. I'm offstage when the show
opens, so I was also in the stage-right wing and making
damn sure to keep out of Goobie's way. But I was there, and
I could see everything he did. First he snapped on the small,
gelled tenser light on the lectern that illuminated the three-
holed notebook that held his script, the pages of which had
been cut from a script just like mine and pasted onto larger
pages which allowed him room to write in the lighting cues.
Then he put on a headset, through which he would whisper
those lighting cues to the faithful Ridley, ensconced in the
lighting booth up above. He snapped out the work lights,
plunging the wings into darkness, except for his small gelled
light and the light from the audience coming through the
crack in the front curtain.

Goobie's lips moved and I caught the whispered words,
"House out."

And slowly, through the crack in the curtain, I could see
the house lights begin to dim. As they did, Goobie stepped
forward from the lectern, took hold of the rope from the
curtain and said, "Stand by cue number one." A beat, then,
"Cue number one . . . go!" As he said it, Goobie pulled the
rope smoothly, hand over hand. The front curtain rose and
the lights dimmed up on the set.

Once again I felt a thrill. Very impressive. Goobie might
be a prick, but he was obviously a very good stage manager.
Ridley might be a fumble-fingered pothead spaceball, but
the kid could run lights. From what I could see, peering out
from the wings, the tech director, lighting and set designer,
whose name escaped me at the moment, had come up with a
pretty classy-looking set.

Being Act One, it was of course Raina's bedroom,
complete with French windows leading to the balcony I was
soon to climb. On the balcony, backlit and silhouetted

against the night, was Margie-poo/Raina in her nightgown, a young Bulgarian woman caught up in the romantic notions of the night.

She was gorgeous. I've said it before and I'll say it again. Much as I'd come to dislike the woman in the short time I'd known her, I had to admit that, standing there on that balcony, she sure looked like every young man's romantic dream.

The tableau lasted just a moment, as if waiting for the audience's applause, then the play began. The door opened and Catherine came in to tell Raina that her fiancé, Sergius Saranoff, had just led a cavalry charge and won a great victory over the Serbian artillery. But she never *got* to tell her, because as soon as she came in, Goobie stopped the scene and jumped them ahead to the next tech cue. Which, it turned out, was only a couple of pages ahead, with the entrance of my roommate, Nellie/Louka, who says that the Serbs are being chased back through town and that they've been told to lock their windows. This leads to a bit of business about fastening the balcony shutter. Catherine wants them fastened, Raina wants them open. Of course, mommie wins. But after Catherine exists, Louka points out slyly that one of the bolts on the shutters is missing on the bottom, and if Raina wants them open she need only give them a push. Important plot point? You betcha. That's how yours truly enters.

Which happens right after Louka's exit, and comes accompanied by numerous tech cues. These consisted of gunshots from street—SFX on tape switched on by Goobie at lectern, Raina blowing out candle—light cue—and hopping into bed, followed by more shots, closer and more furious, and the entrance by balcony of our hero.

Which was by no means smooth. I strike a match and blow it out again. I hold a gun on Raina and make her light a candle. All of which required light cues. Which, of course, had never been rehearsed before and had to be set now. Goobie would stop and say, "Okay, Ridley, cue four is a three count. Let's check those levels, shall we? I have dimmers one, two and four to seven, dimmers three and five to three, dimmers nine, ten and twelve to five. Okay, let's back up and run that one again. Take it from 'Strike a light and let me see you.' "

Which of course had to be done for every light cue. And with so many of them coming just like that, it took a while for the scene to get going. Of course, after the last one was when the scene would have normally cut. But we were running the scene just for me.

And you know what? I enjoyed it. I really did. Because after the torture of the line rehearsal that morning, it was a real joy to be doing something where I basically knew the lines and could play the scene. It was a chance to show the other actors I wasn't so goddamned bad.

And I wasn't. Oh yeah, there were a couple of times I forgot my lines and the scene went right in the toilet while we waited for Captain Kirk of the *Starship Enterprise* to find his place, but it wasn't often that I got so stuck so bad I had to wait for him. Other times, if I didn't have the line exactly right I would paraphrase and bull through, the way I would have to do in performance, if it ever came to that. And, as with the night before, when the scene flowed it wasn't half bad.

And it *did* flow, and what made it flow was I was ignoring the nuances of Walter's performance that Margie-poo had made me learn the night before. Oh, she stopped me the first time I left one out. But when she did, I turned, looked out over the darkened audience and said, "Herbie, I have neither the time nor the inclination to give the same performance Walter would have given. Broad blocking of course must be the same, but as far as these finer points go, I'm a different actor and I have to do it my way. I know that puts an added strain on Margie, but in the long run she'll be more natural if she plays off me rather than off remembering what someone else used to do."

With the house lights off I couldn't really see Herbie, which was good, because I'd just put the man on the spot. From the look Margie-poo was giving him, she'd just been attacked and she'd like her man to defend her. But to do so, Herbie would have had to take an indefensible stand. What was he supposed to do, tell a replacement actor coming in and helping him out that if he didn't perform exactly like the actor he was replacing he was out of the show? No, my request was so reasonable and my argument so logically framed, there was nothing Herbie could do but go along.

And while that really pissed Margie-poo off, as with last night, it really worked well within the context of the play. I was calm, cool, witty and in complete control, while she was exasperated and angry. And, as it never had last night with me forced to be a Walter clone, tonight the scene really started to play.

Particularly my recounting of the cavalry charge. See, in the play, Sergius Saranoff and I are rivals in more ways than one. I am a Swiss soldier fighting as a mercenary for the Serbs and am in the artillery routed by his cavalry charge. In the beginning of the play, when Raina hears Catherine's account of the charge, we get a romantic picture of Sergius as a gallant young hero, fearlessly leading his men to victory. Now we get the story from the other side. Bluntschli, not knowing the man who led the charge is her fiancé, describes him as: "an operatic tenor. A regular handsome fellow with flashing eyes and a lovely moustache, shouting his war cry and charging like Don Quixote at the windmills. We did laugh." And it turns out Sergius's charge was actually ill-advised and should have been a disaster for him and his men, and the only reason it succeeded was because the artillery they were charging had been sent the wrong ammunition and couldn't fire back at them. In Bluntschli's words, "He and his regiment simply committed suicide. Only the pistol missed fire, that's all." Raina, incensed, asks him if he would know the man if he ever saw him again and, when he says he would, hands him a photograph of Sergius and tells him he's her fiancé.

What follows is one of my favorite lines in the play, because Bluntschli gets to play so many things. He takes the picture, looks at it and, with a shock, recognizes the man

he's been talking about. He says, "I'm really very sorry."
Looks at her, says, "Was it fair to lead me on?" Then looks
back at the picture, says, "Yes, that's Don Quixote, not a
doubt of it," and has to stifle another laugh.

Which of course *gets* a laugh from the audience. Which is
one reason I love the line. And the scene was going so well I
was really looking forward to playing it. In fact, it flashed on
me I might even get a laugh from the other actors and
members of the tech crew there. So I was really psyched up
and into my part.

Anyway, we reached that point and Raina handed me the
picture and said, "This is a photograph of the patriot and
hero to whom I am betrothed." I took it, looked at it, and
reacted to recognizing her fiancé as the man who led the
cavalry charge.

In acting, timing is everything, and when it's going well,
you can feel it. I could feel it now. In this instance, I had
reacted just right, and I had paused just the right amount of
time before delivering the line. I opened my mouth and—

From the wings came the nasal monotone of Captain Kirk
of the *Starship Enterprise*. "I'm really very sorry."

And that's when I did the thing I'm not proud of. The
thing I've taken great pains to explain.

I snapped.

I exploded.

I blew up.

I had a tantrum, like any other temperamental actor. I
actually stamped my foot and shouted, "Jesus Christ! I know
the fucking line!"

Of course, shouting embarrassed me and made me feel
worse, which made me react to the embarrassment, which
only compounded the problem. I turned to the audience and
cried, "Herbie, I'm sorry, but I can't work this way. I've
only got a day left to learn this part and I can't do it if I have
to put up with this. It's bad enough when I call "line," I
can't get prompted till the kid finds the right page, but if I
gotta start worrying about every time I take a dramatic pause
he's gonna start droning words at me, I'm gonna have a

nervous breakdown. This is not a normal situation, this is an extraordinary situation and I cannot work like this. I'm sorry."

During my diatribe Goobie Wheatly had emerged from the wings and stood there, hands on hips, waiting for me to finish. When I did, he turned to the audience and said, "Herbie, what do you want done?"

From the audience Herbie's voice floated up. "Goobie, I'm sorry. The actors come first. If Stanley can't work with him, he has to go."

"Yes, sir," Goobie said smartly. He wheeled around, faced the wings. "Captain Kirk. Front and center."

There was a pause, then the creak of the folding chair, then the shuffling of feet, and then the chubby, bespectacled, timid face of Captain Kirk appeared around the corner of the flat.

Goobie snapped his fingers, pointed to a spot on the stage. "*Now*, Captain," he said.

Kirk shuffled out, head down, clutching his prompt script to his chest, giving the impression of a dog about to be whipped.

"Captain Kirk of the *Starship Enterprise*," Goobie said. "I know you are only trying to do your job, to be a good prompter. But you have not. You have failed in your job." Goobie turned, pointed his finger straight at me. "You have offended this actor. You have prompted him at the *wrong time*. You have prompted him when he didn't *want* to be prompted. You have prompted him when he actually *knew* the line. This is not tolerable to this actor. Therefore you cannot prompt him. You are hereby relieved of your duties. You are off the show. Turn in your prompt script."

Captain Kirk looked as if he was about to cry. He was obviously overwhelmed. He blinked twice, dumbly, and gawked.

Goobie snapped his fingers and held out his hand. "The script."

Behind the thick-lensed glasses Captain Kirk's eyes brimmed with tears. But the snap of the fingers spurred him into action. Without a word he thrust the prompt script into Goobie's hand, turned and ran from the stage.

It was a public humiliation of the first order.

No, not of Captain Kirk.

Of me.

In front of Herbie, the tech crew and all my fellow actors, I'd been made to look like a total, selfish, insensitive fool. And it had been done deliberately. Goobie Wheatly had publicly humiliated Captain Kirk in order to publicly humiliate me. As a manipulative act of cruelty it was almost unparalleled.

But, oh, how it worked.

I'd never felt quite the way I felt just then.

I felt terrible for Captain Kirk, of course. But for my own part, I felt humiliated and ashamed. After all, I *had* requested his dismissal—but not like that. Not in those terms. It was Goobie Wheatly who had taken it, twisted it, made it as ugly as possible. Which of course made me furious. And all the more furious in knowing that in what he said, for all his exaggerations, there was still at least a grain of truth. So it was like it was my fault but it wasn't really, but I was being made to feel it was. Though it wasn't, for god's sake, I mean, if Herbie were on the ball he'd have known it was important and seen that I got a competent prompter in the first place. But Herbie wasn't on the ball, he was too busy running around with my leading lady, which left me to deal with an incompetent prompter and a sadistic stage manager, so of course this was the result.

So, all in all, it would be hard to imagine my feeling any more humiliated, ashamed, angry, exasperated, frustrated and helpless than I felt at that very moment.

☆ 9 ☆

"MY ROOMMATE'S GOT NICE TITS."

"What?"

"Pretty nice, anyway. Not big, but firm. Supple."

"Stanley."

"I'm sorry. She's not *really* my roommate. My dressing-room partner."

"Damn it, Stanley."

I'd called Alice for moral support. After the Captain Kirk incident I sure needed it. Before I hit her with that depressing tidbit, I thought I'd fill her in on some of my other adventures in the scant twenty-four hours since I'd arrived at the Playhouse of the Damned.

Nellie/Louka's breasts seemed as good a place to start as any. That was the sort of thing that the longer I waited to tell her the worse it would be, and if I waited until she found out herself, I would have elevated myself to Chump/Moron Husband of the Month. So I explained the dressing-room situation.

Or at least tried to.

"I don't understand," Alice said. "Why aren't you in the star's dressing room?"

"Don't start with me, Alice."

75

"What?"

"There's a TV star playing Sergius. They put him in it."

"Oh really? Who is it?"

"No one you've heard of. He's not really a star, just a guy on TV."

"What's his name?"

"Avery Allington."

"Avery Allington? Sounds familiar. What's he in?"

"A show that got cancelled. He's a nobody, Alice."

"What was the show?"

"I have no idea. It's a show that got cancelled after six episodes. He wasn't the star of it and I'm sure you never heard of him."

"Oh. All right. But the name's familiar. Maybe it's just one of those names that *sounds* like you've heard of him."

"Alice, I don't want to talk about Avery Allington."

"Wanna talk about the girl in your dressing room?"

"Not particularly."

"Couldn't you ask to change rooms?"

"No."

"Why not?"

"I got enough problems. The show opens tomorrow and there's no time for that crap."

"How long could it take?"

"I don't want to do it."

"I'll bet."

"If I asked Herbie to change rooms, he'd think I was ticked off because I didn't get the star's dressing room."

"Aren't you?"

"Maybe a little, but not enough to make a stink about it."

"Think you might if you didn't have breasts in your dressing room?"

"That's got nothing to do with it."

"Right. Couldn't you ask her to keep her shirt on?"

"I'd rather be shot dead. Alice, I'm the oldest actor here. By a wide margin. I don't intend to remind everybody of it by being such a total old fogy as to *object* to an actress changing in my dressing room. *That* humiliation I would like to avoid."

"*That* humiliation?"

I sighed. "Yeah. That's kind of why I called."

"Oh?"

I told her about the Captain Kirk incident. She was, as I'd expected, totally sympathetic.

"That's terrible," she said. "But if the director's an old buddy of yours, why did he let this happen?"

"I'm afraid Herbie's not really on top of things."

"Why not?"

"He has a thing for one of the actresses in the play."

"The one in your dressing room?"

"No. The other one."

"There's only two?"

"There's three. The other young one."

"How young?"

"I'm not good at people's ages."

"Nice try. Closer to twenty, thirty or forty?"

"Probably twenty."

"Jesus Christ. I thought he was married."

"He is."

"Wonderful. What is he running up there, a playpen for middle-aged men?"

"Alice."

"Maybe I should get a baby-sitter and come up there."

"I don't need a baby-sitter."

"I mean for Tommie."

"I know what you meant. Alice, you don't have to come rushing up here because my roommate's got tits."

"Oh, yeah? Well, as I recall, you like them."

"Alice."

"Then you tell me the director—who is just your age—is running around with one of the actresses, and what am I to think?"

"What about, I'm glad that's not *my* husband?"

"You've only been there one day."

"Alice."

"And you're sharing a room with the Playmate of the Month."

"That's not my fault."

"That's not the point. I know how you get."

"I'm too busy to get anything. I'm working practically round the clock. I barely have time for this phone call."

"I'm glad you *took* time. You certainly made *my* day. So what are you going to do about the kid?"

"Kid?"

"Yeah. The prompter. The one you got fired."

"I didn't get him fired, Alice. Jesus, I—"

"Hey, hey. Don't be so defensive."

"Well, why not, for Christ's sake? I just got finished telling you I'm upset because everyone thinks I got him kicked off the show. And here you're saying I got him kicked off the show."

"I'm sorry. Of course you didn't. I'm just using that as shorthand to refer to him cause I didn't know his name."

"Kirk. Captain Kirk of the *Starship Enterprise*, for Christ's sake."

"Oh. Right. Well, what about him? If you're so upset, can't you do something? Can't you get him back on the show?"

That was too much. "I don't *want* him back on the show!" I cried in complete exasperation.

There was a long pause.

Alice exhaled. "Jesus Christ," she said.

"I'm sorry."

"That's okay. Listen, all kidding aside, how are you?"

"All kidding aside?"

"Yeah."

I sighed. "Alice, it's a fucking nightmare."

☆ 10 ☆

THERE IS AN ADAGE IN THE THEATER—BAD DRESS REHEARSAL, good performance. By that standard, *Arms and the Man* was going to be an absolute smash.

Of course, with me plugging into the show on twenty-four hours' notice, there were bound to be holes, but even so. Even if I had been flawless, it would have been a bomb. Because, in point of fact, my fellow actors weren't so hot, either.

The dress rehearsal was the first time I'd ever had a chance to notice. In the line-through they were just feeding me cues. And in the tech rehearsal I'd been too preoccupied with my own lines and with the fate of Captain Kirk.

But in the dress . . .

Oh, boy.

Not that I saw them right away. First we had to get through Act One. No picnic there. Though it was my most rehearsed scene in the show, it was also my longest. And I still didn't have all my lines. Captain Kirk was gone but had not been replaced, which meant I was now being prompted by Mr. Warmth himself.

I dreaded the experience, but I shouldn't have. As I said before, Goobie Wheatly might be a prick, but the guy was one hell of a stage manager. And he wasn't about to screw up his job on purpose just to make me look bad. He was a man who took pride in his work and did every aspect of his job like a pro. He prompted only when needed, anticipated when that was and never made me have to say "line."

I so disliked the man by this time that I sensed an underlying hostility in this. Goobie was being scrupulously careful to do his job flawlessly, so if there was any screw-up in the lines it would be entirely my fault. Be that as it may, his prompting was smooth as silk.

The rest of the show fucked up right and left.

It began with Nellie missing her entrance at the beginning of Act One. Raina and Catherine, left onstage with egg on their faces, attempted a few feeble ad-libs to try to stall till she appeared. But when she didn't, and when Margie-poo, so help me, tried a line as ridiculous as, "I hope my noble Sergius will bring me the head of a vanquished Serb and lay it at my feet," Herbie stood up in the audience and bellowed, "Where the hell is Louka?" and the whole thing ground to a halt.

Which is not entirely kosher. You're supposed to keep going in a dress rehearsal if you can. But once things got as ugly as having decapitated Serbs bandied about, there was no help for it. The show was stopped, a search was instituted and my dressing-room partner eventually proved to have been in the ladies where, she claimed, she did not hear Goobie Wheatly call "places." (A contention, by the way, which Goobie Wheatly strenuously denied, since making sure all the actors knew places had been called was his responsibility.)

At any rate, by the time all that got sorted out we had to start the show again, which had to be a bit of an embarrassment for Herbie, particularly since we had an audience of sorts. This consisted of whatever apprentices were still awake, of which there seemed to be about eight or ten, including, I noted with regret, the ousted Captain Kirk; Amanda Feinstein, Herbie's partner and co-producer, and what she thought of her investment now I hated to guess; a few well-dressed men and women sitting with Amanda, obviously money people of some type or other, being made to feel part of the in-crowd by getting to see the theater in its rawest, purest form, and what a bad idea that was; and last, but not least, Herbie's wife, who must have arranged a baby-sitter for the kids so she could sit in on the dress, and I bet old Herbie had to be thrilled about that.

Anyway, that audience got to see the curtain go up twice, because once Nellie was in place we treated it like a flag on the play and cranked it back and kicked it off again.

Did I mention the scene that preceded her entrance? No, I guess I just mentioned her entrance as the first fuck-up. Well, in the tech, her entrance came after cutting a couple of pages of dialogue. In the dress, I got to hear 'em. They were not good. The woman playing Catherine was not at all convincing as Raina's mother. Oddly enough, she did not project as an older woman, she came off as a younger woman attempting to *play* an older woman. That may not make any sense, but that's what I saw. To me the whole scene rang false. It wasn't very funny or particularly interesting. In fact, as far as I was concerned, the only highlight was Nellie missing her entrance.

The second time she made it, but things didn't improve. That section of the play seemed dull. Everything seemed slightly off. Timing, cues, characters, you name it. Plus the fact that there was a small audience there and they weren't reacting at all. At any rate, the whole thing just seemed bland.

You think I brightened things up? The whole first act I didn't get a laugh. I got through the goddamn scene, which was quite an accomplishment in itself, only requiring two prompts, in both cases administered expertly and unob-trusively by the otherwise malevolent Goobie Wheatly. With his help I got through, but it was a real relief at the end of the act when I finished my monologue and was able to lie down and pretend to go to sleep.

Not much, though, because Raina and Catherine came back in, played a rather unconvincing scene of finding me there asleep, and delivered a couple of lines, at the end of which the curtain came down to dead silence, followed after a few beats by an obligatory and at best perfunctory smattering of applause.

Fortunately, I wasn't really in Act Two.

Unfortunately, I got to watch it.

In my humble opinion it stunk.

In Act Two, Raina's father Major Petkoff and fiancé Sergius Saranoff return from the wars, which are now over, and recount an amusing tale a Swiss soldier told them during the prisoner exchange. It seems in escaping Sergius's cavalry charge, he climbed a balcony and took shelter in a young woman's bedroom. She and her mother took pity on him, let him stay the night and sent him off the next morning disguised in a coat belonging to the master of the house.

This is of course supposed to be funny. And it might have been, if the reactions and looks Raina and Catherine gave each other while Sergius was relating that story weren't so broad and theatrical that they seemed to be straight out of vaudeville. As it was, I cringed, and I couldn't help thinking, good god, did Herbie direct them to do that? I mean, that sure wasn't the way we did the show twenty years ago.

But that was nothing compared to Avery Allington.

Act Two is really Sergius Saranoff's act. First he expresses his undying devotion for Raina, who declares that she thinks they have found the "higher love." Next he asks Louka if she knows what the higher love is, and when she says no, says, "A very fatiguing thing to keep up for any amount of time," and proceeds to make a pass at her. This is of course hilarious any way you play it, and one reason why the part of Sergius Saranoff cannot miss.

Unless you're Avery Allington.

I was sitting in the wings and I couldn't believe what I was seeing. Avery Allington's performance was too big for the American stage. He exaggerated everything—every line, every gesture. And I thought the women's reactions were broad. They were positively subtle compared to this. But nothing Avery Allington did was the least bit real. It was all huge, monstrous caricature.

Yes, he got laughs. I have to admit it. But they weren't *genuine* laughs. What he got was nervous laughter, people laughing because they thought they were supposed to. Believe me, I've been in the theater before and I know the difference. The man was bad, and the people watching could tell.

Yes. I must admit to observing this with a certain amount of satisfaction.

I watched while Avery came on to my dressing-room partner, Nellie. She flirted with him but teased him, saying Margie-poo was interested in someone else also. No, not Herbie—I mean, within the context of the play. And in the play, Louka tells Sergius that Raina is interested in another man, but won't let on it's me. That leads up to my entrance at the end of the act, when I show up to return Major Petkoff's coat, which, as Sergius had related in his story, the women had loaned me to escape. Before I can do that I am spotted by Sergius and Major Petkoff, who are delighted to see me, because they need advice on drawing up the orders to send their regiments home. While this is going on, Raina enters, sees me and exclaims, "Oh! The chocolate cream soldier!" which is what she called me when she fed me chocolate creams in Act One. She covers this slip in a scene that would have been funny in any other production of the play, though in this one it just lay there. The act ends with me being persuaded to stay.

Setting up Act Three.

I hate to describe Act Three, but, unfortunately, it's important. I will try to be succinct.

The act opens with all of us onstage. I am drafting orders for Sergius to sign to send the regiments home. There is a bit of byplay about Major Petkoff not being able to find his old coat, and Catherine telling him it's right in the closet where he left it. The servant Nicola is sent to look and sure enough the coat is there, since I've just returned it.

Eventually the orders are finished, and everyone exits,

leaving me to play a scene with Raina. This is the scene I mentioned before, the one that went well in rehearsal with me on the book.

With me off the book, oh boy, did it bomb. I blew four or five lines, I forget which, and even with Goobie Wheatly's skillful prompting the scene just died. The thing was, for the scene to work, I have to be casual, cool and on top of it, and it's hard to do that when you haven't the faintest idea of what you're saying. Anyway, the best that can be said of it was we got through it, and somehow managed to convey the important plot point that Raina had sent me her picture, inscribed "to her Chocolate Cream Soldier." She had slipped it in the pocket of the coat her father was now wearing, and since I hadn't found it, it must still be there.

At that point Louka enters and I exit.

And not a moment too soon.

I've often had the actor's nightmare of being onstage in a play I haven't rehearsed and of which I don't know the lines. And here it was coming true. The scene I'd just played with Raina was an absolute disaster. The moment I got offstage, I rushed to find my script.

I had stashed it in an alcove near the top of the stage-right stair. I pulled it out and sat on the top step to go over my lines. There was a certain cold desperation in this. My next scene was with Avery Allington, and I didn't want to blow it.

Sitting on the top step, my back was to the stage, but I could hear what was going on just fine. Raina had exited right after I had, but Nicola had entered and was having a scene with Louka. I was too concerned with my lines to pay much attention, but I vaguely heard him telling her she was destined for a life above her station, and he hoped she would patronize his shop when she was a lady.

Though only half listening, I couldn't miss it when Nicola's voice was replaced by another one, booming, theatrical, and way out of line: the impossibly mannered Avery Allington. That incredible prick of misery intruded on my line study by coming on to Louka again in a voice that would have befitted Henry V rallying the troops. (I couldn't help wondering why it had never occurred to anyone that everyone in the house couldn't have helped hearing every word, but, hey, I'm not the director.) Anyway, she responded by telling him he had no chance with Raina, now that I had come back.

As you might imagine, he had a good deal to say about that. But before I even realized it, he had said it and I heard my entrance cue. I dropped my script, sprang up from the steps, ran to the door and walked casually in, just passing Louka going out.

Whereupon Sergius immediately challenges me to a duel: "You have deceived me. You are my rival. I brook no rivals. At six o'clock I shall be in the drilling ground at the Klissoura road, alone, on horseback, with my sabre. Do you understand?"

And I, unperturbed, say, "Oh, thank you: that's a cavalry man's proposal. I'm in the artillery, and I have the choice of weapons. If I go, I shall take a machine gun."

It got a laugh. The first genuine laugh in the play. Admittedly, halfway through Act Three is far too late to be getting your first laugh, but still. What a fucking relief. If you've never been an actor, you don't know how good that felt. It was as if a weight had been lifted from my shoulders. As if a stigma had been removed from my name. I felt like Sally Field at the Oscars.

And the lift that gave me is the only explanation I have for what happened next. No, it didn't go well—I still had to deal with Avery Allington's impossible overacting. And, as I say, the rest of the actors weren't that hot. Me included. But I got through it. And I think I got through it without a prompt. I got through to the end of the act.

If you're not familiar with the play, briefly, here's what happens. Raina and Louka enter and the four of us try to sort out who's in love with who. Major Petkoff and Catherine enter, and he wants to know what the devil is meant by this picture of Raina that says "to her Chocolate Cream Soldier." Which leads to a, one would hope, hilarious scene of sorting

everything out, at the end of which I take charge, admitting
to being the chocolate cream soldier, but saying that there
can be no real harm done since this is just the infatuation of
a schoolgirl of seventeen.

Raina is incensed: Don't I know the difference between a
schoolgirl and a young woman of twenty-three?

I'm astounded, but recover quickly and formally ask for
her hand. I then wrap everything up, click my heels, and
exit, leaving all the other actors still on stage.

I must say I played that last scene well. It did not in fact
get any laughs—and by rights it should—but I got through it
and I got offstage and boy was there satisfaction in that.

There was also satisfaction in that I then got to hear the
play's last line. It was delivered by Avery Allington, so I
knew it wasn't going to be delivered well. But that didn't
matter. What was neat was the line itself.

He looks after me and says, "What a man! Is he a man!" It
is the tag line of the play and ends the show. And much as I
hated to have Avery Allington have the tag line, much as I
knew his performance would suck, I wanted to see the son
of a bitch have to say that about me. So I stood in the wings
and watched.

And Avery Allington turned, looked, then turned back,
struck a hopelessly theatrical pose and said, "What a man!"
He then went through several overdone and outrageous takes
before striking another pose and saying, "Is he a man!"

The performance was so bad I wasn't really surprised
when nothing happened.

Then another beat went by and nothing happened.

It wasn't just that the audience didn't clap. The stage
lights didn't go out. The curtain didn't fall. The actors stood
there, frozen onstage, and nothing happened.

I couldn't believe it.

Goobie Wheatly had missed his cue.

It wasn't his fault though.

Goobie Wheatly was dead.

☆ 11 ☆

"IT'S FROM THE SHOW," HERBIE SAID.

"The show?"

"Yeah. Not this show. The last show."

"The last show?"

"Yeah. *Zoo Story*."

"*Zoo Story*?"

What Herbie was referring to was the murder weapon, which was the knife that was found sticking out of the chest of Goobie Wheatly. It was a switchblade knife which, as Herbie said, was a prop from the last production of *The Zoo Story*. As such, it should have been struck from the set with all the other props from the show. The fact that it hadn't was an oversight, and under normal circumstances the person responsible would have been disciplined. However, in this case the person responsible happened to be Goobie Wheatly.

We were in the auditorium of the theater being questioned by a man in plain clothes who didn't look much like a cop but who seemed to be in charge. Three cops in uniform were prowling around onstage. To my mind, they were probably trampling over whatever clues might exist there, but no one was asking for my opinion. I was merely sitting there with the other actors, waiting my turn to be questioned.

No, I had *not* jumped up when the police arrived and announced that I was a private detective. That's the type of thing that happens in books. In real life, the police don't give a shit. In fact, they prefer it if you aren't. And since my being a private detective was entirely coincidental and not to be inferred, and since Richard Rosenberg was not licensed to practice in Connecticut, and even if he had been he handled accidents not murder, there was no reason to consider me anything more than a civilian like everybody else.

If the cops would let it go at that.

The cop in question was as I said in plain clothes. He was a middle-aged man, plump, balding. Or perhaps he *looked* middle-aged because he was plump and balding. He was one of those people I automatically defer to and then am astonished to discover are younger than me. Anyway, for a small-town cop with a murder on his hands he didn't seem particularly upset, just went about his business with a cool, methodical diligence that I might have found admirable if I hadn't been so damn anxious to have him get on with it, so I could find out just what the hell was going on. The guy seemed in no rush, however; he just stood there and listened patiently while Herbie explained to him about the switchblade knife that had killed Goobie Wheatly being a prop from the previous show.

"That's where it came from," Herbie said.

He and the cop were standing in the audience just in front of the proscenium, and Herbie jerked his thumb over his shoulder in the direction of the stage-right wings. "Can't we get him out of here?" he said.

The cop shrugged. "I called Sy, but I had to wake him up. It's gonna take him a little while to get over here."

"Sy?"

"Medical examiner. Don't wanna move the body till he checks him out." The cop smiled. "Surely you've seen police shows on TV."

"Yeah," Herbie said. "It's just rather awkward."

"Of course."

We in the audience were divided into three groups: the

actors, the apprentices, and Amanda Feinstein and her money people. The cops hadn't segregated us; we had. I guess it was some sort of instinctual class banding in the face of calamity. At any rate, the actors were all in the first two rows, the money people were clumped in the middle, and the apprentices, who started out up front trying to peek into the wings, had been shooed away and herded into the back.

While I watched, Amanda Feinstein detached herself from the money people and glided up to the policeman.

"Pardon me, Bob, I'm sure," she said, "but how long do these people have to stay?"

"It shouldn't be that much longer."

That was not the response Amanda was looking for. "I've got some important people here," she said. "People I was counting on for backing. Getting them detained in a murder investigation isn't going to help."

The cop smiled. "That's why you're over here askin', Amanda. And every one of them watching now can see that their bein' kept here is in no way your fault."

Amanda looked at him stone-faced. I understood her predicament. If she smiled, those people watching her would think their being kept here *was* her fault. Instead she gave the cop a deadpan, elevated her chin and sailed back to her group.

The cop turned back to Herbie as if he hadn't been interrupted. "Now, as I was sayin', we'll get him out of here as soon as possible and we'll get *them* out of here as soon as possible, but back to business. You say you recognize the murder weapon?"

"Yes, I do."

"Can you swear to it?"

"Absolutely."

"How is it you're so familiar with this particular knife?"

"I directed the show. I approved its purchase."

"Purchase?"

"Yes."

"Ah, well, let's rethink that. You can't buy a switchblade knife in this state, and if you can, I'd like to know where."

"Right. Well, all I know is I authorized twenty dollars for the knife."

"Twenty?"

"Yes."

"That's a large knife. Seven- or eight-inch blade. Even if it weren't illegal, twenty bucks is a steal."

"Exactly. It's more like we rented it. Twenty is what I had to pay to have it in the show."

"You rented it from an individual?"

"*I* didn't."

"But you authorized it rented?"

"That's a rather fancy way of expressing it. I said, 'Hey, get me a knife.'"

"Who?"

"What?"

"Who'd you say, get you the knife?"

"Oh. Him." Herbie jerked his thumb.

The cop looked up at the stage. "Oh. Figures. And do you know where he got it?"

Herbie looked at the cop. The cop looked at Herbie. Their eyes met, they smiled slightly, and then, so help me god, Herbie and the cop said together, "In the chest," just as if it had been a vaudeville routine. They looked at each other, shook their heads and smiled.

I'm sitting there gawking, not believing what I just heard, when one of the cops came out of the wings and downstage to where they were standing. "Sir?" he said.

The plainclothes cop named Bob with the casual manner and bizarre sense of humor said, "Yes?"

"I've nothing further to report."

"Oh?"

"We have a stabbing victim found with the murder weapon in place. The acter was not on the scene."

"Right," Bob said, then put his hand on Herbie's shoulder, leading him off to the side of the auditorium. "Let's you and me talk this over," he said.

I was of course sitting in the front row close enough to hear, but my attention was no longer on them. As they moved away I stood up and stopped the uniformed cop, who was turning back to the wings.

"Excuse me," I said.

The cop, a burly type with a beer belly spilling out over his belt, turned around and eyed me with suspicion. "What do you think you're doing?" he said.

"Excuse me," I said. "What did you just say?"

Now he really stared at me. "What?"

"Just now. About nothing to report except the knife still in the body."

He frowned. "Who said anything about a knife?"

"You said a stabbing victim. And the murder weapon in place."

"Yeah. So?"

"What did you say after that?"

"What's it to you?"

"Please. Didn't you say someone was not on the scene?"

"Yeah."

"Who?"

"No one in particular."

"You said the *actor* was not on the scene. What did you mean by that?"

The cop looked at me as if I were a moron. "I mean he was gone."

"No, I mean who?"

"What?"

"You said the actor was not on the scene. Why did you say *actor*?"

"Because he wasn't shot."

I frowned. "What?"

"If he was shot, I would have said the *shooter*. Any other type of weapon—stabbing, strangling—you say the *acter*. The guy who did the act."

"How do you spell it?"

The cop blinked. "What?"

"*Actor*. How do you spell *actor*?"

It was absolutely surreal, the whole thing. I mean, the cop had no reason to talk to me—by rights he should have told me to go to hell. But I'd lucked out, got him started by mentioning the knife, which made him suspicious of me, and before he knew it I'd turned things around so he was answering my questions instead of me answering his. And the only reason I could think of that he was doing it was because they were such innocuous questions he couldn't believe I was that stupid.

So we're sort of sparring with each other and then I ask him this. Now he thinks I'm not only stupid but weird.

He looked at me. "What do you mean, how do I spell it? I didn't spell it. I said it."

"I know. But if you *did* spell it. Like, when you write up this report."

"I don't write it up. The chief does."

"Okay. But if you *did* write it up. How would you write the word *actor*?"

"*A-c-t-e-r,*" he said irritably. "*Acter.* The guy who acted."

I exhaled. "Son of a bitch."

He stuck out his chin. "Now then," he said, "what's this about the knife?"

I was saved from having to answer by the return of Chief Bob, if that's who he was, and Herbie.

The chief strode right up and said, "I understand you found the body?"

"That's right," I said.

"Now, Herbie tells me you're a private detective."

Damn. That was the one thing I was hoping to avoid. As I said, my being a private detective had nothing to do with the situation and there was no reason it had to come up. But good old Herbie had felt he had to mention it. Great. It was bad enough being the one who found the body, but being a meddling private detective was enough to elevate me to the very top of the local law enforcement's shit list.

I took a breath. "That's right, I am."

He nodded. "Good. Glad to have you aboard. Case like this, I can use all the help I can get."

☆ 12 ☆

"HERBIE AND I GO BACK A BIT."

It wasn't me that said that. It was him. The cop, I mean.

"Oh?" I said.

I was in the star's dressing room. Not that they'd given it to me. The cop had commandeered it for his questioning. And I was first up to be questioned, what with finding the body and all. So here I was at last, in the room with the star on the door.

Wondering why the cop was leading off talking about him and Herbie.

"Yeah," he said. "You were close enough to hear, weren't you? What me and Herbie said—in the chest?" He shook his head. "Very unprofessional. Just couldn't resist. See, I've done some work for Herbie. Acting, I mean. Here. At the playhouse. Just cameos, but what the hell, I get a kick out of 'em.

"And Herbie, he gets publicity. What with me being the chief of police and all. Always rates a piece in the paper— Chief Benson to appear in such-and-such. That's me, Bob Benson." He smiled. "Herbie's always kidding me, Bob's no name for an actor, I should call myself Robbie, then he could advertise Robbie Benson to appear, maybe someone would come. Thinkin' it's the actor, you know?"

No, I didn't know. Someone had just been killed, and I'm sitting there with a bald, plump guy in a brown suit and tie who looked more like the vice-president of a bank than the chief of police and who seemed more interested in discussing his acting career than the murder. So I was *not* relating particularly well. In fact, I couldn't think of a single comment and contented myself with smiling and nodding.

As if he read my mind, he put up his hand. "I know, I know," he said. "We have this murder to contend with. First one here in four or five years. And the last one was a husband/wife thing, I knew who did it from the word go and so did everybody else. So much so they found the guy guilty and he's actually doing time." He shrugged. "This case, frankly, I haven't got a clue." He looked at me. "But I got a P.I."

I shifted position in the chair. "I'm not really that type of P.I. I chase ambulance for a negligence lawyer. Handle accident cases."

He nodded. "Most P.I.s do. That's not the point. If you're a P.I., you're trained to observe details. You'll see things other people won't."

"I wouldn't even go that far."

"Doesn't matter. The point is, you were here when it happened, I wasn't. So you're my eyes and ears on this case, and I want to know what happened."

"I know about as much as you do."

He held up both hands. "Fine. But on the off chance you know more than you think you do, I'll ask you some questions, and if you know something, maybe the Socratic method will bring it out."

"Socratic method?"

"Hey, just 'cause I'm a small-town cop don't mean I'm dumb. By the way, I say *don't* by choice, not by education, I know it's incorrect usage. Anyway, let's have it. Tell me how you found the body."

I took a breath. "All right. I was onstage at the end of the play. With all the other actors. I said my last line and I exited."

"Which way?"

"Stage right."

"And how many exits were there from the stage?"

"You saw the set yourself."

"Yeah, but I want your recollection, not mine."

"There were two. Stage left and stage right."

"You exited stage right?"

"Yes."

"The stage manager, Goobie Wheatly's position was where?"

"Downstage right."

"So you walked offstage and found the body?"

"No."

"No? What do you mean, no?"

"I didn't find it right away. See, my exit is not the *very* end of the act. There's one line after it. Sergius Saranoff says, 'What a man! Is he a man!' Then the curtain falls. So when I got offstage, I turned around to watch the last line. He said it, I waited for the lights to go down and the curtain to fall. Didn't happen. I could understand Ridley blowing the light cue—"

"Ridley?"

"The apprentice running lights."

"Oh. Right."

"Yeah, well, I could understand him blowing the light cue, even if Goobie gave it to him. But I couldn't understand Goobie not bringing the curtain down. So I went to look and I found him."

"And where was he when you found him?"

"Right where *you* found him. 'Cause I didn't touch a thing."

"Sitting in the folding chair?"

"Yes."

"Next to the lectern?"

"Yes."

"With the prompt script in his lap?"

"That's right."

"And the knife in his chest?"

"Yes."

"You didn't touch the knife?"

"I didn't touch a thing."

"What *did* you do?"

"The actors were all onstage looking around like, What the hell's happening? I walked out from the wings, put up my hands and said, "Excuse me, there's been an accident. Actors please take your seats in the auditorium. Herbie, come up here."

"Where were you standing when you said this?"

"Downstage right."

"In the doorway?"

"No. The doorway's upstage right. I walked from the lectern straight out through the wings onto the stage."

"You walked between masking flats?"

"Actually, I squeezed out between the proscenium and the front of the set."

"You were standing downstage right, you just walked out on the stage and made this announcement?"

"That's right."

"Did the actors do what you said?"

"Yes, they did."

"Right away?"

I frowned. "I wouldn't say right away."

"Right," he said. "But aside from the usual huh?-what's-going-on? type of bullshit, did the actors leave the stage, or did any of them come over where you were standing and try to look into the wings?"

I frowned again. "Actually, a couple did."

"Who?"

"I'm not sure. But I think the guy playing Nicola and the woman playing Catherine."

"What are their names?"

"I don't know."

"Right. You just got here."

"Yeah. Just last night. Jesus, was it just last night?" I shook my head.

"Right. So aside from those two, what about the rest?"

"I think they crowded around, but I'm not sure."

"And they all went and sat in the audience?"

"That's right."

"They climb down off the front of the stage?"

"Yeah. No one went backstage, if that's what you mean."

"That's what I mean."

"Yes, they climbed down."

"And Herbie climbed up?"

"That's right."

"You took him to show him the body?"

"Actually, first I shouted to Ridley to turn on the house lights, which he did. When they came up I asked everybody to please stay seated for just a moment. Then I took Herbie offstage."

"The body was right where you found it?"

"Yes, it was."

"It hadn't moved in that short time?"

"Absolutely not."

"The knife was sticking out of the chest?"

"Yes."

"You saw it when you first found the body?"

"Yes."

"Or was it the second time, when you brought Herbie into the wings?"

"I *saw it* the second time. But it *was* the *second* time. That was *not* the first time I'd seen the knife."

"The first time was when you first found the body?"

"Right."

"That *was* the first time? You hadn't seen the knife before that?"

"No."

"Really? I understand it was from the show. *Zoo Story*."

"Right. But I didn't see the show. Since I got here, I've done nothing but rehearse."

He nodded. "I see. So what happened then? After you showed Herbie the body?"

"As soon as he saw it, he went and called you."

"Where'd he call from?"

"The box office, I think."

"You go with him?"

"No, I stayed onstage, made sure no one went near the body."

"What happened then?"

"Herbie came back, took charge, relieved me of that responsibility."

"He made an announcement?"

"Yes, he did."

"What did he say?"

"He said what I said. That there'd been an accident, and would everyone please remain in their seats until the police arrived."

"He did not say anyone had been killed?"

"No."

"Or that it was a murder?"

"Not at all."

"But by the time I got here everybody knew. How is that?"

"Obviously somebody talked."

"Yeah, but who? Who knew?"

"Me, Herbie, and the murderer."

He nodded. "Interesting."

"Yeah, but—"

"But what?"

"Amanda Feinstein came up and spoke to Herbie. I didn't hear what was said. They're partners and he probably told her."

He nodded again. "That could be it all right. Too bad." He scratched his head, thought a moment. "Okay," he said. "I know you've only been here twenty-four hours, but can you think of anyone with any reason to want to see this guy dead?"

I shook my head. "Not at all. The man had an abrasive

personality. He probably offended everybody. I don't think anyone liked him much. But that's not the sort of thing you get killed for, if you know what I mean."

"Yeah, I do. Aside from that?"

"As you say, I haven't been here long."

He nodded. "Okay, you're no help as to motive. Let's take opportunity. Who could have done it? Well, you, obviously, because you found the body and you found it alone. But you'd only been here one day, didn't know the man before—you didn't, did you?"

"No."

"So we would have a totally motiveless crime. Not too promising." He smiled. "So, if you don't mind, let's say you didn't kill the gentleman. In that case, who else could?"

"I've been trying to think."

"Any luck?"

"Not really."

"Well, let me help you. You say at the end of the play all the actors except you were onstage?"

"Yes, I did, but I'm not entirely sure of that."

"Oh?"

"The servant, Nicola. He may have exited after his scene."

"You say may have?"

"Yeah. I'm not sure. I did this play twenty years ago. Aside from that, I've rehearsed the whole thing for only one day, and Act Three least of all. He has a bit in the final scene where he explains why he claimed to be engaged to Louka when he is in fact not. He may exit right after that, but I'm not sure."

"Would it be in the script?"

"Yes, of course. Oh, shit."

"What?"

"My script. It's onstage. Well, in the wings, actually."

"Stage-right wings?"

"Yes. I barely know my lines, but I was trying off the book. I had the book offstage, I was looking over my lines every time I got a chance."

"It still there?"

"It must be. I forgot about it when I found the body. It should be right where I left it."

"Which is?"

"Top of the stage-right stairs. You know how there's a railing on the side, with a kind of shelf over the top? Well, it's right on there."

"I see." He strode to the door, bellowed "Felix."

Moments later the cop I'd spoken to upstairs, the one who couldn't spell *actor,* came in. "Sir?"

"This man left his script upstairs. Let him get it. It's at the top of the stairs leading to the stage. Did it have your name on it?"

"Yes."

"It has his name on it. Stanley Hastings. It's a script for the show they're putting on. It's at the top of the stage-right stairs. Now I know that's the crime scene, but I said it's okay. You can go with him, make sure all he touches is the script. When he's got it, take him out in the audience with the others, then start bringing 'em down one at a time. Start with the actors. I don't care whose nose gets out of joint, I want to see them first. You got that?"

"Yes, sir."

"After the actors bring me the trustees—that's the money people. They're the ones clamoring to go home. If you wanna tell 'em anything, you can tell 'em they can leave after they're questioned. But that won't win you no points, since I'm takin' the actors first. They can leave after they're questioned too." He jerked his thumb. "Except him. I'm sorry, but I'll need to see you again.

"Last of all, you bring me the apprentices. No problem with them. They're either asleep or they think it's fun."

"You got all that?"

"Yes, sir."

"Okay, let's do it." He stretched out his arms, then clasped his hands together. He shook his head.

"Looks like a long night."

☆ **13** ☆

"WE'RE GOING ON WITH THE SHOW."

"What?"

Herbie was holding onto my arm with what I think was supposed to pass as camaraderie and support, but which came across as if he were afraid I might suddenly vanish.

"That's right," he said. "I already told the others. But I spoke to Bob—that's the chief—before he took you down. He says to go ahead. As far as he's concerned, we can open." He took a breath. "Now, I know that's rough on you. There was little enough rehearsal time as it was, and now this. Plus Bob says he wants your help."

"Herbie—"

"I'm sorry, but I had to tell him. It's not just that I've gotta live in this town. He's a friend."

"So he said."

"Did he? Well, it's true. And he's acted for me. Cameo roles, you know. The King in *Imaginary Invalid*, or the Royal Messenger in *Threepenny*. And it's a lot better I tell him than it comes out in the questioning, you know?"

"Yeah, Herbie. But it's not like there's anything I can do."

We were interrupted by Amanda Feinstein. Out of the

corner of my eye I'd seen her pestering Felix, obviously to no avail, and as he exited with Avery Allington in tow, she turned her sights on me.

"Well," she demanded, "what did he say?"

"Who?"

I shouldn't have said that. Amanda Feinstein's social graces had been stripped bare by the situation, and she made no attempt to hide her annoyance.

"Who?" she snapped. "Bob, of course. The cop. What did he say?"

I sighed. "I hate to tell you this, but the last thing he said was, 'It's going to be a long night.' "

Amanda exhaled noisily. "Did he say anything *concrete?*"

I shook my head. "No. I don't think he has any ideas yet. He has to talk to everybody."

"Well, the trustees should come first," Amanda said.

So, they actually *were* trustees. I, of course, being totally ignorant of any corporate structure, had no idea what Herbie's setup actually was.

"They may be more important," I said, "but they're peripheral. The actors were onstage and had a better chance to have seen or heard something."

"If they're so damn peripheral, I don't see why they can't go home."

That was when Margie-poo horned in. She insinuated herself between Herbie and Amanda and said in a half-pouty, half-whiny voice, "Herbie, what do I have to tell them?"

"Tell them?"

"Yes. What are they going to ask me, Herbie? What do I have to say?"

Herbie frowned. "Huh?"

Margie-poo said, "Do I have to tell them *everything?*"

Herbie did a double take. You see them in movies all the time, but it's not that often you see one in real life. There was a beat while he looked at her, then suddenly his mouth dropped open and his eyebrows launched into orbit.

Herbie knew what she meant. And I knew what she meant. And from the look on her face, Amanda Feinstein knew what she meant.

I wondered if Herbie's wife, who came bustling up at that very moment, would have known what she meant if she had been there to hear it. But she missed that statement, arrived instead just in time to see him standing there with his mouth open and his eyes bugging out of his head, looking very much like something one might see in the window of a fish store.

She grabbed him by the arm. "Herbie," she said.

He managed to close his mouth, but his eyes were still wide. Behind his thick-lensed glasses they looked enormous. "Yes, dear," he croaked.

"What about the kids?"

Poor Herbie's mind was obviously blown. "Kids?" he said stupidly.

"Yes, the kids. They won't let me leave, and the baby-sitter has to go home."

Herbie's wits had returned. "I know, I know, dear. But it's an emergency."

"I know it's an emergency, but this is a sixteen-year-old girl. She was supposed to be home by now. What am I supposed to do, call her parents?"

"Maybe you should."

"What?"

"Yes. Good idea. Call her and call her parents. You can call from the box office. If they're upset with her being there that late alone, maybe one of them can go over there and stay with her."

"They're not going to like that."

Herbie spread his arms wide. "What can I do? Tell 'em if they got a beef, they can take it up with Bob. This is not our doing."

Herbie turned imploringly to Amanda Feinstein. "Amanda, take her to the box office, let her make the call."

Amanda gave him a look, but put her arm around

Herbie's wife's shoulders—Christ, I gotta learn these people's names—and led her off up the aisle.

Margie-poo watched her go almost triumphantly, then turned back to her man.

But Herbie was having none of it. He took me by the shoulders, said, "Excuse me," and piloted me off into the corner.

"As I was saying," Herbie said, "the show must go on. I talked to Bob and it's okay. Right now the stage is a crime scene, but he assures me by tomorrow all this will be gone."

As if on cue, two young medical-assistant types emerged from the wings carrying a stretcher with a body bag on top.

The full type.

The audience, which had been abuzz with little pockets of chatter scattered throughout the auditorium, suddenly fell deathly quiet.

The two medics stopped in the middle of the stage, looked around. A white-haired man carrying a medical bag came out from the wings, and the other two looked at him for guidance. He in turn looked around and spotted Herb.

"Herbie," he said, and it occurred to me how strange it was for a New Yorker that, in this small town, all these people seemed to know each other. "How do we get out of here?"

The loading door sprang to mind, and I had a vision of them bumping Goobie Wheatly down the loading dock, as if he were a flat, but Herbie said, "You'll have to lift it down off the stage, then up the aisle and out the back."

There was once again dead silence while they accomplished this. Every eye in the place watched spellbound, while the body went up the aisle into the lobby and out.

As the lobby doors closed, Herbie turned back to me. "All right," he said. "Here's the thing. This is a tragedy and I'm real upset and all that, but the fact is, I got a show to put on." He looked at the book in my hands. "I see you got your script. Good. If you're gonna be stuck here anyway, you might as well work on your lines."

Good lord. I held up my hand. "Herbie, I'm not gonna be able to concentrate on the script."

"Of course not, I'll get someone to cue you."

He looked toward the back of the auditorium where the apprentices were. I could sense his eyes stopping on Captain Kirk.

"Herbie," I said. "I'll kill you."

He looked at me.

"Poor choice of words," I said. "But you get the picture."

"Right," he said. "You want Margie to run scenes with you?"

About half-a-dozen responses came to mind. I stifled all of them, contented myself with a simple no.

My roommate, Nellie/Louka, who'd been chattering away with Nicola, Catherine and Major Petkoff, none of whose names I knew, chose that moment to break away and descend on Herbie. He intercepted her smoothly. Before she could even open her mouth he said, "Nellie, please, do me a favor. We're all screwed up, we're gonna lose rehearsal time. Cue Stanley, will you? At least till you're called. It's a tough thing and we all gotta hang together."

She looked at him. "You're serious, aren't you? We're really going on with the show?"

Herbie took a breath. He looked out over the audience at the trustees, most of whom were looking in our direction. He exhaled, looked back at us and smiled grimly.

"You better believe we are."

☆ 14 ☆

CHIEF BOB, AS I'D COME TO THINK OF HIM, LOOKED NONE THE
worse for wear. I'll bet *I* did. It was four in the fucking
morning. Please excuse the expletive, but it was the second
night in a row I'd happened to see that particular hour, and
it's not one of my favorites. In fact, as a time of day, I'd
have to rank it pretty damn low.

I was not happy to be there. I had sat in the auditorium all
night long while every stinking actor, trustee, apprentice,
director, producer, director's wife or what have you, had
been led out one at a time, never to return, leaving me all
alone in the audience of an empty theater—well, empty
except for the bored-looking cop sitting dangling his legs
over the front of the stage. And much of that time I had been
prompted on my lines by a seemingly endless procession of
people, each one, upon being called, passing on the prompt
script to the next outwardly helpful person, whom I couldn't
help viewing, however, as yet another sadistic Grand
Inquisitor. In the course of the evening I must have been
prompted by a good ten to fifteen people, none of them,
praise the lord, the dreaded Captain Kirk. He was the first
apprentice chosen to be questioned, and therefore mercifully
and rapidly gone. But most of the rest of them had a whack

at me, for all the good it did—unless there's something to sleep-teaching, I don't think I learned a single line.

At any rate, at four in the morning, barely conscious and my mind mush, I was summoned once again into the presence of Chief Bob, who, as I said, looked none the worse for wear. Of course, if you're bald, your hair can't be out of place, but still. The guy didn't look a bit fazed. He waved me in, motioned me to the big, overstuffed chair. He was sitting in the straight-backed makeup chair himself, as he had in our first interview, and this time it struck me as a ploy on his part—going the Spartan route himself, so the witnesses, given better, couldn't complain. Anyway, he waved me to the chair and said, "Thanks for sticking around," as if that had been a conscious decision on my part.

I slumped in the chair, said wearily, "What can I tell you that I haven't already?"

He smiled. "Not much, I'm sure. I imagine you checked your script to see if that actor left the stage after his scene. I asked him myself, and he says he did. But he says he exited stage left."

I frowned, tried to think. "Yes, I guess he would have."

"Then I would think he did. There's no real reason to doubt him. He says it's penciled in his script, 'Exit DL,' for down left. He didn't have it with him, but offered to bring it in if we want. Of course he could erase it and change it if it said 'DR,' but I'd be looking for that. Besides, I'll be in the audience tomorrow night and see which way he goes."

"The show is really going on?"

"You bet. It's not just that Herbie's a pal of mine. I want to see it." He shrugged, grinned. "You know, like the cops always do in books. Reconstruct the scene of the crime. I mean, I can question the actors all night long about where they were and what they did in Act Three, but it'll be a lot clearer to me to just watch 'em do it."

"Do you think it's one of them?"

"Well, it's somebody. Who else was there?"

"Anyone could have come up the stairs and killed him while we were all onstage."

He nodded. "Absolutely. No doubt about it. And if that happened, I'd certainly like to prove it. The one sure way I could would be to prove that none of the actors could have done it."

"True," I said. "Another way would be to find someone who saw someone going up the stairs."

"Yes, wouldn't *that* be nice. The eyewitness always makes circumstantial evidence that much more convincing. But failing that, we have to think out this crime."

"You'll pardon me, but it seems like you don't have much to go on."

"I've got you."

"I beg your pardon?"

He smiled. "To help me, I mean. To think this thing out."

There came a knock on the door.

Chief Bob called, "Come in."

Herbie entered carrying two Styrofoam cups.

"Ah, thanks, Herbie. Just what we need," Chief Bob said.

Herbie handed one of the cups to him, one to me.

"Thanks, Herbie," I said. "Where did you find coffee this time of night?"

He jerked his thumb. "Mary Anne's got a hot plate. It's just instant, and there's no milk and sugar. But it *does* have caffeine."

I took a sip. It was terrible, but very welcome.

"You gonna be long?" Herbie asked.

Chief Bob shook his head. "No, we can close up shop soon. I just need a few minutes with your boy."

Herbie nodded and went out, closing the door behind him.

Chief Bob said, "Good man. Too bad this had to happen to him."

"Right," I said. I took another sip of horrendous coffee. "All right, look, this may have caffeine in it, but frankly I'm fading fast. What's this evidence you want me to evaluate?"

"Well, to begin with, I have a problem with the knife."

"Oh?"

"Yeah. The murder weapon. I told you it's a prop from the show."

"Yeah. *Zoo Story*. So?"

He jerked his thumb. "You know the prop room's right next door?"

"Right."

"You've had reason to go there?"

"I beg your pardon?"

"To get props, perhaps? For your show?"

"No."

"No? You didn't have any personal props? For the dress rehearsal?"

"Actually, there was a gun I used in Act One."

"But you didn't get it from the prop room?"

"No. It was on a prop table backstage."

"I see. So you've never had occasion to go to the prop room?"

I hesitated.

"Well?" he said.

"The night before this. Strike night. I rehearsed till three in the morning, couldn't sleep, wandered over here to check the place out. I happened to notice the prop room then."

"At three in the morning?"

"Between three and four. Why?"

"That's the problem. The switchblade knife should have been struck with the props from the show. The apprentice in charge of props—his name's Jack—says it was. Says he got it back from the actor and gave it to Goobie Wheatly. Right after the play. And right after that it should have been taken down to the prop room and left on the shelf with all the other props from the show." He jerked his thumb again. "There's a shelf in there marked *Zoo Story*. Did you see that?"

"Actually, I did."

"Really? You recall seeing the knife on it?"

I shook my head. "I didn't notice."

"Damn," he said. "You sure of that? I mean, maybe you don't remember seeing the knife. But do you remember *not* seeing it? Like it wasn't on the shelf?"

"I just don't know. I wasn't looking for it, you know? All I saw was the pistol I use in Act One."

"Was the door locked at the time?"

"No. It was closed, but not locked."

"You open it and go in?"

"No, I just looked through the screen." I looked at him. "What's the problem with the knife?"

"Same one I got with you. I can't find anyone who recalls seeing it on that shelf."

"Oh."

"And by rights it should have been there. With all the other props. Except for one thing."

"What's that?"

"It's a switchblade. Which makes it illegal. As such, Goobie might have hung onto it. Not put it with the other props."

"I see."

"Now if it *was* in the prop room, it's no problem for the murderer. Cause the door's unlocked. It was unlocked when I got here, and apparently it was unlocked during the show. So if the knife was there, it's no problem for someone to go in and take it. Plus, with that chicken-wire door, you could see it lying there on the shelf just walking by." He looked at me. "It's a wonder you didn't see it."

"I had other things on my mind."

"So it would seem."

I took a breath. "All right," I said. "I'm sorry I didn't see the murder weapon, but the fact is I didn't. If there's nothing else, I'd really like to get to bed."

"I know," Chief Bob said. "Just one more thing."

"Yeah? What's that?"

He looked at me and cocked his head.

"What's this about Captain Kirk?"

☆ 15 ☆

I STARED AT CHIEF BOB IN UTTER DISBELIEF. "WHAT?"

"Captain Kirk. Tell me about Captain Kirk."

"The prompter?"

"Yes, the prompter. I understand you had some trouble with him."

"Oh, good lord."

"Am I misinformed?"

"There is an apprentice called Kirk. Goobie called him Captain Kirk. He was the prompter on the show. I don't know who assigned him to it, but he never should have been, because he was absolutely incompetent."

"Which I understand you pointed out."

I took a breath. I was trying to control myself, but I was having a hard time. I was beginning to feel as angry and frustrated now as I had been when actually confronted with the problem of Captain Kirk.

"Yes, I pointed that out," I said. "I'm fitting into the show on two days' notice. I'm learning the lines cold. It's a tough enough task without a bad prompter always fouling me up."

He nodded. Held up his hand. "I understand. It was incredibly frustrating for you, so you had to ask for relief. Which you did. And what happened then?"

"I gather you've heard this story."

"Yes, I have, but I'd like to hear it from you."

I took a breath. "All right. It was during the tech rehearsal. Captain Kirk jumped my line and I blew up. Said I couldn't work this way. Which was true, but I regret how I said it. At any rate, when that happened Herbie told Goobie Wheatly that I couldn't work with this guy prompting, and Goobie proceeded to boot him off the show."

"In front of everyone?"

"Yes. He called him out on the stage and let him have it. Told him he was being fired for doing a lousy job."

"And what is your personal opinion of the way Goobie did this?"

I took another breath. "He did it to ridicule and humiliate me."

"That's how you saw it?"

"Yes, I did."

"Make you angry?"

"Not angry enough to kill him."

"I'm glad to hear it. But you *were* pretty steamed?"

"Wouldn't you be?"

"Yes, of course." He smiled. "This doesn't require that much explanation. I've worked with Goobie Wheatly myself, I know how he can be."

"Then why are you doing this?"

"I'm a cop. I have to ask my questions. And this is something that came up."

"Came up how?"

"I naturally asked everyone who'd want to see Goobie Wheatly dead. You'd be surprised how many votes you got."

"Oh, shit."

"Well, it's natural. New kid in town. Let's blame him before we blame one of us. Plus Goobie gunned you down onstage in sight of all. There were a lot of witnesses to that scene. Anyway, let's get on with it. That happened in Act One?"

"Let me see. It was my scene with Raina and—that's right, Act One."

"Yes, in the voting, that *was* the most likely time it happened. But witnesses are not always accurate."

"So," I said, "this happened in the tech rehearsal, I let it fester inside me all day till the dress, and then did the sucker in?"

"You don't like that theory?"

"Why would I do that?"

"Well, there's a wrinkle."

"Oh?"

"Yeah. This Captain Kirk. He was prompting you from offstage. Next to Goobie Wheatly. Sitting there in that folding chair."

"Yeah. So?"

"He's there in Act Three, Goobie Wheatly doesn't die."

"Son of a bitch!"

He put up his hands. "Hey, I'm not trying to load you up with guilt. But that's the situation. The only reason Goobie Wheatly *could* be killed in Act Three was because he was alone. Because there was no prompter there."

"You're saying I got rid of Captain Kirk so I'd have a clear shot at Goobie Wheatly?"

"That's the wrinkle."

"Yeah, but, Jesus Christ."

"What's the problem?"

"I killed Goobie Wheatly for publicly humiliating me. To do so I had to get rid of the prompter. But getting rid of the prompter is the thing he publicly humiliates me for. See what I mean? It's out of order. When I gave myself the opportunity, I had no motive. So I had no motive to give myself the opportunity."

"There's no reason to get upset."

"Oh, no? You're sitting here accusing me of murder."

"No such thing. We're merely evaluating possibilities."

"But they all come back to me."

"Funny about that."

I opened my mouth to protest, but he put up his hand.

"Please. Let's not have a childish argument. These things come up and they have to be discussed. That doesn't mean I think you did it."

"Thanks for your support."

"I'm merely telling you how it is. To give you a chance to help yourself while you're helping me."

"What do you mean?"

"Well, if you could come up with anything conclusive that could prove you *didn't* do it, it would be a big help to both of us."

I looked at him. "How the hell could I do that?"

"I don't know. Maybe if you saw or heard something. Anything that might help. Of course, I don't have the medical report yet. Once I get that, pin down the time of death, we'll be in a lot better shape."

He jerked his thumb at the notebook on the makeup counter. "Anyway, I got a lot of statements to go over. A lot of stories I want to check with you. But not tonight. And not tomorrow, either. Herbie needs you to rehearse the show. So for now, let's just hit the high spots. When was the last time you saw Goobie Wheatly alive?"

I exhaled, shook my head. "I've been trying to think, and you know, it's tough. I know he was alive at the beginning of Act Three."

"You saw him?"

"No, I didn't. I heard him, but I didn't see him. I was sitting on the top step of the stage-right stairs, cramming my lines. I heard him call, "Places, please." I put down the script where I told you before and went out onstage. I'm seated at the desk when the curtain goes up. Now I know he was alive when I walked out on the set. And I know he was alive when the curtain went up."

"How do you know that?"

"Because it went up. That was him. He pulled it."

"Anyone could have pulled the curtain up."

"Yeah, but the lights went up too. Ridley wouldn't have brought 'em up unless Goobie said, 'Go.' "

"Over the headset?"

"Yes."

"A murderer couldn't have picked up the headset, whispered 'Go'?"

"Yes, he could, but it's a moot point. You'll recall he'd taken over the prompting—my motive for the killing, right? Well, he was prompting, I'm shaky on my lines, and he must have prompted me three or four times during the act."

Chief Bob nodded. "Yes. Now we're coming to it. That fact is testified to by almost all of the witnesses. You were prompted several times during the act. Now, can you swear it was Goobie Wheatly feeding you the lines?"

I hesitated. "Let me be very careful here. Swear to it? I don't know. But just between you and me, I'm sure it was. Prompters are very different, they all have different styles. Now, what I heard each time was just a few whispered words—not enough for a voice ID—but I'd gotten used to Goobie's style, and I'm sure it was him."

"Could someone imitate him?"

"Maybe, but I don't think so. It would be easier to imitate his voice than to imitate his style of prompting. As a prompter he was very good. I don't know many prompters who *are* that good. To pass for him while prompting that well—I can't imagine anyone doing that. For my money, it was him."

"Then I'm sure it was. I value your statement. For my money, an opinion like that's more likely to be right than some schmuck says, 'Oh yeah, had to be Goobie, no doubt about it.' A jury may not feel that way, but I sure do. So let's take it for granted it was Goobie giving you the lines.

"Okay, let's talk this through. As I understand it, when Act Three begins you're onstage. You have a scene with everybody, they all exit except you and the young girl. That's Margie, right?"

"Right."

"You play a long scene with her, then the other girl enters." He consulted his notes. "That's Nellie Knight?"

"I believe so."

"You're not sure?"

"I'm just learning this, remember?"

"Indeed I do. But according to my notes, that's what happens. Of course, we can always check the script. But that's not important now. All right, she enters, gives you a letter. You read it and exit. Then Margie exits, and she plays a scene with the other servant. Then the other guy, this TV actor, enters, plays a scene with her. The other guy went out when he came in. At the end of that scene you come in as she goes out. You start off playing a scene with the TV guy. More and more people keep entering after that, one at a time—we don't have to sort it out now, but they do—and that takes us right up to the end of the act." He stopped, looked at me. "Is that right?"

"I think so."

"So you're onstage for two long stretches in Act Three. At the beginning of the act and at the end. In the middle you're offstage."

"That's right."

"You come offstage in the middle of the act, you didn't see Goobie Wheatly?"

"No, I didn't. He's downstage right, the door is upstage right. If he'd been at his lectern, I'd have seen him. But he was sitting in the folding chair with the prompt script."

"Exactly," Chief Bob said. "That's the whole problem. The chair was behind a masking flat. At least from your point of view. Actually it was in front of it. Downstage of it, I mean. Anyway, the point is, with him sitting there, you couldn't see him from the door. Or from the top of the stairs. Or anywhere else in the wings, for that matter. The only way you could see him was if you walked all the way downstage to the lectern and looked around the corner of the flat. And given Goobie's personality, who would do that? He wasn't exactly the type of guy you'd go and schmooze with."

"No kidding."

"Which is too bad. Anyone else, with so many actors going in and out, *someone* would have seen him. It bein' Goobie, no one did."

"Shit."

"Yeah. So, anyway, you came offstage, didn't see Goobie, and what did you do?"

"I came out of the door, went right to the stairwell to get my script. I'd been blowing lines right and left and wanted to cram for the end of the act."

"Which you did?"

"That's right."

"Until just before your cue?"

"*Until* my cue. I was actually sitting there and heard it. I throw down the book, jump up and hurry in."

"So you went onstage then, were onstage for the rest of the act, came off and found Goobie Wheatly dead?"

"That's right."

"Did he prompt you?"

I sighed, shook my head. "I saw where this was going, and I've been waiting for you to ask."

"What's the answer?"

"I don't think so. I know he prompted me a lot in Act Three. But the only lines I can remember him prompting me were in the beginning."

Chief Bob nodded. "That's right. I can't find *anyone* who remembers you being prompted at the end of the act."

"Damn."

"Yeah. It would be nice. Real nice. If you'd been prompted, I mean. Particularly if we could pinpoint the line. Because, as I said, after your entrance the actors came onstage one at a time, and with the exception of this servant—what's his name? Nicola—except for him they all stay onstage until the end of the act. And they're all standing out there when you find the body. So anyone who was onstage when you got your last prompt couldn't have done it."

"Shit."

"Right. If and only if you were prompted at the end of the act. And I can't find anyone who thinks you were."

"That's bad."

"Actually, it's worse."

"What do you mean?"

"It's not just that you didn't get a prompt. According to the other actors, there were times you might have *needed* a prompt, but instead you ad-libbed, paraphrased your lines, and managed to get through without it."

"Of course. Because that's what I'll have to do in performance. I won't be letter-perfect. I'll say the lines the best I can."

"Of course. But the fact is, that's what you did tonight. You paraphrased, invented, covered, whatever you want to call it. You did everything in your power to make sure you wouldn't need a prompt. Which you would have had to do if you knew Goobie Wheatly *couldn't* prompt you, because you knew Goobie Wheatly was dead."

"Oh, come on."

"Hey, I'm not saying you did that, I'm just telling you how it looks."

"That's how it looks to you?"

He put up his hand. "Let's not get hung up on semantics, shall we? I'd like very much to clear you of this crime. So we can get on to what *really* happened. I bring all these things up so you know what people are saying and people are thinking. Would you prefer it if I kept all this from you and investigated you in secret?"

"Of course not."

"Well, there you are. So stop griping and getting all offended when I mention how you could have done it. That's part of my job. You're a detective, you ought to know that."

"I'm not that kind of detective."

"You're a college graduate. Went to school with Herbie, right? You can think. You can reason. So think and reason. Help me out here. It's late, we're tired, we can get through this a lot faster if you don't fly off the handle and get defensive all the time."

"Fine," I said. "Here I am, sitting here, not taking it personally when you suspect me of murder. What can I do for you next?"

Chief Bob smiled. "That's more like it. That's the attitude

that will get you through this. What can you do for me? One thing in particular. You say you can't recall Goobie Wheatly prompting you in the last half of the act. The next time you sit down and go over your script, I want you to look at Act Three real careful and I want you to remember the last line Goobie Wheatly *did* prompt you on. If you're right, it's in the first part of the act, before you go offstage for the long break in the middle. But whenever it was, I'd like to know that line. Can you recall it offhand?"

"Not right now."

"I didn't think so. But later, when you go over the script, try to recall which line it was. Neat assignment, huh? Try to remember what you forgot. Maybe you can do it, maybe not. But try to remember all the lines in Act Three he prompted you on. Every one helps, and the later the better. We can pin down the last time this guy was alive."

"Didn't *anyone* see him after Act Three started?"

Chief Bob shook his head. "No. A lot of actors saw him during the break. And of course the set crew."

"Set crew?"

He looked at me. "You really *were* in your own little world, weren't you? Between Act Two and Act Three is a set change, right? It didn't happen by itself, magically, while you sat there reading your script. A set crew of four apprentices made the change. Goobie Wheatly supervised. And they all saw him, cause he was right there holding the clock. The intermission's ten minutes, they were running the change at speed to see if they could get it done. According to the kids on the crew, they came in under eight minutes. That didn't please Goobie none, since he was shooting for five." He shook his head. "I'm amazed you didn't see them with all that activity going on."

"I was aware of it, but not aware of it, you know. I was into my lines. Were these kids backstage when the act started?"

"No. Tough luck there. Since it was just dress rehearsal they let 'em watch the show. They were out in the audience till just before the set change at the end of Act Two. Actually, your entrance onstage was their cue to go backstage and take their places. When you came on, the four of them got up, went out the back doors to the lobby, then downstairs and through the greenroom to the stage. Two of them went up the stage-right stairs and two of them went up the stage-left stairs, and they were there waiting in the wings when the curtain went down."

"Which is when I grabbed my book and went to sit on the top stair."

"Right. And went over your lines while the kids changed the set. When they finished, Goobie bawled them out for being too slow and they went back downstairs—must have walked right past you on the step—and were back in the audience when the curtain went up. No help there. But they are, to the best we can determine, the last people to have seen Goobie Wheatly alive."

I sighed. "Oh, good lord."

"Exactly. So you see how important these lines become."

"I'll try to remember."

"Do that. I got a lot more stuff for you to go over, but for now, concentrate on that. Because that's what you'll be doing anyway, learning your lines. So concentrate on the show. Open the thing tomorrow and let me take a look. With luck, maybe I'll have cracked the case by then. But if not, come Saturday, the show's open, you got no rehearsals and we got some time, we'll sit down and go over it. Okay. Let's call it a night."

We rounded up Herbie, locked up the theater, Chief Bob took off and Herbie drove me home.

We didn't talk much on the way. It was late, we were tired, and there wasn't much left to say.

But I couldn't help thinking, of all the witnesses Chief Bob had questioned tonight, Herbie included, just how many of them actually thought I'd done it.

✩ 16 ✩

FRIDAY WAS ROUGH. WE HAD A TEN O'CLOCK REHEARSAL, which meant once again I was operating on insufficient sleep. Really insufficient. Herbie actually had to come and wake me up. Ten-fifteen he's knocking on my door, wondering where the hell I was. I was sound asleep, thank you, and not at all happy to go to rehearsal. But I rolled out of bed, splashed water on my face—after a trip down the hall, of course, not having running water in my room—pulled on my clothes and let Herbie lead me out to the car.

When we got to the theater I was still barely conscious. Herbie poured a good deal of coffee down my throat—terribly bad and probably whipped up in the costume room by Mary Anne—and managed to get me through rehearsal.

You think I was shaky on my lines? Good guess. And I didn't have Goobie Wheatly to feed 'em to me anymore. They did not, praise the lord, reassign Captain Kirk—I don't know how I would have dealt with that. But what's-his-name, the tech director, lighting and set designer, who was now functioning as stage manager, had inherited the prompting job as well.

He was not good. He was not as bad as Captain Kirk, of course—that would be hard to imagine—but after Goobie

Wheatly, *anyone* would seem bad. Since he *was* bad, he seemed terrible.

At first this threw me, but after a while it had the opposite effect. Knowing I was going to be prompted in a heavy-handed and obvious style that would destroy the pace of the scene, I took care not to let that happen. As the caffeine kicked in, I found myself more and more on my toes, tap-dancing away from the offending prompts.

Not that I was always successful. Sometimes I'd ad-lib myself into a corner from which there was no getting out and be forced to call "line." But often as not I'd escape and carry on.

When lunchtime rolled around the actors all broke and went out. All except for me. I didn't because Amanda Feinstein brought in a cheeseburger and a Coke so I'd be able to stay in and go over my lines. I suppose this was thoughtful, but I must say by this point I was beginning to feel like a social leper, and I would have just as soon said screw it and gone out.

I don't know if it was because he sensed this, or if it was entirely coincidental, but Herbie happened to assign the most attractive apprentice in the theater to stick around and cue me. I don't know how I missed her before—though being desperate about my part and getting mixed up in a murder might have had something to do with it. But the girl was gorgeous. Being an apprentice, she probably wasn't more than twenty, which made me old enough to be her father, and what a disturbing thought that was. She was a baby-faced blonde with large breasts, long legs and a derriere to die for. That last sounds like a book title, if I ever got back to writing. Anyway, she was dressed in cutoff shorts and a cutoff tank top, the type that stops at the bottom of the breasts and leaves the midriff bare. On a girl with breasts that large the effect was quite something—head-turning if not mind-boggling. All I know is, while having Nellie Knight as a dressing-room partner was pleasant, had this girl been in there pulling the topless routine they'd have had to scrape me off the ceiling.

At any rate, Beth—as I later found out her name was—made being left behind for lunch bearable.

Toward the end of the break I excused myself and called Alice, who was understandably shocked. I hadn't been able to call her last night, and this morning I'd been unceremoniously yanked out of bed and dragged to rehearsal, so that was the first she'd heard of Goobie Wheatly's death. A somewhat difficult concept not knowing who Goobie Wheatly was. I reminded her of the Captain Kirk incident, but played that down as my motive for the murder. Still, Alice offered to arrange a sleepover for Tommie so she could come up.

I talked her out of it. In the first place, I was so wrapped up in opening the show I wouldn't have time to see her. In the second place, I was so nervous about my performance I didn't want the added pressure of knowing she was out there in the audience.

Alice wasn't happy about it, but she finally agreed to hold off and come up later, once the show was running.

While I was still on the phone the other actors started dribbling in. Then Herbie showed up and I had to get off and get back to rehearsal.

Believe it or not, being cued by Beth—every man's secret-fantasy apprentice—had not substantially improved my mastery over my lines. However, dealing with what's-his-name tech-director-new-stage-manager sure did. I kept ahead of him as best I could and somehow limped through the afternoon.

When we broke for dinner I would have objected to a brought-in sandwich, any incredibly endowed prompters notwithstanding, but that had never been intended. Instead, Herbie and Amanda took me out.

It was a small, quiet restaurant in the village, though it occurred to me in that town *any* restaurant would have been small and quiet. We sat down at a table, a waiter appeared and we ordered drinks—a martini for Amanda, a Scotch for Herbie and a diet Coke for me. When it arrived Herbie lifted his glass, said, "Cheers," then took a sip as if he needed it.

He grimaced as the whiskey went down, then smiled, said, "Well, this is it. Another openin', another show."

"Yeah," I said. I pulled out my script. "Maybe I should be working lines."

Herbie waved his hand. "Ah, take it easy. You know 'em as well as you're gonna. The opening is inevitable—there's nothing to do but relax and enjoy it."

"That's an obnoxious, sexist remark," Amanda said.

Herbie shrugged. "Yeah. Isn't everything?"

"That's for sure," Amanda said.

She smiled, and it suddenly occurred to me the two of them actually liked each other.

I wondered what Amanda thought of Margie-poo.

The least of my worries.

I took a sip of Coke, put the glass down. "Can I ask you something?" I said.

Herbie and Amanda looked at me. I hadn't directed the question at either of them in particular.

"What's that?" Amanda said.

"Who do *you* think killed Goobie Wheatly?"

Amanda and Herbie looked at each other, then back at me.

Amanda pursed her lips. "You want an honest answer?" she said.

"Of course."

She shrugged. "Then the answer is, Who gives a shit? I'm sorry, but I'm a producer and I've got a show to put on." She looked at me. "So do you."

"I know it."

"I know you do. So let's concentrate on that."

Amanda took her martini glass, held it up and looked at Herbie. "Come on, Herbie. A toast for the gentleman. He's opening tonight."

Herbie picked up his glass and clinked it against Amanda's. They smiled, turned to me and said it together.

"Break a leg."

☆ **17** ☆

I WAS GOOD!

Don't get me wrong. I am by no means a great actor. I can't do accents and character parts at will the way some actors can. If cast in a role like that, it takes me a month to work my way into it. And I find myself talking like that all day long—at home, at work, or whatever. I can't go in and out of different characters the way stand-up comedians can.

But my timing is good, I project sympathetically, and in a relatively straight role like Captain Bluntschli I can hold my own perfectly well.

And I did.

And they liked me.

I should start from the beginning. Half hour, I'm in the dressing room. Putting on costume. Putting on makeup.

Having a nervous breakdown.

Stage fright?

You bet.

Butterflies?

Just count them.

I was having trouble with my makeup. My hands weren't shaking, I was just so insecure I was sure I was putting it on wrong. I wasn't, of course, it was all in my head. At least that's what I told myself. Only trouble was, I didn't believe me. I just knew I was going to fuck up my makeup and have to start over. As a result I'd be late and miss curtain. And I swear to god, it actually occurred to me I was damn lucky Goobie Wheatly wouldn't be there to bawl me out.

Of course none of that happened. My makeup went on just fine. But I think a pretty good indication of my state of mind would be that, while I was doing this, my roommate Nellie Knight was putting on her makeup too and I barely noticed her at all.

Barely.

At any rate, I was all dressed and ready when whatever-the-fuck-his-name-was called, "five minutes"—I'm starting to curse a lot, I must be really nervous. I was out in the greenroom when he called, "Places, please."

I had my script in my hand. No, I wasn't going to take it onstage, I just wanted to hold it. Like Linus's security blanket. I probably wasn't even going to look at it. I just wanted to know where it was.

I went up the stage-right stairs, took my place in the wings. I was all alone. The door to Raina's bedroom was stage left, so she, Nellie Knight and the woman playing Catherine had gone up the other stairs.

I stopped at the top of the stairs, took a big breath, exhaled. I took my script, stuffed it where I always had on the shelf over the stairwell. I stepped away from it, a conscious action, then stood there with my arms slightly out, as if free-falling. Then I turned and looked around.

The work lights were on, so I could see everything backstage perfectly. I took a few steps downstage so I could look around the masking flat and see the lectern and prompt script where the stage manager would stand. It occurred to me I'd better learn his damn name. Along with half the cast.

Along with half my lines.

That brought a rush of fear.

So did the murmur of many voices. I'd heard it of course when I'd first come up the stairs, and I'd been ignoring it. But now it was as if the rush of fear at the flash of not knowing my lines had opened the floodgates, let it in. The cacophonous mumble of many voices.

There's an audience out there!

I took a breath, tried to calm down. I could feel my heart beating very fast. But my eyes were wide with wonder. And I felt myself drawn downstage. Inexorably, as if pulled by a magnet, I felt myself walking. Downstage. To the lectern. And beyond.

To the curtain.

And the gap.

The gap between the curtain and the proscenium arch.

That's right. I confess. Confess to the most amateurish of all possible moves an actor can make.

Peeking out at the audience from behind the curtain.

Holy shit.

The theater was packed. From that angle I couldn't see all the way to the back, but every seat I saw was filled. And the noise from this far downstage was deafening. A huge lively crowd.

Good lord.

I was still looking when he tapped me on the shoulder. The what's-his-name tech director, etc., etc.

"Yeah, I know," I said sheepishly. "I shouldn't be doing that."

He smiled good-naturedly. "I don't give a shit, but places please."

I went back upstage to the masking flat. As I did I saw that he had gone out onstage to check on the actors on stage left. Then he came back offstage and switched the work lights off. He put on the headset; his voice was slightly louder than Goobie's, so I could hear the words, "Stand by, cue one." He took ahold of the curtain rope and, "Cue one, go!"

The curtain and lights went up.

I felt a huge rush of adrenaline, even though it was five minutes or so before I had to go onstage.

They were the toughest five minutes of my life.

As I've said, the opening scenes are not particularly

funny. They did not in fact get a single laugh. But there was an audience out there, ready to laugh, ready to go with the show, ready to like it. I could feel the presence. Expectant. That was the feeling in the air. One of expectation. The audience was waiting for something.

And I was it.

And suddenly it was upon me. Bingo, lights out, alarms, offstage shots, and yours truly strides out from the wings and trips over something in the dark that shouldn't have been there and falls flat on his face.

The audience couldn't see me. It was dark to begin with, and I hadn't cleared the window frame yet. But they could hear the crash. Well, no matter, a crash is right in keeping with the scene. But it sure as hell jumbled my wits.

What there was left of them.

I scrambled to my feet, wondering if I'd blown my cue, which of course I hadn't. I couldn't. Raina was alone onstage, shrinking from the noise and hiding, and nothing could possibly happen until I came in.

Which I did. I clambered through the window. My knee hurt from where I'd fallen on it, but that was the least of my worries. I had a sudden panic attack that when I'd fallen I'd lost my gun. I hadn't of course, it was right in my hand. I came through the window crouching, wheeled around on Raina and delivered my first line, "Shh. Don't call out or you'll be shot!"

And suddenly I was fine.

Which was again perfectly understandable. The anticipation was far more terrifying than the deed. Now that I was doing it, it felt absolutely right. Of course it helped that the first scene called for nervousness, high tension and anxiety. Hey, no problem. Just tap those emotions, they're there.

The first scene played like gang busters. And I could feel the audience warming toward me. And then when the soldiers came to search the house, and Raina relents and hides me from them, I could feel them going with it. And afterwards, when she gives me back my pistol and says ironically, "Pray take it to defend yourself against me," and I smile and tell her it's not loaded, cartridges are no use in battle, I always carry chocolates instead—I knew they were mine.

But what really sold them was the cavalry charge.

When Raina finds out I was routed in the cavalry charge, she of course wants to hear all about it. I tell her a cavalry charge is like throwing a handful of peas against a window—first one comes, then two or three close behind him, then all the rest in a clump. With her eyes shining with thoughts of her hero Sergius, she says, "Yes. First one. The bravest of the brave." My line, said prosaically, is, "Hm. You should see the poor devil pulling at his horse."

The audience roared.

Now, I know the credit belongs to George Bernard Shaw, not me. But the fact is, I got it. And there's nothing that compares to that immediate response of an audience to an actor's line.

I can't tell you what that meant to me. That first laugh. That first stamp of approval.

After years and years and years.

I had 'em, and I wasn't gonna let 'em go.

I played the hell out of that act.

Before I knew it, it was over and Raina was gone off to fetch her mother and I was left onstage to do my monologue. I did it slowly, easily, naturally and with complete confidence, not to mention a few small but welcome laughs, and tumbled blissfully into bed. Raina and Catherine reentered, found me there and the lights and curtain went down.

To thunderous applause.

Son of a bitch.

I did it.

Son of a bitch.

I really had.

So far.

One down and two to go.

☆ **18** ☆

ACT TWO STUNK.

I know that's horrible for me to say, since I'm not in Act Two till the very end. That's like saying Act Two stunk because I wasn't in it. And what a horribly self-centered, egotistical, conceited thing that would be. But it really was bad. And it wasn't bad because I wasn't in it so much as because Avery Allington was.

As much as Bluntschli carries Act One, Sergius has to carry Act Two. And Avery Allington couldn't carry my luggage. I mean, he'd been bad in rehearsal, but in performance he *stunk*. It was as if seeing me get laughs in Act One had blown every fuse in his nervous system. The guy came onstage this hyper mass of nervous energy, not to be believed. He rolled his eyes, he rolled his voice, he postured, he posed. He strutted, he strode. All in an outrageous, outlandish, overblown performance that wasn't believable for a second.

Yes, as in the dress rehearsal, he got laughs, but once again, they weren't genuine laughs. They were at best nervous, embarrassed laughs. And I hate to say this, but when I made my entrance at the end of the act, I really felt like I'd come back to save the show.

Which brings us to Act Three.

The dreaded Act Three.

When I took my place onstage at the beginning, I couldn't help thinking, I couldn't get it out of my mind: *This is when it happened. This is when Goobie Wheatly died.*

I knew Chief Bob was in the audience. He'd be watching, in case there was a clue hidden in the act. It wasn't up to me to look. I had other things to worry about and didn't have the time. But I couldn't help thinking, all the same.

But when the curtain rose and the lights came up I took charge. I was Captain Bluntschli, smooth, cool, efficient, back to put everything in order. Quick as a wink I straightened everything out, and before you know it, all the other actors were offstage and Raina and I were playing the scene.

And I hadn't been prompted yet.

The scene with Raina went well, got laughs, and I knew I had the audience back again. Before you knew it, it was over and I was out the door.

Again without a prompt.

I'm only human. The first thing I did when I got offstage was look to see that the stage manager was still sitting there.

Which he was.

I stood in the wings while Louka and Nicola did their scene. It was competent, but frankly dull.

Then Sergius and Louka did their scene. It wasn't dull, but it wasn't theater either. I don't really know what it was, but the show went right in the toilet again.

And suddenly that scene was over and suddenly it was my turn to come onstage and stick it to him.

Which I did. First I skewered him with the "I shall bring a machine gun" line, and the audience roared. Then Margie-poo entered and the three of us went at it and I kept zinging them and the audience kept roaring. Then everyone else entered, one at a time, and I kept firing off lines and the audience kept eating it up, and before you know it I'm delivering my last line, clicking my heels and walking offstage.

To thunderous applause.

Sergius still had his last line to say, but with all due apologies to Shaw, if I'd been the director I'd have cut it. Besides, Shaw might have felt different about it if he'd known Avery Allington.

As it was, I turned around and suffered with the audience through an excruciating line reading of, "What a man! Is he a man!" then watched the curtain fall, once again to thunderous applause.

It was the best of all possible worlds.

We'd gotten through the play.

The audience liked it.

And nobody died.

☆ **19** ☆

THE CAST PARTY WAS AT MORLEY'S, A BAR ON THE OUTSIDE of town. It wasn't *really* a cast party, I mean, nothing official, it's just that's where the actors went to hang out. The bar was a moderately nice place, with booths, tables, TV and pool table. It seemed to cater to the theater crowd. The actors were all there, as well as Herbie and Amanda and a few people who looked like trustees, and a few others who just looked like theatergoers, though which were which I couldn't tell you.

The apprentices were there too, occupying the booths and apparently trying to look old enough to drink. Half of them were having Cokes, but a few of them were having beers, and it appeared to me the Coke drinkers were occasionally sipping from the beer drinkers, and the bartender was doing his best not to notice.

The actors were congregated around the bar and the pool table. Herbie was buying a round for all of us, and Amanda was digging her elbow into his ribs and whispering something to him, probably that he *personally* was buying this round of drinks and not the theater.

Aside from that, good will was just bubbling out all over. I almost couldn't hate Avery Allington.

Almost.

The son of the bitch was at the bar, pontificating to anyone willing to listen about the theater in general and his niche in it in particular. His audience consisted of a couple of trustees, the actor playing Nicola, the actress playing Catherine and the actor playing Major Petkoff. In other words, all of those whose names I didn't know.

I suppose you could count me in his audience too, since I was at the bar close enough to hear, but I was really in Herbie and Amanda's group, which included a few trustees, Margie, and Nellie Knight.

In our group, it was Herbie who was holding forth. "Sold out," he said. It was not the first time he had said it, either. "We're sold out for tomorrow and we're sold out for Sunday."

One of the trustees, a well-fed type in a three-piece suit who made Herbie look positively slim, said, "Not surprising, really, with press like this."

He held up a folded-up newspaper he had been carrying under his arm.

Herbie didn't even look at it, just waved his hand. "A sellout's a sellout. Doesn't matter why they buy the tickets, just so they do."

I pointed at the paper. "What's that?"

The trustee looked at me as if I were from Mars. "You mean you didn't see?"

Herbie put his arm around my shoulders. "Hey, Stu, give the guy a break," he said. "Stanley's the fill-in. I guarantee you, the last two days he hasn't read anything but his script."

Stu the trustee said, "Oh, yeah? Two days? Is that right? Very nice job."

"Thank you," I said. "What is it I didn't read?"

Stu handed over the paper. I took it, unfolded it and looked.

It was the *Daily Sentinel*, evidently the local paper. The page-one headline was PLAYHOUSE MURDER. Underneath it were two pictures, one of Goobie Wheatly and one of the playhouse. The playhouse photo was obviously recent, since the sign on the side read *Arms and the Man*. The picture of Goobie Wheatly was obviously *not* recent, since it showed Goobie Wheatly alive.

"Yeah," Stu said. "Can't help selling out, publicity like that."

"We've sold out before," Amanda pointed out.

"Yeah, but never so quickly," Herbie said. "It's only Friday night, and the weekend's *already* sold out. We've never done that before. And you know what that means? People calling up tomorrow and Sunday looking for tickets aren't going to get 'em. They'll have to take weekday nights instead. Come Monday, Tuesday, you'll see."

I looked at Herbie and couldn't imagine what it was like to be a producer. Because, in spite of the murder, in spite of me filling into the show, in spite of everything, he was looking at the attendance figures of this show's run as a vindication of his theory of opening shows on Friday night. That was more than I could deal with at the moment.

So was the article.

It was long, taking up half of page one and then being continued on page fourteen. I was still riding a high coming off the show, and there was no way I could concentrate on reading it now. And not in front of all of them. But I sure wanted to read it.

"Where can I get a copy of this?" I said.

Stu waved his hand. "Keep it, please. It's from the office, I got another copy at home."

"Thanks a lot," I said.

I felt someone standing behind me, turned and found myself face to face with Beth, the dream-girl apprentice I'd met just that afternoon. She was evidently twenty-one, since she'd just bought a beer at the bar. Oddly enough, I found that thought somewhat disconcerting.

It also flustered me when she put her hand on my shoulder, gave me what seemed to be a very warm and genuine smile and said, "You were *great!*"

My ears must have turned red.

Believe me, I had not had a girl say that to me in an awfully long time. Certainly not a girl like that. I was dumbfounded, embarrassed and terribly self-conscious, and for a split second I was afraid I wouldn't even be able to croak out the words, "Thank you." Then I smiled and said smoothly, "Well, you taught me the lines."

She mugged at that and said, "Oh, sure, it was all my doing."

She smiled me a dazzling smile and walked off back toward the apprentice tables.

Hot damn.

I hate to say it, but that felt good. Really good.

And you know what else felt good? Avery Allington had been standing at the bar, and she hadn't told him *he* was great. But he was close enough to hear her tell me. And he was watching her now on her way back to her booth.

Oh boy, did that feel good.

I must have still been blushing pretty splendidly, because Herbie said, "Well, well, Stanley, you have an admirer."

That jerked me back to reality.

I don't think I would have minded that so much, coming from Amanda. But from him? All I could think of was, "Yeah, Herbie, screwing around with young women *is* on your agenda." Which took all the joy out of what I'd just been feeling.

Well, let's not go overboard. I was still high as a kite over the show. And it didn't hurt any when several of the trustees chimed in to second Beth's opinion of my performance. The momentary damper was just that, momentary, and in no time at all I was back in the stratosphere again.

So was Herbie. "I tell you," he said. "This show can't miss. Ticket sales are through the roof already. They *loved* it tonight, so word of mouth is going to be terrific. Plus we should get a dynamite review."

I blinked. Looked up. "Review?"

"Sure," Herbie said. "Be in tomorrow's *Sentinel*." For a second I saw a look of doubt, almost panic, cross his face.

"If he was there, for Christ's sake. Was the reviewer there?"

"Sure he was," Amanda said.

"Really?" Herbie said. "Anybody see him?"

"I saw him," Stu said. "Relax. Harvey was there."

Herbie exhaled. Grinned nervously. "Thank god for that. If he missed that performance, it would be a crime."

Crime.

Nice choice of words.

I'm a writer, albeit a failed one, so words fascinate me. Like the word *actor,* however you want to spell it. And now Herbie's use of the word *crime.*

I knew it meant nothing, just like the word *actor* didn't. But it set me off, started my mind going over the whole thing. On Goobie Wheatly's death. The seemingly pointless murder of a spiteful but otherwise harmless, elderly stage manager.

Crime, indeed.

Was it, like many of the crimes of New York City, a pointless, mindless crime?

No. Not backstage during a dress rehearsal. Someone wanted Goobie Wheatly dead. And if there was a reason, there was a way to find out why.

All of that excess baggage was tied up in the simple word *crime.*

But it wasn't that important to me.

I hate to admit it, but from the moment Herbie mentioned it, all I could think about was the review.

☆ 20 ☆

IT WASN'T IN THE MORNING PAPER.

When I pulled the *Daily Sentinel* out of the vending machine on the corner of Main Street at nine-thirty the next morning, I discovered the headline PLAYHOUSE MURDER.

Déjà vu?

Good god. My mouth dropped open.

Another one?

I'm not at my best in the morning; still, it didn't take me *that* long to realize there had *not* been another murder, what I was holding in my hands was another copy of yesterday's paper. Evidently today's paper wasn't out yet.

A woman passing by confirmed the fact the *Sentinel* was an afternoon paper and wouldn't be out for hours.

She also directed me to the police station.

Chief Bob had stopped by my dressing room right after the show to say, "Nice job," and to invite me to drop in at ten o'clock this morning to discuss the case.

I was happy for the praise and skeptical of the invitation. I suspected Chief Bob of being a postgraduate of the Columbo school of investigation—he had latched onto me as the most likely suspect and would therefore be constantly popping up to solicit my opinion of the crime, until such time as I either managed to incriminate myself or confessed. It occurred to me that, since I hadn't *committed* the crime, this could take quite a while.

Anyway, since the review wouldn't be out for hours, I set off to meet Chief Bob.

There was not, as I'd expected, anything quaint about the police station. It was a perfectly substantial, white stone building, granted not that large, but simple, functional, solid and somehow reassuring.

Inside I found the uniformed cop who couldn't spell *actor* sitting at a desk. He didn't have to ask who I was, just told me Chief Bob was waiting for me and pointed to a door in the back. I was on my way in before I realized he had actually said, "Chief Bob." It was the one light touch in an otherwise formal setting.

I went in and found Chief Bob sorting through a mound of papers piled up on his desk.

"I'm boiling it down," he said. "Too unwieldy. What am I going to do with this? Witness statements, evidence, everything concerning the case. I'm trying to make some order of it." He motioned me to a chair. "You can help."

"How?" I said, sitting down.

"I'll bounce ideas off you, you tell me right or wrong. Let me know if I got my facts jumbled up."

"You learn anything from seeing the play?" I asked.

He nodded. "Absolutely. I know who came in when in Act Three, and I know where they came in and where they went out. It's all in here," he said, pointing to the pile. "And in here." He pointed to his head. He indicated the papers, shook his head, chuckled. "I would think we got enough data here to figure *anything* out."

"Too bad you don't have a computer," I said.

It was a facetious remark, but Chief Bob took it seriously. "We do," he said. "Only I'd have to type all the data in, and once it was there, what would I do with it? There's no program for it, you see. Make a fortune if I could come up with one. What would you call it, *Cop Write?* No, too close to *copyright. Murder Write?* Too close to "Murder, She

Wrote." *Suspect Hunt*? Sounds like a Nintendo game. No, I'm afraid we have to do it the old-fashioned way, which is why I need your help."

I pointed to the pile of papers on the desk. "With that?"

He shook his head. "No. Let's start with something simpler." He picked up a book from his desk.

"What's that?" I said.

He held it up and I recognized the *Arms and the Man* script.

"Where'd you get that?" I said.

"Peter Constantine."

"Who?"

"The actor who plays the servant Nicola. You don't know his name?"

"I'm poor with names."

"Right," he said. He frowned, as if reevaluating his assessment of me as a private detective. "Anyway, it's his. I borrowed it from him because I needed one to study. And because I wanted to see what he'd written in it."

"And?" I said.

"And it's just as he said. Where he goes out, he's penciled in 'Exit DL.' I looked at it closely and I can't see any erasures. Frankly, I don't think there are any. He certainly exited down left last night. If that was any change from dress rehearsal, I'd think someone would have noticed.

"He also entered down left, by the way. Which is still a factor, since we haven't pinned down the last time Goobie Wheatly was alive."

"I think I can help you there," I said.

"I was hoping you could. What have you got?"

"I can remember for sure four times when he prompted me."

"All in the first half of the act?"

"Yeah."

"Damn."

"I know, but the facts are the facts. Want me to give you the lines?"

"Please."

We went over the lines I'd been prompted on, Chief Bob stopping to locate each one and mark it in the script.

"Okay," he said. "So the last one you know for sure is, 'It doesn't matter, I suppose it's only a photograph. How can he tell who it was intended for? Tell him he put it there himself.'"

"That's it."

"That is referring to the picture she left in the coat pocket, the one she wrote 'to her Chocolate Cream Soldier' on?"

"That's right."

"And are you sure it was Goobie Wheatly who gave you the line?"

"Pretty sure. Like I said, he has his own style. That's a long line, and he didn't just read it to me, like ninety-nine prompters out of a hundred would have. He threw a key phrase."

"Can you remember what?"

"Sure. He threw me 'doesn't matter.' And that's significant."

Chief Bob frowned. "Why?"

"The line begins. 'It doesn't matter.' He left off the word 'it.'"

"So what?"

"It was the right thing to do. The key words are 'doesn't matter.' The word 'it' is unnecessary. He throws, 'doesn't matter,' and I supply the 'it.' I come right in with, 'It doesn't matter.' Plus the word 'it' has a hard t sound. If he throws the three words, "It doesn't matter," there's much more chance the audience hears it than if he leaves the word 'it' out."

Chief Bob frowned. "You're kidding."

"Not at all. Plus, the word 'it' tells me nothing, so when I hear it I don't start my line. I can't till I hear the words 'doesn't matter.' So, aside from being heard, the word 'it' actually creates a hole in the dialogue."

"My word."

"I know, but it's true."

"How could Goobie think all that out? I mean, in time to do it?"

"He couldn't, of course. I had all night to think about it and analyze it and that's what I came up with. And I think it's right. As a prompter, Goobie was instinctively brilliant. I think he did everything I just told you absolutely correctly out of instinct. I don't think anyone could have possibly duplicated that, and that's why I'm sure it was him."

I can't say Chief Bob looked terribly convinced. But at least for the time being he seemed willing to concede the point.

"All right," he said. "Say that was Goobie Wheatly. Could he have prompted you at any time after that?"

"He could, but I don't think so. I go out a page later. I've looked at every line after that, and I think I knew them all. I certainly don't remember getting stuck on any of them."

"Then you probably didn't." Chief Bob referred to the script. "So, the last line he gave you was when just you and Margie were onstage?"

"That's right."

"You exit a page later, but not before the entrance of . . ." He ran his finger down a page in the script. ". . . Louka. Nellie Knight."

"Right. She comes in bringing me a letter. I read it and exit."

"Exactly. Leaving the two women onstage. They play a short scene, then Margie exits. Stage right, like you." He looked at me. "You didn't see her?"

I frowned, thought a moment. "It's possible, I just don't remember. I'm sitting on the top step, facing away from the stage, going over my lines. It's possible she went by me and down the stairs. That would make sense, because she's off for quite a while; she could want to go back to her dressing room."

"But you don't recall if she did?"

"I'm not sure."

"If she *had* gone down the stairs, would you remember her coming back up?"

"I don't, but I wouldn't necessarily, because I go onstage before her. So I could have gone onstage before she came back up."

"But you're not sure?"

"No."

"Too bad."

"I'm giving it to you the best I can."

"I understand that. Why should you remember? You were concerned with your lines, and it wasn't important. How were you to know someone was going to wind up dead?" He shrugged. "Still . . ."

"Yeah, I know," I said. "It would be nice."

"Well, let's get on with it," he said. "Whatever you *do* remember helps. So Margie came off stage right and either did or did not go downstairs. If she didn't, that leaves her in the stage-right wings to kill Goobie Wheatly."

"Why? Why would she do that?"

"Why would *anyone* do that? The fact is, somebody did. Right now we're not doing motive, we're doing opportunity. If she didn't go downstairs, she's in the wings, she had the opportunity. Okay, that's her. Let's see what happened next. Onstage, Louka is playing a scene with Nicola. That's Nellie Knight and Peter Constantine. Peter entered down left, by the way, penciled into his script nice and proper.

"Anyway, they play the scene until they're interrupted by the entrance of Sergius Saranoff—Avery Allington—who comes in from up right." He cocked his head at me. "Did you happen to see *him?*"

"I don't remember," I said. "I saw him in performance, but in dress rehearsal . . . again, I'm sitting there on the stairs reading my lines."

"Well, did he come up the stairs and walk by you?"

"I have no recollection. It's entirely possible. Any number of people could have come up the stairs and walked by me and I wouldn't have even known it. In Avery Allington's case, I have no recollection whatever."

"Which is too bad. But, he *did* enter from up right. Which

means at some point in time he was in the stage-right wings."

"Obviously."

"It would be nice if we could establish how long he was there."

I took a breath. "You're making me feel like I'm not doing my job. Maybe I'm not. But I'm doing the best I can, and believe me it isn't easy."

Chief Bob held up his hand. "Hey, I never said it was. Believe me, no one's blaming you. And I'm certainly not drawing any inferences from your lack of knowledge. You know, like you *would* know who'd gone up and down the stairs if you'd actually been sitting there and weren't downstage killing Goobie Wheatly with a switchblade knife at the time. You don't hear me saying that."

"I just did."

"Certainly not. I was just telling you what I'm *not* saying. No reason to take offense at that. Now, then, where were we? Ah, yes. Avery Allington enters the stage. From upstage right, presumably after having an opportunity, though we do not know how long, of having killed Goobie Wheatly first. He comes onstage and finds both the servants, Louka and Nicola. Nicola exits one line later. Again, down left.

"Now then, Avery Allington and Nellie Knight play that scene until your entrance. As I recall, you claim you're sitting there on the stairs going over your script and you hear your cue line. You spring up and run onstage. Is that right?"

"That's what happened."

"Up until your entrance you were sitting at the top of the stairs?"

"That's right."

"Because of the window in the set, looking out over the garden, there is no crossover from stage left to stage right in Act Three, is there?"

"No, of course not. The audience can see all the way back to the cyc."

"So anybody exiting stage left who wanted to get to stage

right would have to go down the stairs, through the green-room and up the stage-right stairs, is that right?"

"Yes, of course."

"So this Peter Constantine, who keeps coming on and off stage left, for him to have killed Goobie Wheatly he would have had to go downstairs through the basement and up the stage-right stairs, presumably passing you at the top."

"That's right."

"Unless he waited till your entrance. See what I mean?" Chief Bob said. "He could have gone down the stage-left stairs, through the greenroom to the stage-right stairs and waited at the bottom for you to get up and go onstage. Then he could have crept up the stairs, killed Goobie Wheatly and gone back down the stairs the way he came."

"Yes," I said. "Except . . ."

Chief Bob actually clapped his hands together, a big smile on his face. "Yes, yes," he said. "Except for Louka. Miss Nellie Knight. Who exits upstage right immediately after your entrance. If Peter Constantine had come up the stage-right stairs he'd have run into her. And since he wasn't supposed to be there, since his entrances were all from the other side of the stage, his presence would be unusual enough to make her wonder. Or at least to remember it. Which, according to her statement, she doesn't."

"Unless they were in it together," I said.

Chief Bob put up his hands. "Oh, please," he said. "Do not let this be an Agatha Christie plot where *everyone* in the cast had a reason for hating the man and they *all* did it."

"No chance of that," I said dryly.

"Oh, present company excluded, of course," he said. "Anyway, let's hold any conspiracy theories in abeyance. For now, take it that Nellie Knight's presence inhibits Peter Constantine's opportunities for murder. So where does that leave us?"

"I'm onstage with Avery Allington, to be joined shortly by Margie. Followed by Nellie Knight. Then Major Petkoff. Then the woman playing Catherine. Then what's-his-name, Peter Constantine. All except him entering up right. And, aside from him, they all stay onstage until the end of the act."

"Except for you, of course."

"Right."

"And since you were not prompted during that time, there is no one who can testify that Goobie Wheatly was alive."

"What about Ridley?"

"Huh?"

"Ridley. The electrician. The apprentice running lights."

"What about him?"

"Goobie Wheatly was on the headset. So was Ridley. So anything he said, anything that happened, Ridley should have heard. I mean, hell, Ridley should have heard him being killed."

Chief Bob nodded. "Yeah, but he didn't."

"Why not?"

Chief Bob cocked his head at me. "You know what a six-cue show is?"

As it happened, I did. "Sure," I said. "A show with no light cues. Just up at the beginning of the act and down at the end. Most shows are three acts, so that makes six cues."

"Right," Chief Bob said. "Now *Arms and the Man* isn't. Act One's at night and there's a lot of cues, lights on, lights off, striking a match, candles and all that. But Acts Two and Three are just up and down. There's no internal cues. So Act Three, after he turns the lights on, this apprentice's got nothing to do till the end of the act, so he takes off his headset."

"Shit."

"Yeah. Now he doesn't say he takes his headset off, I just conclude he does. From seeing what kind of kid he is, and from the fact he claims he heard nothing. Nothing at all. And if he'd been wearing his headset, he'd have heard Goobie Wheatly prompt you."

"Yeah, unless Goobie Wheatly took *his* headset off."

"He was found with it on."

"True."

"Which looks like he was wearing it the whole time.

Unless he had just put it on because it was the end of the act."

"I don't think I like that theory."

"I didn't think you would. Anyway, if he was wearing his headset and this kid Ridley didn't hear you being prompted, then he wasn't wearing his."

"Makes sense."

"Anyway, there we are. So we got a schedule to pin down. We know the last time Goobie Wheatly was alive. From your line, 'doesn't matter.' From that point on, we know who came and went till the end of the act. Somewhere in there, someone killed him." Chief Bob shrugged. "We just gotta figure out who."

I sighed. "Yeah."

"So," he said. "You got any insights to offer?"

"I don't know. Can I ask you something?"

"Of course."

I jerked my thumb. "The officer at the desk. What's his name?"

"Felix."

"Right. Felix. The night of the murder he came out and told you about the crime scene. You remember? He said we had a stabbing with the murder weapon in place and the actor was not on the scene?"

"Yeah. So?"

"Funny choice of words. In a play, you know. The word *actor*, I mean. So I asked him why he said *actor*, and he said that's what cops said when it wasn't a shooting. Call the guy the *actor*. So I asked him how he spelled it, he said a-c-t-e-r."

Chief Bob did not seem inclined to comment, but when I paused and waited for a reaction, he said, "So he's not a Harvard man. So what?"

"Do cops really do that? Call the guy the *actor*?"

"I suppose we do."

"How do you spell it? If you had to type up a report, I mean. How would you spell *actor*?"

Chief Bob looked at me a moment. "I don't know that

I've ever done that. If I did, I would spell it a-c-t-o-r. Just like you would. What's your point?"

I had none. I just wanted to know. It had been driving me crazy ever since I heard it. It was a confusion of cause and effect. Somehow I had the crazy idea that if I could unlock the riddle contained in that statement, if I could figure out how cops really spelled *actor,* that I could solve the crime.

Rationally, I knew that didn't make sense. I still couldn't help asking.

I tried to explain this to Chief Bob, but I think all I did was elevate myself five or six notches on his suspect list. He certainly seemed to be favoring me with a look one usually reserved for the criminally insane.

"That's very interesting," he said. "And not to pooh-pooh that particular idea, but do you have anything *else* you'd care to ask me?"

"Actually, yes."

"What's that? How do you spell *cop*?"

"No. When does the paper come out?"

☆ **21** ☆

IT WAS STILL ON THE FRONT PAGE. BUT THE HEADLINE TODAY WAS NO LEADS IN PLAYHOUSE MURDER.

I wouldn't want you to think me hardhearted, but I'd had enough with Goobie Wheatly's death. I didn't read the front-page story. I turned to the back for the review.

It's hard to explain. If you've ever been an actor, you'll understand, but if not, I don't know if I can really get across how I felt.

The thing is, dreams die hard. And they come in all shapes and sizes. They're not all winning the Academy Award. For instance, one of my dreams has always been becoming a successful enough actor to get on the Johnny Carson show, so I could ask him if he really did a Carnac joke I once heard attributed to him but could never quite believe he'd actually done on the air. Carnac, if you'll recall, is the bit where Johnny wears a turban and is the sage, seer and soothsayer who divines the answers to questions in sealed envelopes. The answer to this particular Carnac was "Cock Robin." The question was, "What's in my mouth, Batman?"

With Johnny retiring, that dream had to die. But others

149

would live on. And one of my dreams has always been to be reviewed by the *New York Times*.

All right, so this wasn't the *Times*, it was just some crummy little local paper.

But still.

Anyway, I have to admit, as I turned the pages I was excited. Like a kid on Christmas morning. Wondering, could it be, was it really there?

It was there, all right.

I couldn't miss it.

STAR SHINES ON PLAYHOUSE STAGE was the headline.

Underneath was a picture of Avery Allington, in full costume, striking a hopelessly theatrical pose. The picture was captioned, "TV star Avery Allington as Major Sergius Saranoff in *Arms and the Man*."

The reviewer, one Harvey Frank according to his byline, began by alluding to the murder, which I guess was unavoidable.

"Wresting triumph out of tragedy," the review began, "the playhouse has mounted a superb production of George Bernard Shaw's *Arms and the Man*." It continued:

> The tragic death and apparent murder of stage manager Goobie Wheatly could not diminish the opening-night audience's enjoyment of this delightful farce. The packed house of what one would assume were largely curiosity seekers—if the intermission conversation is any guide—saw no extracurricular theatrics develop. Instead, they were treated to one of the most delightful evenings this reviewer has seen in a long time, a thoroughly enjoyable production of *Arms and the Man*.
>
> Every aspect of the production shines, from the sets and lighting of designer Joe Warden to the authentic period costumes of Mary Anne. The play is performed by a first-rate ensemble acting troupe under the skillful direction of Herbert Drake.
>
> Leading the way is Avery Allington, star of the

late, lamented ABC–TV series "Sink or Swim." Mr. Allington plays Sergius Saranoff, a part which allows him to demonstrate his considerable talent and versatility. In the play, Major Saranoff, a dashing young military officer, is engaged to Raina Petkoff, a beautiful young Bulgarian woman, fetchingly portrayed by attractive young Margie Miller. Professing that they have found 'the higher love,' Mr. Allington twirls his moustache and sets his sights on Raina's maid Louka, portrayed by pert young Nellie Knight. It is a situation fraught with comic possibilities and loaded with potential laughs, and Avery Allington delivers every one of them. Demonstrating a range far beyond what he has been able to show due to the constraints of television, Mr. Allington masterfully depicts the multifaceted Saranoff in all his bravado and bluster in a way that can only be described as achingly funny. Indeed, the audience howled throughout.

So great in fact was the hilarity, that it was not until the final curtain fell that this viewer, for one, recalled the tragedy that had resulted in this opening-night sellout. Mr. Allington had happily made me forget all that with his superb performance.

At that point the review was "continued on page fourteen."

My fingers were numb as I turned the page. I felt like I'd been hit over the head with a sledgehammer. Good god, had Harvey Frank seen the same show I had? Had this ass-kissing, TV-star-loving son of a bitch *any idea* what he'd seen? All right, never mind the man's partiality for Avery Allington. But even putting that aside, I couldn't imagine even the world's worst Journalism 101 student writing that review. I mean, was it possible to write a review of *Arms*

and the Man without mentioning "the Man," Captain
Bluntschli? Had Harvey Frank really done that?

He hadn't.

"Also good," Mr. Frank continued on page fourteen,
"were David Rothwell as Major Petkoff, Julie Katz as his
wife, Catherine, Peter Constantine as the servant Nicola, and
Walter Penbridge as Captain Bluntschli."

☆ 22 ☆

THE SHOW THAT NIGHT WAS BAD. NO REAL SURPRISE. SECOND nights often are. But compared to last night's smash opening, tonight's was a real downer.

What made it worse was Alice was there. She'd scared up a sleepover for Tommie and driven up to see the show.

I'd taken her out to dinner and told her about it. Or at least tried to. It's hard to tell somebody you're good. Even your wife. Yes, Alice and I are tuned into each other and we understand, but there's understanding and there's understanding. I could make her see it through her eyes but not mine.

I showed her the review. Explained why it was so unfair. And not just unfair—dead wrong. While Alice sympathized and agreed, I always felt I hadn't *quite* got my point across. That she couldn't *really* understand, as I could, what a kick in the crotch this was. And as I sat there at dinner, not quite being able to explain it to her, the thought that finally came to me was, she'll have to see for herself. That was the saving grace. We could talk about it after she'd seen the show.

I'd forgotten about second-night jinx.

Don't get me wrong. Nothing disastrous happened. I didn't forget my lines or screw up my blocking or do any-

153

thing else horrendously bad. The show went reasonably
well. It even got laughs—not as big or as frequently as
opening night, but it still got them. It's just the whole show
was a little flat.

Of course, Alice had no way of knowing this, having
nothing to compare it to. "You were great," she said, when
she came back to my dressing room right after the show.

I was in the process of changing out of my costume with
the speed of light in an attempt to forestall a head-to-head
confrontation between Alice and a bare-chested Nellie
Knight, who had fortunately been waylaid in the greenroom
by guests of her own. So I was too preoccupied to deal with
such a difficult concept—no, I wasn't great, but last night I
was. I merely nodded thanks and kept on dressing, and got
us the hell out of there while Nellie was still chattering away
in the greenroom. But from my point of view that show
sucked.

Aside from that, the evening was smooth as silk. Alice
missing the "Nellie Knight Show" was just part of it. She
also accepted my introduction to Herbie with perfect grace
and didn't say anything along the lines of, "Oh, you're the
cradle robber, aren't you?"

Herbie positively beamed at Alice, then pointed to me and
said, "Wasn't he good?"

"He sure was," Alice said.

I knew better, but it was not the time to argue. I contented
myself with a small smile.

Perhaps mistaking my lack of enthusiasm, Herbie said,
"I'm sorry about the review."

I frowned. "Don't be silly."

"You gotta understand," Herbie said. "You came in so
late, and the programs had already gone out. We should
have had an insert, but there wasn't time. Anyway, I know
Harvey was told; he must have just forgot."

Oh. That's what he meant. For a moment I'd thought he
was apologizing for the review being all about Avery
Allington. "Don't worry about it," I said.

"I'm really sorry. If it's a problem . . ."

"It's no problem, Herbie."

"I could get him to print a retraction. I know that doesn't help much. Not the sort of thing you want to put in your scrapbook. Say, I know. Amanda, don't you know that editor over there? I bet you could get him to reset the column with the name Stanley Hastings. They wouldn't print it again, but they could run you a copy and then you'd have one."

It was humiliating at best, and I declined as politely as possible under the circumstances. I also declined the invitation to accompany Herbie and Amanda out to Morley's for a postshow postmortem. There were a lot of reasons, but near the top of the list was that I couldn't really bear the thought of Avery Allington modestly accepting compliments on his review.

That and the fact I hadn't seen Alice for some time.

I took her to my humble abode. I wasn't aware of how humble it really was until I had the benefit of Alice's assessment of it. I'd expected Alice to be eloquent, and she did not disappoint.

"We could go to a motel," I suggested.

Alice cocked her head, gave me a look. "Do you know of any?"

"Not offhand."

"I don't recall seeing any between here and the highway."

"We could call information."

"From what phone?"

If there was a phone in the apprentice house, I wasn't aware of it. There was a pay phone on the corner downtown, near the box from which I'd purchased the paper with the scurrilous review, but that didn't seem worth mentioning.

"It's not that bad," I said.

Alice raised her eyebrows. "Not that bad?" She pointed. "That's a single bed."

It was indeed. Which hadn't been a problem up till now.

"I know, I know," I said.

"And there's no bathroom."

"It's down the hall."

"Great."

"No fair on the bathroom. You knew that before you came."

"That doesn't make it any better."

"Granted. But that's the way it is. So why don't we make the best of it?"

"You can make the best of it," Alice said. "Me, I'm going back to New York."

"Not just yet," I told her.

It was like being in college again. A single bed. I think, after her initial reluctance, even Alice got a kick out of it. Not that she was willing to stay the night, and there I couldn't blame her. But she stayed long enough to soothe the savage beast. Or is it savage breast? Or do I just have breasts on the mind lately?

Could be.

As I waved good-bye and watched her drive off in our Toyota, it occurred to me, aside from missing Nellie Knight, I was damn lucky Alice hadn't come popping out of our communal bathroom and encountered my next-door neighbor, who just happened to be the even more nubile and attractive young apprentice, Beth.

☆ **23** ☆

SUNDAY MORNING FOUND ME BACK IN THE POLICE STATION.

"I got the medical report," Chief Bob said.

"Oh?"

"Yeah, I know. Little late to be getting it. Sy works at his own pace. Can't hurry him. He'll get it done in his own good time." He shrugged. "His own good time turned out to be this morning. So we finally have the medical report."

"What does it say?"

"Not one damn thing useful. Gilbert N. Wheatly was killed by a knife wound in the heart. What a surprise."

"Gilbert?"

He cocked his head. "You think his given name was Goobie? Yeah, it's Gilbert. And that's about the only thing interesting in the report."

"What about the time of death?"

"Nothing we don't already know." Chief Bob consulted his notebook. "Here's how I dope it out. Dress rehearsal had an eight o'clock start, actually went up at eight oh four. No guesswork there—Goobie Wheatly logged it in his book. And, yes, I've checked out his watch and, wouldn't you know it, it was right to the minute. Checking it out was a mere formality—with Goobie Wheatly I would have

157

expected nothing less. So dress rehearsal went up at eight oh four.

"Act One came down at eight thirty-six. Again, according to Goobie. There was a ten-minute intermission scheduled but, being dress rehearsal, it actually ran fourteen. Because Goobie's got Act Two logged in as taking off at eight fifty.

"Act Two ran thirty-eight minutes, came down at nine twenty-eight. There's another ten-minute intermission that ran thirteen, then we have Act Three starting at nine forty-one.

"All those times appear to be in Goobie Wheatly's handwriting, and there's no reason why they shouldn't."

He looked up at me. "There's no time listed for when Act Three ended, and we know why. But it ran thirty-seven minutes opening night, so the dress rehearsal was probably in the ball park. That would bring the curtain down at ten eighteen. Only it never came down, of course. But that would make ten eighteen the time you found the body. Which corresponds with everything everybody else said."

Chief Bob lifted a paper off his desk. "And with the medical report. Which, as I say, helps not one bit.

"To continue our schedule, Herbie calls in by ten twenty-six. They reach me at home by ten thirty, I'm at the playhouse by ten thirty-seven."

Chief Bob looked up, shook his head. "Except I'm not the medical examiner. And Sy cannot be hurried, and Sy takes his own sweet time. By the time he shows up, it's after eleven, and by the time he gets the body temperature taken it's eleven fifteen. Almost an hour after the body was initially found.

"And when does he estimate the time of death? In his opinion, when he examined the body it had been dead from one to two hours. Which, of course, encompasses all of Act Three. Which is no help at all."

"Yeah," I said. "All right, look. That's his official report. That's on the record. Off the record, is the guy willing to do any better than that?"

Chief Bob grimaced. "You don't know Sy. He only does

that because it's required of the job. But to be helpful just to be helpful? Forget it."

"I find that hard to believe," I said.

"Of course," he said. "You're from New York City, where all doctors are totally competent and everyone does everything exactly right."

"I'm sorry," I said. "You're right. I don't find that hard to believe at all."

"Exactly," Chief Bob said. "In New York City a guy like Sy would be lost in the shuffle. You'd never notice him. A small town like this, we only got one and he shows.

"Anyway, even if he was some colossal, super-duper, best fucking medical examiner in the world, it wouldn't do us a bit of good, because how accurate can you get? Certainly not more than the half-hour leeway that would allow *any* of those actors to have killed him."

"You figure it's an actor?"

"However you spell it?" Chief Bob said. "Well, they're the most likely. That's what I'd like to do today. Discuss the relative merits of the people who were there."

"What do you mean?"

"I mean, aside from the actors, I'm talking about everyone in the theater."

"Well, you can toss out a whole bunch right away," I said.

"Oh yeah? Who's that?"

"The audience. They were sitting there when the act ended and couldn't have done it. That's Herbie, Amanda, the trustees, the tech director, and most of the apprentices. They're all off the hook."

"I wish they were," Chief Bob said.

I looked at him. "What do you mean?"

"Exactly that," he said. "I wish there were one stinking one of them I could definitely cross off the list. The closest I can come is Amanda. She's highly visible, she was sitting with the trustees, and I got at least two or three of 'em think she was there all the time.

"Of course, the operative word is *think*. But when you add

in two or three separate recollections, it starts to get convincing.

"Besides, I know Amanda. I know it doesn't mean anything legally. But just between you and me, I know Amanda, and she wouldn't kill anybody for any reason."

"Not even to protect her family?"

"She *has* no family."

"How about her reputation?"

"Spotless, I assure you."

"That's exactly the kind that needs protecting."

He looked at me in surprise. "You suspect Amanda Feinstein?"

"Not at all," I said. "I just categorically reject your assumption that she has to be innocent because you know her."

He gave me a pained look. "Please. I'm not scratching her from the list of suspects, I'm giving you a personal opinion. I'm pointing out that, of all the people who were in the theater that night, her alibi was the best." He cocked his head. "You read murder mysteries?"

"Yes, I do."

"Me too. But I know the difference between what I read and what I do. Now, in a murder mystery, her having the best alibi would make her the prime suspect. In real life, it's the other way around. Things aren't that convoluted. She probably has a good alibi because she *didn't* do it."

I smiled.

"What's so funny?"

"There's a sergeant named MacAullif on the NYPD who's always pointing things like that out to me."

"Then I shouldn't have to. Let's move on. Where were we? Oh, yeah. Who could have done it—people in the audience. Okay, next least likely would be Joe Warden."

"Who?"

"The tech director. He's sitting there surrounded by apprentices. Almost all of them saw him sitting there, none of them saw him get up, and according to some of them he was actually asleep."

"I wouldn't be surprised."

"Me either. He'd been up all night. The problem is, so had they. It's a good bet at least some of the apprentices vouching for him dozed off too."

"Great."

"Hey, like I say, none of these are perfect. Take Herbie, for instance. He should have the best alibi of all, since he's directing the show. But it's dress rehearsal. He's not *doing* anything, he's just watching it. Watching and taking notes. And I know Herbie, cause I've been in the shows. And I know without even asking, his habit in the dress rehearsal is to sit in the very back row. Because he doesn't want the actors to look out and see him sitting there. He sits in the very back of the theater taking notes in the glow of the exit light. Where no one would be apt to notice if he got up in the middle and slipped out the back door."

"You're kidding."

"Not at all. He goes out through the lobby, down the stairs, through the greenroom, up the stage right stairs, kills him, and goes back the way he came."

"Without anyone seeing him?"

"Who? Everyone's in the audience watching the show. Or onstage. Think about it. They all enter, one at a time. After Catherine's entrance, they're all onstage until you exit. That's a good four or five pages. Plenty of time for him to kill Goobie Wheatly, then make his way downstairs through the greenroom, upstairs through the lobby in time to be sitting there in the back of the theater when the curtain doesn't come down."

"Jesus Christ."

"What's wrong with that?"

"What about Nicola? He comes on and off after that."

"Yeah, but from stage left. No reason for him to see what's happening stage right. So there's no reason Herbie couldn't have done it."

"Good lord."

Chief Bob held up his hand. "Hey, don't get me wrong. I'm not saying he did. Herbie's my friend. I don't think he did it for a minute. I'm just saying he could have. For that matter, so could everybody else."

"What about his wife?"

"Who?"

"Herbie's wife. She was there. She wasn't sitting in the back row, and if she'd gotten up to go out someone would have seen her."

"They did."

"What?"

"They *did* see her. The middle of Act Three, she got up and went out the back door."

I stared at him. "Are you kidding me?"

"No. She admits she did. The play was running longer than she'd expected, and she went out to the box office to call the baby-sitter."

I frowned. "Is that true?"

"I don't know if it's true, but the baby-sitter confirms it. She doesn't remember the exact time of the call, but she remembers Martha Drake making it.

"But what the hell. That got her out there, and if she wanted to, she could have gone backstage and killed Goobie Wheatly too."

"Why would she do that?"

Chief Bob held up his finger. "Again with the motive? I still want opportunity here. But that is a valid point. I can't imagine Martha doing Goobie Wheatly in." He shrugged. "If it was Margie Miller lying there, I might have second thoughts. But Goobie Wheatly?"

"That's interesting," I said. "You concede she has a motive for killing Margie Miller?"

"I should think that was fairly obvious."

"Yes. Do you think she *knew* she had a reason for killing Margie Miller?"

"There I can't be sure."

"Did you ask her?"

"No. It has nothing to do with the current investigation."

"But it is a matter to consider."

"Sure. In your wildest dreams. We're talking realities

here. Anyway, who else could have killed him? The whole damn audience, for my money. Every stinking apprentice, every stinking trustee. They try to alibi each other, but there's no two of them do a good enough job of it to cross anybody out.

"Then there's the people in the playhouse but *not* in the audience."

I frowned. "Who would that be?"

"Actually, just two. Ridley up in the light booth, and Mary Anne."

"Mary Anne?"

"During the dress rehearsal she was in the costume shop, sewing."

"Sewing? For what?"

He looked at me. "For the next show. I know you have a limited viewpoint, but wake up and get with the picture. *Arms and the Man* is not the last show of the season. They're rehearsing right now for *Glass Menagerie*."

"Yeah, I know," I said. "I just didn't think of it in terms of our dress rehearsal. I mean, that she'd be working on something else."

"Yeah, well, she was. She was down there sewing dresses all night. Or so she says. She also could have been climbing the stage-right stairs and killing Goobie Wheatly. Just between you and me, I doubt it. Anyway, if she really was there as she claims, and some unauthorized person had come up the stage-right stairs, he would have had to go right past the costume shop and she might have seen him."

"I take it she didn't?"

"So she says. Granted she wasn't looking for anything like that. But still, if some unauthorized person had come by, she probably would have noticed. It's a small point, but possibly a valuable one."

"You'll pardon me, but they all seem small points right now."

"Sure, 'cause we're just getting started and we don't know what we're looking for. Anyway, that's her.

"Then there's the kid. Ridley. He's up in the light booth.

On the headset but as I said, he probably took it off. If so, he
could go out of the light booth, down the ladder to the balcony, down the steps to the lobby, downstairs to the
greenroom, upstairs, kill Goobie Wheatly, then retrace his
steps and be up there on the headset in the light booth
waiting for a cue he knew would never come."

"Why in the world would he do that?"

Chief Bob looked at me. "Are you going to ask that about
every person we discuss?"

"Sorry. Yeah, you're right. He could have."

"There you are. Far as I can see, everybody in the theater
could have done it."

"I guess so."

"But the word is *could*," Chief Bob said. "The most likely
to have done it are still the actors."

"Of course," I said.

Chief Bob nodded. "And of all the actors, the most likely
of all is you."

☆ 24 ☆

To a New Yorker like me, the words "domestic disturbance" conjure up images of minorities in housing projects armed with guns and knives involved in, at best, brawls and, at worst, hostage situations.

At the reported domestic disturbance Chief Bob and I checked out that morning, I found myself sitting at the kitchen table having coffee and homemade doughnuts pressed on me by both Mrs. Etheridge and her husband, while Chief Bob tried to mediate their differences. The exact cause of the dispute never surfaced, but by the time we took our leave—armed with a bag of homemade doughnuts—the Etheridges were smiling and waving good-bye just as if it had been any other social occasion.

I was not as easily placated. Back in the police station, I took Chief Bob to task.

"I'm sure you'll pardon me," I said. "But before we were so rudely interrupted, you had just accused me of a crime."

Chief Bob, who had been digging into the bag of doughnuts, looked at me in surprise. "No such thing."

"Didn't you say I was the most likely suspect?"

"Oh, that," Chief Bob said. He bit into a doughnut. "There's no reason to take offense. You *are* the most likely

165

suspect. In terms of opportunity, I mean. After all, we were only talking opportunity. And in that category you've got the others beat hands down. You had, after all, two separate and equally good opportunities to kill the man. At the end of the show, while all the rest of the actors were onstage at the time you claim you found the body."

"Claim?"

Chief Bob held up his hand, "Please. We're having a hypothetical discussion here. We'd get a lot further if you'd discuss it rationally instead of taking offense at every statement. Look, we're taking the overall hypothesis here that you committed the crime. I'm not saying you did, I'm just saying, for the purpose of this discussion. But take it for a given that's what we're discussing and don't fly off the handle every time you realize that it is."

"Fine," I said. "You've made my day. In terms of this hypothetical discussion, at the end of the play when I *claim* I found the body, would you mind if I pointed out that all the evidence suggests that that's exactly what I did? I mean, opportunity, hell. It's not like I had this wonderful chance to kill Goobie Wheatly. You saw the show. I walk offstage, there's one more line, 'What a man! Is he a man!' by Avery TV-star Allington, and the show is over. Now, how long could that take? Even with Avery Asshole emoting and doing six outrageous takes before speaking, we're talking a few seconds at most."

"Till the end of the act, yes. But the lights and curtain didn't come down at the end of the act. There was a pause, a hole where nothing happened. Then finally you appear onstage and say there's been an accident.

"Well, now, witness statements vary. But the time between when the curtain should have come down and the time you appear onstage has been estimated at as long as fifteen seconds."

I looked at him. "Oh, for Christ's sake."

"Plenty of time for you to walk up behind the gentleman in question and stab a knife in his heart."

I put up my hand. "No," I said. I shook my head. "Doesn't fly."

"Why not?"

"Goobie Wheatly was found sitting in the chair with the headset on and the prompt script in his lap."

"Yeah. So?"

"That's all wrong. For a lot of reasons."

"Why?"

"We're talking now about me killing him at the end of the act. After my exit, right? Well, that's what I mean. Couldn't have happened that way."

"Why not?"

"First off, he was wearing his headset. Now, you will agree that after my exit there were only a few seconds until Avery Allington delivers the line, 'What a man! Is he a man!' It doesn't matter if there were fifteen seconds *after* that. The point is, there were only a few seconds *before* it. And that is the cue for lights and curtain. So even if Ridley took his headset off in the light booth, by the time I exit he's got it back on because it's the end of the act and he's only seconds away from his light cue. So if I stabbed Goobie then, Ridley would have heard it on his headset."

"Unless you turned it off. Isn't it possible to turn those things off?"

"I suppose so, but—"

"So you sneak up behind Goobie Wheatly, click his headset off and stab him in the heart. When you're finished you click it on again so no one will know."

"Yes, but you can tell the difference. Ridley would hear it being clicked on and off and he'd report that. It's just the sort of thing a kid like that would be sure to remember."

"Yeah, if he wants to. A kid like that generally wants nothing to do with the cops, he just wants to get out of there. He didn't see nothing, he didn't hear nothing. So if it *had* happened, he wouldn't talk about it because he'd figure it could get him in trouble."

I frowned. "That's really stretching."

"Hey, we're talking hypothetical here."

"All right, fine," I said. "Forget Ridley. It still won't wash."

"Why not?"

"Just like I say. He was sitting in the folding chair with the prompt script in his lap."

"What's wrong with that?"

"Everything. It's the end of the act. Just like Ridley's got the headset on, ready for it, Goobie Wheatly would be ready for it. Now, in the middle of the act he might have been sitting there in the folding chair with the prompt script in his lap ready to throw me cues, but not at the end. At the end of the act the prompt book is back on top of the lectern, and he's standing up next to it with the headset on, ready to give the light cue and pull the curtain."

"That's the way you see it?" Chief Bob said.

"Yes, it is."

He nodded. "Very good. That's the way I see it too. And I think it's a very convincing argument. Frankly, I don't think there's any way you could have killed him when you came offstage at the end of the act."

"I'm glad to hear it," I said.

He shrugged. "Unfortunately, you could have killed him in the middle of the act just fine." He smiled and held out the bag. "Care for a doughnut?"

☆ **25** ☆

THIS TIME IT WAS—I KID YOU NOT—A CAT UP A TREE. CHIEF
Bob captured it with the aid of a ladder dragged out from a
two-car garage, suffered only superficial scratches bringing
it down, and delivered it to its owner, a sweet old lady who
was so grateful it was all we could do to escape without
another round of coffee and doughnuts.

"I thought it was the fire department did that," I said as
we drove off.

"It is," Chief Bob said. "But they're volunteers. And it's
Sunday. Why should some poor salesman have to leave his
barbecue and get out the hook and ladder on his day off
when I can handle it?"

"Nice guy."

"Yeah. I finish last," Chief Bob said. He hung a left,
headed out of town.

I frowned. "Where we going?"

"Just down here a ways."

There was a billboard near the edge of town. Chief Bob
pulled in behind it.

"You're kidding," I said.

He shrugged. "Gotta pay the rent. Let's see if we can nab
us a speeder."

Chief Bob had brought along the bag of doughnuts. At the time, I'd wondered why. He pulled one out, took a bite. "So, as I was sayin'. About the murder. We've made admirable progress so far, knocking out the possibility of you killing Goobie Wheatly at the end of the show. Now, let's suppose you killed him in the middle."

"I didn't. I was sitting on the steps studying my lines."

"So you say. But we have only your unsubstantiated word for that."

"Didn't anyone see me there?"

"Actually, I believe Margie Miller did. She comes off-stage a few lines after you. She claims when she got offstage she went down to her dressing room and passed you sitting on the top of the stairs with your script."

"There you are," I said.

"Yeah, but that's when you first got offstage. Well before your reentrance. Look what happens next. Louka, who came onstage before your exit, plays a scene with Nicola. Who enters from stage left. So they're both out of the picture. He also exits stage left, so he would never see you at all. And she is onstage till your entrance, so she's out of the picture too. The only other actor to enter before you do is Avery Allington."

"He enters from up right," I said. "Didn't *he* see me?"

"Yes, he did, but it doesn't help you at all. He claims he came up the steps, saw you sitting at the top with your head in a book. He walked right by you and took up his position at the door. You recall no one exits before his entrance—he walks in on the two servants and then Nicola goes out. So he's in position by the upstage door, waiting to go on."

"You'll pardon me, but why doesn't that help me?"

"The masking flat."

"What masking flat?"

"The one in the doorway. Look, I checked this out myself. When you're in position to enter by the upstage-right door, that masking flat screens you off from the rest of the wing. With Avery standing there, it's perfectly possible for you to walk from the stage-right stairs to the downstage wing where Goobie Wheatly was without anyone seeing you at all."

"Oh, come on," I said. "I'm going to trust my murder to masking flats and sight lines with the guy standing right there?"

"We're talking possibilities here. The fact is, it was possible." Chief Bob shrugged. "Possible, but not necessary."

"What do you mean?"

"Well, as soon as Avery Allington goes onstage, you could have killed Goobie Wheatly, no problem. I mean, he's got the whole scene to play with Louka before you come in. Nicola goes offstage left, no problem there. You'd have plenty of time to do it."

"Yeah, but why?"

Chief Bob gave me a look. "Slow learner? Okay. I'll give you a break. We're gonna get to why. Promise. But for now, play what-if. What if you had a reason—could you have done it? You gave me a great explanation for why you couldn't have done it at the end of the act. Can you give me as good a one for why you couldn't have done it here? How about it? What was there to prevent you from killing Goobie Wheatly before you went onstage in the middle of Act Three?"

I took a deep breath, blew it out again. "I don't know."

Chief Bob shook his head. "I don't either. It's a shame, but there you are. I'd really like to cross you off the list. But the sad fact is you could have done it. You could have done it just fine."

A blue Nissan with New York plates whizzed by.

Chief Bob pulled out and nailed him. I stayed in the car, but I could see the entire operation. The driver was a young jock type, and he was pissed. Tough luck for him. Chief Bob took his license and registration and wrote the ticket.

"You nail him 'cause he was from out of state?" I asked, as Chief Bob climbed back into the driver's seat.

"No. I nailed him for doing fifty-two in a thirty-five-mile-an-hour zone." Chief Bob shifted into gear and pulled out.

"Okay. I got my speeder. Whaddya say we go back to the station and celebrate?"

"Celebrate?"

"Yeah," Chief Bob said. "We'll do what you've been dying to do all along."

"Oh? What's that?"

"Discuss the motive."

☆ 26 ☆

CHIEF BOB PICKED UP A PAPER FROM THE STACK ON HIS DESK. "I have here a list of people involved in this case. The suspects, if you will. I've attempted to put them in order, ranging from those who had the most reason to kill Goobie Wheatly to those who had the least." He shrugged. "Once again, you head the list."

I looked at him. "Are you kidding me?"

"Hey, there's the whole Captain Kirk episode. It was highly dramatic and highly visible. Hell, everyone saw it. So you had a motive. You may not think it's much of a motive, but it gains force from the fact that virtually every person in the theater commented on it."

"Yeah, but—"

Chief Bob held up his hand. "Hey, we've been over this before. I don't want to beat it to death. That's your motive. At least your obvious motive. You may have had some other motive we don't know of yet. But in terms of popularity, if this were "Family Feud," that's the one would have been voted the number-one answer.

"Next on the list is Captain Kirk himself. That's Kirk Mitchel. He's fifteen years old. Lives in the apprentice house. His dream is to be a stage manager someday."

"Shit."

"Yeah, I know. It's hard to torpedo someone's dream. Even such an apparently unrealistic one. Anyway, the humiliation of being fired gave him a motive for killing Goobie. Or you, for that matter. If we grant the kid the power to reason, you can say he killed Goobie instead of you because he recognized Goobie's action as malicious, while yours was merely expedient. Frankly, I don't grant the kid that much power to reason. I think it much more likely he killed Goobie Wheatly because when he got backstage you were onstage and Goobie wasn't. Personally, I find that far more likely than any more complex theory."

"What theory?"

"That he actually *did* resent you both, so he killed Goobie Wheatly and framed you."

"What?"

Chief Bob shrugged. "As I say, I find that highly unlikely."

"So do I. Tell me. Are there any motives that are *not* related to the firing of Captain Kirk?"

"Oh, sure," Chief Bob said. "As I said, those are merely the most obvious. Let's see, there's the prop man."

"Who?"

"The apprentice running props. Jack Dent. He worked with Goobie on the last three shows and didn't like him. Not surprising—not many of the apprentices did. Goobie was a real tyrant. A royal pain in the ass. Goobie overworked the kid. Even made him miss the apprentice party."

"Apprentice party?"

"They did a musical, ran two weeks. That meant one week there was no strike night. The apprentices threw a party. Jack couldn't go because Goobie made him inventory props."

"Why?"

"To be a prick, basically. You gotta understand, Goobie Wheatly got off on being a prick. There are people like that, they enjoy doing cruel things."

"Yeah, but something as petty as that."

"Sure, you say that now. But this is something that never would have come up if that man hadn't been killed. Here's a man who spent his life doing petty little things. Then he gets killed and you ask people to remember them and they do."

"This apprentice doesn't come running up and say, 'Hey, I hated the son of a bitch, I have a motive.' "

"No, of course not. But the other apprentices remember him missing the party and some of the comments he made about Goobie Wheatly at the time," Chief Bob held up his hand. "I'm not saying he did it. It's terribly farfetched that he did it. In fact, there's only one thing that points in his direction."

"What's that?"

"He was the prop man, of course."

"So what?"

Chief Bob looked at me. "For a detective, you're unusually dense. The murder weapon was a prop."

"Oh. Right."

"Of course he claims he gave it to Goobie Wheatly on strike night. But we've only his word for that. Unfortunately, we can't question Mr. Wheatly on it."

"True."

"Anyway, that's Jack Dent. He had more motive than most, and the access to the murder weapon. But almost all the apprentices had reason to hate Goobie Wheatly. As I say, the man was a general prick. Jack's just a standout because he worked directly with him and had access to the knife.

"Aside from him, the most likely apprentice is Ridley."

"And why is that?"

"Goobie ridiculed him too."

"What about?"

"The lights, of course. Not this show so much. As I say, it's a simple show. But some of the others. Especially the musical. They did *The Fantasticks*, you know, largely 'cause it's a small-cast show, easy and inexpensive to do. Abstract set, do a lot of suggested settings in pools of light. Well, that makes for a show with a zillion light cues, all of which are important. Goobie reamed the kid out over it. Really made him feel like shit. Enough so that a lot of people commented on it."

"Son of a bitch."

"That's for starters. For another thing, I don't know if you noticed, but this Ridley smokes dope. Which is probably why he wasn't on the headset in Act Three, by the way. From what I gather, he had a habit during the show of sneaking up in the attic to blow a joint. Anyway, that's one reason Goobie Wheatly picked on him. Goobie was hard on drugs, and if he'd actually caught Ridley with 'em he might have booted him out. As it was, he just came down on the kid pretty hard."

"That's a motive for murder?"

"Hey, none of these are great. But suppose Goobie *had* caught Ridley with drugs. He isn't gonna can him the day of the dress but, once the lights were set and anyone can run 'em, was planning on booting him out the next day. Maybe you got a motive there."

"Anything to suggest that was the case?"

"No, just speculation. That's all. Take the statements from all the witnesses, glean what few facts you can get from them and then speculate on 'em. I know it's not much. It's where we are at this point in time.

"Anyway, that's Ridley's motive. Who's next? Let me see. Ah, yes. Beth Scott."

To my surprise, I actually felt a catch in my throat. "Who?"

"By far the most attractive apprentice. Surely you've noticed her."

"Oh, her," I said.

"Yeah, her. She's hard to miss. Well, Goobie noticed her too."

"Oh?"

"No, I don't mean like that. Goobie wasn't like that. Pretty much of an old woman, you know?"

"You mean he was gay?"

"No, not gay. Just asexual. A noncom, you know? Like he was too old and beyond it. Not that he *was* too old, I'm just saying that was his attitude. Sex was the province of the young and foolish and existed expressly for him to ridicule."

"What about this apprentice?"

"Well, that's the point I'm making. It's not like *he* was coming on to her or anything. It was one of the apprentice boys. A Phil Epstein. From the tech crew. That's who this Beth Scott seemed sweet on. Anyway, Goobie found that out and rode it. That's what I mean by *old woman*. A gossip, you know. And not just gossip behind her back. I mean to her face. Snide. Catty. Insinuations. Double entendres. Anything to embarrass or demean. So she'd have every reason to hate his guts. So would he. The kid from the tech crew, I mean. Do you know him, by the way?"

"Not by name."

"Yeah, well, he's in the show. He's the soldier who searches the house in Act One. You knew that was an apprentice, right? The soldier, I mean. Well, that's him. He's also on the set crew, by the way, that does all the scene changes. So he'd be backstage."

"And you say he had a motive?"

"Yeah. Because the way I understand it, she broke it off. And the way I get it, the *reason* she broke it off was Goobie Wheatly running his mouth. Which may or may not have been true. But that doesn't matter, because at least this Phil Epstein seemed to think so. Which gives him a motive."

Chief Bob put the paper down on the table and looked up at me. "You'll be happy to know that's all the apprentices. With specific motives, I mean. The others may have hated him in general because he was a prick, but there's no specific instances that stand out."

Chief Bob picked up another paper. "That brings us to the actors. Excluding you, of course. We've already discussed you as the man most likely. As to the rest, let's start with the resident company."

"Which is who?"

He looked at me. "You don't know?"

I took a breath. "Look," I said, "I'm getting a little pissed off at your sarcasm over my lack of knowledge. I came up here as a favor for a friend to do a specific part. I'm sorry this happened, but it's not my doing. I'm not here of my own accord, I'm here because you asked me. I don't know if you really want my help or if I'm just your chief suspect. Either way, I don't care. But if you want to tell me something, tell me. You don't have to make such a fucking big deal over the fact I don't know it."

Chief Bob smiled. "That was not my intention. I am genuinely amazed that you don't know. If that ridicules you, I'm sorry, but it happens to be the fact. Anyway, let's go over it now.

"There are only four actors in the resident company. That's why most of the shows are small-cast shows. Those four actors are Peter Constantine, who plays Nicola; David Rothwell, who's Major Petkoff; Julie Katz, who plays his wife, Catherine; and Nellie Knight, who plays Louka. All the other actors are jobbed in for a specific show."

"You mean Margie's not in the company?"

"No. She's local, she was brought in just for this play."

"Who brought her in?"

He looked at me. "Do you really have to ask me that?"

"You mean, Herbie knew her before the production?"

"That he did."

"Son of a bitch," I said. "And what, may I ask, did Goobie Wheatly think of that?"

"There you are," Chief Bob said. "It was a situation made in heaven for Goobie Wheatly. The lead actress in the show and the producer/director of the theater, and he's got something on both of them."

"Are you saying he'd *use* something like that?"

"Sure he would."

"Against his own producer/director?"

"Especially against him. The bigger the target, the greater the fun. Petty sport to torture some apprentice. But the head of the whole playhouse? The man who hired him?"

"Yeah, but even if Goobie would tease him about it, that's not motive for murder."

"Tease him, no. But threaten him?"

"With going to his wife?"

"Of course. And you must remember, she was there that night."

"Are you saying you suspect Herbie?"

"Of course not. No more than I suspect you. I'm merely attempting as rationally as I did against you to lay out the case against him." He smiled. "Only in his case, Herbie's not here to take offense. Though I gather you're prepared to take offense for him."

"No, I'm just trying to make some sense out of this, and it doesn't."

"Because the facts aren't all in yet. But we have to evaluate the ones we have. Anyway, that's Herbie's motive. And Margie's."

I frowned. "Why Margie? A young actress like her, a little bit of scandal isn't going to hurt her any."

"Yeah," he said. "But she's married."

My mouth dropped open. "What?"

"That's right," he said. "You didn't know that either? Well, she is. She's married to a young used-car salesman. He'd probably have hit the roof if Goobie Wheatly had given him the news."

"Good lord. He wasn't there that night, was he?"

"No. Thank goodness for small favors. But that wouldn't have stopped him from walking right in through the lobby any time during the act. There was no one in the box office that time of night."

"Shit."

"Right. Of course, why *he* would kill Goobie Wheatly is beyond me. He and Herbie's wife. Same difference. Definitely interested parties, but no motive."

He frowned, rubbed his head. "Let me see now. Where were we? Oh yes, the resident company. The jobbers. The four I mentioned, they're the permanent company, they're in every show. They're rehearsing *Glass Menagerie* now." He picked up another piece of paper from his desk. "Julie Katz is Amanda, Nellie Knight is Laura, Peter Constantine's the gentleman caller, and David Rothwell's Tom.

"Now, the last show was two one-acts. The two guys did *Zoo Story* and the two women did *White Whore and the Bit Player*." He shrugged. "Bit racy for us folk, but there you are. I understand attendance was about the same as the other shows. I guess as many as stayed away from the smut, others came to be titillated. Anyway, the same four actors were in that.

"Avery Allington, of course, was jobbed in for the one show. Big TV star up from New York for the production. This Walter Penbridge whom you replaced was the same deal. Though a much lesser light. Anyway, the point is, being jobbed in for the show, this Avery Allington hasn't been here that long. I know you only had two days, but they only had a week's rehearsal in all.

"So, anyway, out of the members of the cast, Avery Allington and Margie Miller were new, and the rest had been here all year. Margie rates more consideration because she's local and had a previous relationship with Herbie Drake. But with Avery Allington up from New York only five days before, a motive is sort of hard to fathom."

I frowned. "I see."

Chief Bob smiled. "I can understand why that might not please you. For what it's worth, I've had some experience in the theater—granted, not that much, but still quite enough to say that Avery Allington is a terrible actor, and I can understand how you must feel, and sympathize with you entirely over that review."

I think it's a testament of how much I wanted to hear that that I couldn't even resent Chief Bob anymore for thinking of me as a murder suspect. I blinked my eyes and found they were almost tearing. "You know," I said, "you're the first person who told me that."

"A shame," he said. "You did an excellent job and he stinks."

It was amazing, but I felt as if an enormous weight had been lifted from my shoulders. Because it was true, no one had told me that before. Not Herbie. Not Alice. Beth had told me I was great, but that was *before* the review. No one had said specifically the review was wrong.

I grinned. "All right, Chief," I said. "Let's solve this fucking crime."

☆ 27 ☆

THAT AFTERNOON THERE WAS A MATINEE.

I'd forgotten about matinees. In more ways than one. I'd forgotten what they were like, and forgotten that I had one. Actually, I hadn't even *known* I had one. In fact, newly promoted stage manager whatever-the-hell-his-name-was had to come screeching up in a station wagon and rip me out of the snack bar where I was sitting over a cheeseburger and a diet Coke, with no idea that I had any obligation any earlier than that night.

Guess again. It was two-fifteen, the show went up at two-thirty, and I'd just missed half hour.

Fortunately, everything in town was within a couple of minutes' drive of everything else and I was back in my dressing room with a good ten minutes till show time. I'd missed the "Nellie Knight Show," but still had time to throw on costume and makeup, particularly since I'm not onstage at the opening curtain. I wanted to be backstage when it went up though, and not sitting in my dressing room listening to the lines wafting down over the ancient, squeaky, squawky intercom system which had speakers in the greenroom to let the actors know what was going on

182

onstage. It was close, but I made it up the stage-right stairs just in time to see the lights come up onstage.

To squeals of laughter.

Laughter?

Hold the phone. Reality check. Not to brag, but I happen to know there are no laughs in this play till I get onstage.

I edged downstage to see what was going on. I came around the masking flat to where I could see the lectern where the new stage manager stood with his headset. He was grinning from ear to ear, and when he saw me he smiled and nodded.

I stepped down to him, whispered, "What are they laughing at?"

He jerked his thumb at the audience. "Kids," he said. "They're laughing at she's in her nightgown."

I peered out from behind the curtain. Very unprofessional again, but then the stage manager had just invited me to do it. The audience was a sea of young faces. That's what I'd forgotten about matinees. They attract the young and the old. This being Sunday, the audience was composed largely of camp groups. And young ones, at that. Preteen, by the looks of some of them. Young enough to laugh at a night-gown.

And at Avery Allington.

I'm telling you, the gods could not have devised a more exquisite torture than that matinee. Because the audience was too young to appreciate the subtle humor of my performance but laughed uproariously every time Avery Allington mugged.

I had not been in a good mood when the performance began. By the time it ended I was ready to bite somebody's head off. Unfortunately, it was Herbie who grabbed me when I came offstage.

"I heard you almost missed curtain," he said.

"That's right," I said. "It's lucky they found me."

"I almost had a nervous breakdown," Herbie said. "I need you here at half hour."

"You're lucky I got here at all. No one told me there was a matinee."

"There's always a matinee on Sunday," Herbie said.

That did it.

"What do you mean, *always?*" I snapped. "There's no *always* in my case, Herbie. I just *got here.* All I know is what you tell me. And you never told me."

"It's on all the posters," Herbie said.

"So there's no reason to tell me, I should find out for myself," I said. "Great."

I turned on my heels, stomped off to my dressing room.

Nellie Knight was changing into sweater and jeans.

"Oh, you looked pissed," she said.

"I just got bawled out for missing half hour. I'd certainly have been here if anyone had bothered to tell me we had a matinee."

"Well, don't take it personally," she said. "Anyone mention we had an evening performance too?"

"That I knew about," I told her.

"Well, see you then," she said. She smiled. "Hey, don't let it get to you."

I tried not to. I'm not good with anger to begin with, and I can't hold a grudge long. Not against a friend. My instinct is to make up as quickly as possible.

I did that now. I went and hunted up Herbie and apologized for snapping at him. He seemed somewhat distracted but otherwise took it well. Then I went and hunted up the stage manager and apologized for missing half hour. He acted like he couldn't really give a shit, which he probably didn't. But basically they were both hail-fellow-well-met and all conciliatory smiles, and everything was just fine again.

At least until I walked out of the theater and saw Avery Allington on the front steps, smiling, mugging, posing for pictures and signing autographs for the camp kids.

That was more than I could deal with. I didn't want to come walking out the door into that group of kids, none of whom would have given a flying fuck about me, assuming they recognized me at all. That humiliation I didn't need to go through.

So I retreated back into the lobby and went down the stairs in order to sneak ignominiously out the side door.

That's when I saw them. Or half saw them. They were the length of the hallway away, and when I saw them they ducked back into a doorway so I really couldn't be sure. Not without walking the length of the hall and staring, which I wasn't about to do.

But unless my eyes deceived me, what I had just seen was none other than Margie-poo Miller, my young co-star and the apple of producer/director/married-man Herbie Drake's eye, in a close encounter with tech director, lighting and set designer, newly appointed stage manager, what's-his-name.

☆ **28** ☆

THE SHOW THAT NIGHT WAS GOOD. THAT SOMETIMES HAPPENS too. After the second-night letdown, the next night is good. It's an up-and-down sequence, almost predictable. Extended, it's bad dress rehearsal, good performance, second-night letdown, third night good.

The matinee doesn't count, by the way. Matinees aren't really performances, they're a different kind of animal. Just something to get through. Of course there are good matinees and bad matinees, but they tend toward the latter. And they don't figure in the overall scheme of things.

Or maybe I just wanted to forget that one, but *I* sure wasn't counting it. Anyway, Sunday night's show was good. Not as good as the opening, but nowhere near as bad as the second night. And much better than the matinee.

For me, Sunday night's show was a bit of a vindication. To reinforce the impression I had had from opening night, which every subsequent performance had tended to tear down, that I was quite good and Avery Allington was quite bad.

Well, that's the way the Sunday night crowd saw it. The scenes went great. I felt great. They liked me. I got laughs on all the right lines and I had the audience in my hip pocket.

Avery Allington gave his usual overblown performance, which got the lukewarm reception it deserved.

Sometimes life is good.

Anyway, by the time the final curtain came down, I was all pumped up from the performance and was once again a bloodhound on the scent. My meeting with Chief Bob this morning had inspired me to investigate the crime. The surprise matinee had thrown a monkey wrench into that, and then been such a downer to boot. But tonight's show was a real lift. It was kind of a reaffirmation, a yes-I-can. Solve a murder? No problem. Lead me to it.

Besides, what better time to investigate the actors than right after the show when they didn't have a rehearsal and when I knew where to find them?

Sure enough, when I got to Morley's, the actors were there. At least enough of them to suit my purposes. I didn't see Herbie and Margie-poo, but then again you can't have everything. I didn't see our new stage manager either. It occurred to me maybe the three of them were off somewhere and the guys were fighting a duel for her affections.

Avery Allington was there, of course. To my distaste I saw that he was coming on to Nellie Knight. I don't know if she was buying it or not, but she appeared to have accepted a drink from the fellow. I have to admit that lowered her considerably in my eyes.

Anyway, Margie-poo and Avery Allington weren't my main targets anyway. After my talk with Chief Bob I was more concerned with the resident company.

Peter Constantine, standing alone at the bar, seemed as good a place as any. I squeezed in next to him and said, "Good show tonight."

He looked at me rather coolly. I wondered if it was just that we hadn't had any real conversations before, or if he had some other reason.

To my surprise, it turned out he had.

"I suppose so," he said. "Not that it matters in my case."

I was still smiling, but my brow furrowed. "What do you mean by that?"

"Nicola's not the funniest part in the world, now is it? Fairly thankless task."

"Oh," I said. "Well, I guess it is one of the straighter roles in the play."

He looked at me. "Straighter roles? I suppose you could call it that. The fact is, I feel like I'm doing some deserving apprentice out of a part."

My smile was becoming somewhat fixed. "It's not as bad as all that."

"Oh, yeah?" he said. "How'd you like to be in the resident company—be here all summer long, go through the grind, do every show, back to back, no time off? It would be fine if the parts were worth doing, but what happens? Any decent part comes along and they get some big-shot actor from New York to come play it."

That was too much for me. "Hey, look," I said. "It's not like I came up here to ace you out of a part. I'm here filling in on two days' notice because somebody died."

"Right," he said. "The New York actor they brought in to play the juicy part to begin with."

I took a breath. "Okay," I said. "But that's just one show. Aren't you playing the gentleman caller now?"

"Oh, sure, in the small-cast shows. The ones nobody goes to see. But in the big shows . . ." He shook his head. "We did *The Fantasticks*, you know. Think I played El Gallo? You think Dave did? Not that he's right for it, of course, but what's wrong with me? But you think I got it? Hell, no. They brought in some singer from New York, couldn't act his way out of a paper bag. They always do with the musicals. As if acting don't mean shit, they just go with a voice. They brought a kid in to play the boy, and Dave and I wind up playing the fathers. Plant a radish. Whoopdedo."

"*Glass Menagerie*'s a good play," I said. "I did it myself."

"Sure you did. Twenty years ago, right? All the shows Herbie does are at least twenty years old. You notice that?

You know why? He only directs things he's already been in. He's afraid to try anything new."

I frowned. "I wouldn't know about that."

"Yeah, well I would. I'd like to do *The Foreigner*. It's perfect for summer stock—small cast, one set. And I'd love to play that part. Only Herbie won't do it. You know why? He's never been in it and he's never seen it, so he doesn't know how to do it."

Things were not going exactly as planned. I was trying to shed some light on the murder. Instead I'd run into an actor with a personal ax to grind.

Well, so much for subtlety. Time to take the bull by the horns.

"All right, listen," I said. "I wanted to ask you something. What do you think about this Goobie Wheatly thing?"

He frowned. "What do you mean?"

"Who do you think might have done it?"

He frowned again, deeper this time, and looked away, and I could see his mind going. Of course. He along with everyone else in the cast had already suggested to the cops that *I* was the most likely person to have done it.

"That's hard to say," he said. Then, counterattacking, "Why are you interested?"

"No particular reason," I said. "I just happen to have spent the last two mornings being grilled at the police station. The fact is, the cops have no real suspect, so they're picking on me. Since I just got here and don't really know what's happening, it's hard to know what to tell 'em."

"Tell 'em the truth," he said.

"Right," I said. "The truth is, I don't know shit. Somehow that doesn't seem to satisfy them."

"Too bad."

"Yeah. So I was wondering if you could help."

"How?"

"You're in the resident company, right? Been here all summer. So you'd know what's going on."

"Whaddya mean? Nothing's going on."

"It's a figure of speech. Look, Goobie's been here all summer too, right? Running all the shows?"

"Yeah. So?"

"So what he did to me about the prompter—hauling the kid out onstage and firing him to make me look like an asshole—he ever do anything like that to anybody else?"

He frowned. He hesitated a moment, and I got the impression Goobie probably had humiliated *him* at some time or other.

"Goobie was always a pain in the ass," he said. "Offended almost everyone. That's no reason to kill him."

"I'm glad to hear it," I said. "I thought I had this terrific motive. You mean I probably *didn't* commit the crime?"

The minute I said that I realized I'd just flunked Private Detective 101 again. Christ, what an asshole. One sarcastic remark and you could just *see* the guy shut down. I'd never get anything out of him now.

Too bad. Take your lumps, learn your lesson and move on.

I looked around the bar for fresh game.

Avery Allington was still hitting on Nellie Knight. No matter there—I could always talk to her in the dressing room anyway.

Farther down the bar, David/Major Petkoff and Catherine what's-her-name were sitting talking together. Fine. I'll take 'em on both at once.

I moved on down the bar to see what they were talking about, to see how I could edge into the conversation. It wasn't going to be easy. They seemed to be having a heated conversation about the movies. That puzzled me. I hadn't seen any movie theaters in town, and we didn't have time to go anyway.

Stranger still, what they were saying sounded vaguely familiar. Then I realized. It was *Glass Menagerie*. They were running lines.

That let me out. I'd have butted into just about any conversation at that moment, but not two summer-stock actors trying to learn their parts.

Well, that took care of the whole resident company. Great. Who should I tackle next?

As if on cue, Beth apprentice-that-launched-a-thousand-ships Scott detached herself from a table of her peers and bellied up to the bar.

I slid in next to her smoothly. "How's it going?" I said.

She smiled. "Not bad. Good show tonight."

"Oh? You saw it?"

"I see 'em all. It's what I'm here for. You think I'm here to learn to sew? I wanna be an actress. I watch the shows every chance I get."

"You see the matinee?"

"No, I missed that."

"You didn't miss much. It was the Avery Allington fan club. Average age eight to ten."

She grinned. "Yeah. Matinees are a hoot."

The bartender came and she ordered a beer. I realized when it came she'd be gone, so I had to move fast.

"Listen," I said. "I could really use your help."

"Oh? How's that?"

"You know I haven't acted in a long time."

"You wouldn't know it to see you onstage."

"Thanks. But the point is, I've been doing other things. For the past few years—well, I happen to be a private detective."

Her eyes got very wide. She sank down on the bar stool and looked at me in a goofy but totally enchanting way. "You're a private eye?" she said.

I put up my hand. "Do me a favor," I said. "Keep it to yourself. Don't spread it around."

She frowned. "Why?"

"The Goobie Wheatly thing. The murder."

Her eyes got all wide again. "You're here to investigate that." She frowned. "No, you were here when it happened. You're here to play the part." She shook her head. "I don't understand."

"Coincidence," I said. "I mean me being a P.I. I'm here to play the part. But since I am a P.I., I'm doing a little investigating. I sort of have to. Because the cops haven't got a clue in this case, so they're leaning toward me. New kid in town. Plus that whole business of getting the prompter fired. And I was the one who found the body. So you could kind of say I'm investigating this thing in self-defense."

I know I had TV to thank for the buildup, but I have to tell you, Beth was absolutely thrilled.

She lowered her voice conspiratorially. "What do you want me to do?"

"I need information," I said. "Because I haven't been here that long. I don't know what the relationships are—the people in the theater. I don't just mean with Goobie Wheatly—who had reason to hate him. From what I understand, everybody did. I hate to speak ill of the dead, but unfortunately he wasn't a very nice guy. He pissed everybody off, and they all resented him. I understand he even hassled you."

"Oh? What did you hear?"

"That he broke up some relationship or other."

She made a face. "Oh, that isn't true. Phil and I were just friends. It's not like—well, it wasn't anything. I stopped seeing Phil because the relationship wasn't going anywhere, you know? So Goobie starts acting like he broke us up. Which he didn't. Because there was nothing to break up, see?"

"Yeah, I do. But tell me something. What other relationships were there where there *was* something going on? Some juicy bit of gossip Goobie might have got his hands on? Somebody he might not have liked? How about the actors in the company, for instance? You know anything interesting about them?"

"Actors in the company?"

"Yeah."

She frowned. "Not likely. There's only two guys and look at 'em." She looked around to see who was in earshot, spotted Peter Constantine sitting at the end of the bar. She lowered her voice. "Peter Constantine. He's gay."

That hadn't occurred to me. I frowned. "You sure?"

"Pretty sure. I mean, it's not like he ever says anything, ever talks about it. But here he is, a young actor in summer stock, and he's not coming on to the apprentice girls, you know?" She put her hand on my shoulder. "Don't get me wrong. It's not like he's coming on to the apprentice *boys* either. He just acts like he's not interested. Keeps to himself. The quiet type. A loner, you know?"

I did, and I felt a shudder. That was just the way mass murderers were always described by their neighbors after they were caught. Beth might not think much of him as a suspect, but I figured I could set my sights a notch higher on Peter Constantine.

"So he wasn't having a relationship with anyone that you know of?" I said.

She shook her head. "No."

"Not with this other actor, this David what's-his-name?"

The beer had long since arrived. She had taken a sip and now she nearly spit it out giggling. "Him? No way."

"Well, why not?"

"He's not gay. Just fat."

Ah, youth. When perceptions were so cut and dried.

"What about Goobie Wheatly?" I said.

"What do you mean?"

"Think there was anything between them?"

"Between him and Peter?"

"Yeah."

She wrinkled up her nose. "You mean sexual?"

I shrugged.

"Come on," she said. "Give me a break."

"You're saying there wasn't?"

"Of course not."

"Do you remember what kind of relationship he *did* have with Goobie Wheatly?"

"None at all."

"Well, that's strange, isn't it?"

She frowned. "What?"

"From what I hear, Goobie pissed everybody off. Are you telling me Peter Constantine wasn't one of them?"

"If so, it was nothing special. Nothing worth talking about. I'm sure Peter didn't like him."

"Why?"

"Like you say, nobody did."

"The other actor. David. What about him?"

"What *about* him?"

"Did he have any relationships, anything to hide? Or any particular grudge against Goobie Wheatly?"

"Not that I know of. If you ask me, I think you're on the wrong track."

"What do you mean?"

"About the resident company. I can't imagine them doing *anything*."

"What about the women?"

"In the company?"

"Yeah."

"No way. Not them." She looked around. "You see Nellie there, talking to Avery Allington? You know why he's buying her drinks?"

"I have a pretty good idea."

"No, I don't mean that. Sure, he's trying to get her into bed. I mean, why is he trying? It's because he's new. Cause he's jobbed in for the show, so he doesn't know her yet."

"So what?"

"She's a cock-tease. All talk and no action. Likes to lead guys on. Then when they find out they're getting nowhere, they drop her like a hot potato." She jerked her thumb in Avery's direction. "He doesn't know it yet, but he'll see."

"How do you know?"

"Huh?"

"How do you know she does that? Who did she do it to?"

"Oh. Well, Phil for one. That's the one I told you about, the one Goobie said he broke us up? Well, afterwards Phil made a play for her and she pulled the whole routine." She shrugged. "I could have told him. But he wouldn't have listened."

"You're saying she'd done it before?"

"Yeah."

"To who."

"Our producer/director."

My eyes widened. "Herbie?"

"I shouldn't be saying this, should I? He's a friend of yours, right?"

"Yeah, but we're talking murder here. You saying there was something between him and Nellie Knight?"

"No, there wasn't. He might have thought there was, but it never happened. A cock-tease, see?"

"Good lord," I said. "And this was before the thing with Phil?"

"Oh yeah. Way back. The beginning of the summer."

"And nothing since?"

"What do you mean? The two of them? No, why would there be, when he found out it wasn't going anywhere?"

"Was there anybody else?"

"You mean with Nellie?"

"Yeah."

"Not that I know of. Isn't that enough?"

"Yeah," I said. "It certainly is. What about the other one?"

"Who? Julie?"

"If that's her name. The woman who plays Catherine."

"Yeah, that's her. Julie Katz."

"Well, what about her? Anything interesting going on?"

"I wouldn't think so. She's a little old for that sort of thing."

Ah, youth. The woman had to be younger than me. But Beth didn't seem to notice that what she'd just said could be construed as rude.

"She had no special problems with Goobie Wheatly?" I said.

"No. I really think you're on the wrong track. With this resident-company bit. But if you're looking for scandal . . ."

"Yeah?" I said.

She looked around to see who was in earshot, then turned back and whispered, "Margie Miller."

I took a breath. That's what I thought she wanted to tell

me. Herbie wasn't that discreet, and his affair was most likely public knowledge. Chief Bob knew about it, and probably most everybody else did too.

It wasn't going to help much, but I figured I'd better hear about it as if I hadn't. "Margie?" I said. "What about her?"

"Well, this is the juicy stuff," she said. "I mean, forget the resident company. But Margie, she's something else. I mean, she's having an affair with Herbie, right? Everybody knows that—it's how she got the part in the play, for god's sake. So here she is, having this affair with the producer/director of the whole theater, and you'd think she'd be discreet. At least until the play was over. But no, she's gotta have something on the side."

I blinked. Jesus Christ, Margie's little fling with the tech director was public knowledge too?

I frowned, "What do you mean?" I said.

"I mean, here she is having her affair with Herbie, and at the same time she's fooling around with someone else."

"Oh? And who might that be?"

"Walter Penbridge."

"Who? Oh, you mean the actor?"

"Yeah. The one whose part you're taking. I suppose it's to be expected. Co-stars, they have a fling. It always happens in the theater. It's a wonder she's not coming on to you."

I rubbed my head. "Oh, good lord."

"What is it?"

"Well," I said. "That's interesting as all hell, but it's not what I want. I mean, maybe they had a relationship. Fine. But it was over. I mean *really* over. The guy died. This was a done deal. It doesn't really tie in with Goobie Wheatly and the general scheme of things."

"Well, maybe not."

"Well, what about him?"

"Who?"

"Goobie Wheatly. Did Margie Miller ever come on to him?"

Her eyes widened. "Of course not. He—"

"Was too old," I finished for her.

I was feeling pretty old myself. After a few more questions I let Beth escape back to the apprentices.

For my own part, I had a lot to think of. What Beth had told me was rather disturbing. And not just the opinion that old men couldn't find love. All that schoolgirl chatter about Peter being gay, David being asexually fat, Nellie being a cock-tease, Catherine woman-whose-name-I-missed-again being too old and particularly Margie-poo being a nympho—god, how had she missed *that* word?—well, all that was a lot to mull over.

There were some pretty good clues in that, I thought. Either that or it was all gibberish. I'm not sure Beth was entirely accurate, but she sure did have a nice smile.

Plus the show had gone well.

So all in all, it was a pretty good night.

☆ 29 ☆

SERGEANT MACAULLIF WASN'T PLEASED TO HEAR FROM ME.
No surprise there. I can't recall a time he ever *was* pleased
to hear from me, or at least let on he was. MacAullif was an
NYPD homicide sergeant, and I'd worked with him on a
number of investigations. If that's the right word for it. It's
not, really, but I don't know how better to say it. Anyway,
he and I had a sort of friendly adversarial relationship. A
little long on sarcasm, but still comfortable, if that makes
any sense.

At any rate, he voiced what had become his routinely
obligatory displeasure at hearing it was me. For my money,
his irritation became much more genuine when he learned
there was a murder, then escalated when I told him where I
was.

"Connecticut?" he said. "What the fuck you doing in
Connecticut?"

I explained about doing the play. As expected, that did not
cheer him.

"Jesus Christ, what a moron," he said. "Can't you do
anything right?"

"This was not my doing," I said.

"Yeah. You wanna know what your problem is? You

have the Midas touch in reverse. Everything you touch turns to shit."

"Thanks a lot. You want to waste a lot of time blaming me for this, or could we discuss it rationally for a minute?"

"What's to discuss? You're in Connecticut, aren't you? I got no jurisdiction in Connecticut. Whatever the hell you want, I can't do it."

"I don't want anything."

"Then why'd you call?"

"To ask you a question."

"See, you *do* want something. You want advice."

"Not advice. Just a simple question."

"With you, nothing's simple. Look, I'm up to my ass in work this morning. I ain't got time to fuck around. You got a question, ask it and let me get on with my life. But it better be important. If it's not important, I'm gonna be pissed."

"It's important."

"Fine. Fire away. What's your question?"

"How do you spell *actor*?"

There was a long pause. I could practically hear Mac-Aullif's teeth grinding. I could imagine a cartoon character doing a slow burn.

"What . . . did . . . you . . . say?" MacAullif said ominously.

"I know it sounds stupid," I said, "but I gotta know. Look, in a homicide, if it's a shooting, the cops call the perpetrator the shooter. If it's not a shooting, they sometimes call him the actor. Instead of the perpetrator, they say the actor. Referring to the guy who did it. Don't you sometimes do that?"

There was a pause. I could hear the tension in MacAullif's voice, like he was about to explode.

"Yeah. I sometimes do that. So?"

"So how do you spell it?"

The explosion came.

"Who the fuck cares!" MacAullif bellowed. I think I could have heard him without the telephone. "What the fuck difference does it make?"

"I need to know," I said. "See, I'm here with a group of actors, and the cops are referring to the killer as the actor. I don't know how to take that. I asked them how to spell it. The investigator at the scene says a-c-t-e-r. The chief of police spells it a-c-t-o-r. So what's the real way?"

There was another pause. "Real way?"

"Yeah. When you type up an official report, how do you spell *actor*?"

"Who the fuck cares!" MacAullif bellowed again. "Jesus Christ, what the hell difference does it make how *I* spell it. How *I* spell it isn't official. How any other cop spells it isn't official. What, you think there's some guide with the legal definition and proper spelling in it? I spell it any goddamned way I feel like it. And so does any other cop in New York City. And that doesn't make it official and that doesn't make it right.

"But even if there *was* some goddamned official spelling of the fucking word, what the hell difference could it possibly make in a fucking homicide? I mean, how could it possibly matter?"

I didn't know. I just knew it mattered to me. Ever since I'd heard the cop say it the night of the murder I'd been obsessed with the idea. And even knowing it was stupid, it was something I couldn't get out of my head until I'd resolved.

Which was why I'd braved calling MacAullif. Knowing the extent of the abuse I'd have to endure. Or perhaps needing the abuse to snap me out of it, to stimulate me and get my thoughts back on track.

But it hadn't helped. The phone call to MacAullif had not exorcised the demons.

I could not get the phrase out of my head.

"The actor was not on the scene."

Actor.

Acter.

Any way you spelled it, it bothered the hell out of me.

I had a feeling it always would.

☆ **30** ☆

CHIEF BOB WAS OUT WHEN I STOPPED BY, AND FELIX SAID HE wouldn't be in till after lunch, so I strolled over to the playhouse to check out the *Glass Menagerie* rehearsal. Only when I got there, the house and work lights were off and there was no one there.

I went out in the lobby and bumped into Rita, the box-office girl, who was busy hanging up posters for *Glass Menagerie*. I asked her why they weren't rehearsing and was told in a tone of voice that implied I was a moron that they *were*. Me being a stranger in these parts who had never attended a rehearsal other than the dress, and Rita not being the swiftest individual ever to grace god's green earth, it only took a few minutes for me to glean the information that the rehearsal wasn't onstage, that there was a rehearsal hall in one end of the scene shop and that the rehearsal was up there.

The jerk of her thumb Rita used to punctuate "up there" was rather vague, but I figured I could find it. Before I went, it occurred to me she was another person I hadn't thought to question since the murder. In fact, I wasn't even sure if she was there that night.

It turned out she was, though not in the box office. She'd been sitting in the audience with everybody else.

That stirred a chord in my memory. It took me a moment to put my finger on it.

"Wait a minute," I said. "You were in the audience for all of Act Three?"

"That's right."

"But Herbie's wife made a phone call from the box office. Called the baby-sitter. Didn't you have to go out and let her in?"

She shook her head. "No. Why would I? It was open."

"You leave the box office open when there's no one there?"

She looked at me as if I were an idiot. "Why not?"

I *felt* like an idiot. Why should I debate the subject with her? If she did, she did.

I was just turning to go when Amanda came rushing out of the box office with some papers in her hand.

"I'm glad I caught you," she said. "You came late, so we never signed you in."

I frowned. "Signed me in?"

She smiled. "So to speak." She thrust the papers at me. "Here. If you wouldn't mind, just be an angel and do it now."

"What's this?" I said, taking them.

"W-4 and a health form," she said. "You do want to get paid, don't you?"

I certainly did. I accepted the pen, quickly filled out the W-4.

The health form was harder. A full page, both sides, seemingly hundreds of questions.

I frowned. "What's the purpose of this?" I said. "Doesn't a doctor have to do it?"

Amanda shook her head. "No, no. It's just for insurance purposes. We need your general background, plus the names and addresses of the doctors who would have your medical records."

I took a breath. What a pain in the ass.

"Look," I said. "Could I fill this out and hand it in tomorrow? I'm going to have to call my wife to get my doctor's address, you know. I mean, I know where it is—I can find it just fine—but the street number?"

I could tell Amanda would have liked to have had the form right then, but what could she say? I escaped from the lobby with the form unfilled, and set out in quest of the rehearsal hall.

I followed a dirt road through the meadow in the direction from which I'd seen the apprentices carrying a flat on strike night, and soon came to what had obviously once been a barn but now served as the theater's rehearsal hall and scene shop.

A half-dozen apprentice girls were painting flats on the lawn outside. One of them was Beth, who smiled and waved. It was a hot sunny morning and she was wearing a bikini bathing suit, which made my day. At least until I looked by her and saw who else was sunbathing on the lawn.

Avery fucking Allington. TV star and ham *extraordinaire*. With no rehearsal of his own to go to, he had donned a bathing suit, set up a deck chair out on the lawn, and was lounging in it and obviously flirting with the apprentice girls.

When he saw me, he smiled and nodded, a regal, condescending nod that I had to either acknowledge or look like a schmuck. I gave him a wave but otherwise ignored him and walked up to Beth.

"Hi," I said. "I wanted to check out the rehearsal. Where is it?"

She smiled, pointed to steps leading up to the far end of the barn. "In there," she said, then lowered her voice and smiled. "But I hear it's boring."

"Oh yeah?" I said. "Who said that?"

"Avery."

"Oh? Has he been in there?"

"No. But he says it's a boring play."

"I'm sure Tennessee Williams is rolling in his grave," I

said. "I hope Avery won't mind if I make my own assessment."

I walked over, climbed the steps to the rehearsal hall.

It was like a theater without the audience or wings. A small raised stage, with just enough space in front of it for the director and a few other people to sit.

Today, those few other people were Margie-poo. Back from her dalliance with the tech director, no doubt.

The four actors, Peter Constantine, Nellie Knight and the man and woman playing Major Petkoff and Catherine (mental note to learn their names #403) were all onstage doing the scene at the dinner table where the lights go out. It occurred to me that made life easy for Herbie—no blocking. It also occurred to me to wonder if, when there *was* blocking, Margie-poo would open her mouth and chime in.

Herbie saw me, motioned me over.

I went over, bent down by him, whispered, "What?"

"Do you want something?" he whispered.

"No. Just thought I'd look in on rehearsal."

He frowned. "Look, I'd rather you came back when we're running. Right now we're blocking things, and it's slow as hell. Also, it's distracting for the actors."

I put up my hand. "No problem, Herbie. Since I never got in the rehearsal hall myself, I just wanted to see where it was." I nodded, eased my way out the door.

Right, Herbie. Distracting for the actors. And I suppose Margie isn't.

I came down the steps, walked by the flats on the lawn again.

Avery Allington seemed to have distracted Beth, at least enough for her to be chatting with him while she painted. I walked on by and followed the sound of power saws through the wide double doors into the other end of the barn, where the apprentice boys were busily assembling more flats.

The tech director, lighting and set designer, stage manager, and Margie-poo seducer was supervising the construction. I wondered if he realized she was in the rehearsal hall in the other end of the barn. I wondered if he cared.

While I watched, Ridley came by carrying a coiled-up length of electrical cable. He appeared, as always, to be in his own little world. He walked right by me, with no recognition whatsoever, to a ladder at one side of the shop leading up to what must at one time have been a hayloft. He climbed the ladder, disappeared from sight.

A voice said, "Excuse me."

I looked up, saw two apprentice boys carrying a newly constructed flat. One of them looked familiar, and after a moment I realized it was because he was the one who played the officer who searched Raina's bedroom in Act One. Which made him the one who'd been involved with Beth. The one Goobie had broken up. The one who'd tried to hit on Nellie Knight.

I wasn't standing there like a clod thinking all this, by the way; I'd stepped aside to let them pass. I was looking after them thinking all this.

"Can I help you?"

I turned, found myself face to face with the tech director.

In that moment it occurred to me that, aside from Mary Anne, in the space of the last half hour I had just seen every single person connected with the theater.

Which meant I had seen the murderer.

If I could only figure out who.

I took a breath, blew it out again. Shook my head.

"Christ, I wish you could."

✫ 31 ✫

THE HEADLINE THAT AFTERNOON WAS PLAYHOUSE MURDER BAFFLES POLICE. The paper was out early, by one o'clock, so I read it during lunch at the snack bar, then strolled over to the police station to see what Chief Bob thought about it.

He didn't think much. "No big deal," he said, waving it away. "Hell, you can't have a simple break-in or car theft without the paper suggesting I'm not doing my job. It's small-town politics. It's the same all over."

I wished I shared his lack of concern. It occurred to me Chief Bob might not be so damn indifferent if *he* were a suspect in the case. I didn't voice the thought—no reason to remind him that *I* was. Though I'm sure he knew that well enough. Instead I filled him in on my conversations with Peter Constantine and Beth Scott.

"Excellent," he said. "Now you're doing what I hoped you would do. Mingling with the suspects and keeping your ear to the ground."

"Not that we got anything useful," I said.

"Maybe not, but it all helps. You see patterns. This one actor may be gay—though this apprentice girl's opinion on the subject is not necessarily right. The guy isn't admittedly gay, so there's room for error. But it's interesting, because if he *is* gay and isn't admitting to it, there's a whole dynamic there that could mean something. Add that to his insane jealousy of any visiting actors—guest stars, if you will."

"How does that add up to murder?"

"I didn't say it did. But you put it all together and we begin to get a picture.

"Then this stuff about Margie," Chief Bob added. "If she really did have a fling with this Walter Penbridge . . ."

"I think she did," I said.

"Oh? Why is that?"

I told him what I thought I'd seen of Margie-poo and the tech director.

He nodded. "There you are. This is just the sort of thing I need."

I looked at him. "Why?"

He frowned, thought a moment. "I know, I know. It's the type of stuff soap operas are made of. But you know, I like that. The intertwining patterns. The more you learn about them, the more you know of motives. They don't have to be motives for the murder. Just normal, everyday motivations. The more you learn, the better chance there is something in there that will help."

"Yeah," I said, somewhat dubiously. I must say I was beginning to feel uncomfortable. What Chief Bob had been saying was not reassuring me. In fact, I had visions of the investigation dragging on for weeks. Months, even. While Chief Bob leisurely investigated the everyday motivations of everyone in town.

As if he read my thoughts again, Chief Bob suddenly reverted to crisp efficiency.

"But enough of that," he said. "We have work to do here. First I'm going to outline the basic problem, then I'm going to need your help."

"The basic problem?"

"Yes. Aside from who did it, of course, which is the *real* basic problem. No, the basic problem here is that we know what everyone was doing at the time of the murder. Or the approximate time of the murder. Because the murder took place during Act Three and we know what each and every actor did during that act. Unfortunately, the murder is entirely consistent with the actions of those actors. In other words, any of them could have done it and still maintained the strict schedule required of them by their performance in Act Three." He paused, frowned, shook his head. "Except . . ."

I looked at him. "Except what?"

"They had to act."

"What?"

Chief Bob rubbed his chin. "See, I've been an actor myself. I've been onstage. So I know. It's not easy, acting. It requires concentration, skill. That's why I tend to think it *wasn't* an actor."

"Why not?"

"Think about it. To kill someone, and then walk out onstage. Remembering your lines, your blocking, your part. Keeping in character. Not letting the fact you've just killed someone show." Chief Bob pursed his lips and shook his head. "That would really take concentration, wouldn't it. Be some hell of an acting exercise."

I frowned. "I see what you mean."

"Yeah. And the fact is, none of the actors seemed any different than usual. We know that because nobody's mentioned it. Not one person has commented on anything out of the ordinary with regard to that act." He smiled. "With the exception of you, of course. Actually, several people have commented on the fact that you seemed particularly fired up toward the end."

"Yeah, I was. Because it was going well, the lines were coming and I was getting into it. Not because I'd just killed the stage manager."

He held up his hand. "No need to protest. I'm just telling you we have nothing useful in that regard.

"Same goes for the audience. If Herbie's wife, for instance, had gone backstage to kill Goobie Wheatly at the same time she slipped out to call her baby-sitter, you'd expect her to be somewhat frazzled-looking coming back. Or you would expect the baby-sitter to find her somewhat distracted on the phone—either because she has just killed him or because she was about to, depending on when she made the call.

"Same with the rest. No one, for instance, can remember Amanda going out and coming back during the act. Where, if she had come back from just having killed Goobie Wheatly, you'd expect her manner to have been such that people *would* have remembered it.

Chief Bob broke off and looked at me. "Do I seem to be going around in circles? If so, it's just because I am. The problem with the crime is, from the evidence we have here, no one could have done it. At least, is *likely* to have done it.

"The motive, if any, is obscure. Opportunity was open to all. We have no way of narrowing this thing down. We are, in effect, no closer to solving this crime than we were three and a half days ago when the murder was committed."

My thoughts exactly. It was nice to have Chief Bob voicing them, so I didn't have to.

"So what can we do?" I said.

"Take a different tack, that's what we can do. We can stop focusing on the murder as such. You've taken a good step in that direction, questioning the actors. That was good work with Constantine. Now I'd like to see you get the others. Why didn't you, by the way, when you were into it last night?"

"The ones who play Major Petkoff and Catherine were busy running lines. It would have been tough to disturb them. And Nellie Knight was being hit on by Avery Allington."

He raised his eyebrows. "Really? You didn't mention that. Now, that's interesting. That's just the sort of stuff we need. Did he get anywhere, by the way?"

"I don't know for sure, but according to Beth he wasn't about to."

"Oh?"

I told him what she told me about Nellie being a cocktease.

He smiled, shrugged and held out his hands. "See?

There's a wealth of information here. You think anybody mentioned any of these things during *my* questioning? Of course not. Because they have nothing to do with the investigation. No one thinks they're important. No one mentions them. But how the hell can I get a picture of what happened unless I know the personalities of the parties involved?

"This is excellent stuff. You get any more tidbits like that, don't keep it to yourself, pass it right along.

"Now, where were we? Oh, yeah—what can we do? As I say, we gotta broaden our scope. Stop concentrating just on the murder. All this little stuff will help, but let's try to be specific. Pin people down. When you talk to people now, steer them *away* from the murder. Get them talking about the things that happened prior to it. Relationships, arguments, fights, disputes. Anything at all.

"Once you got that—and this is something you should ask everyone—try to find out if anyone remembers anything prior to the murder—anything at all and I don't care what it is—but anything that struck them as strange, unusual, out of the ordinary."

I frowned. "What do you mean?"

"Just that. Anything worth commenting on. Anything worth remembering is something I want to hear. Anything they tell you, tell me. I really want to know if there was anything that happened before Goobie Wheatly's murder that was the least bit strange."

My eyes widened. "Oh, good lord."

He frowned. "What is it? You remember something?"

"Yeah."

"What?"

"A light almost fell on my head."

☆ 32 ☆

I FOUND RIDLEY WORKING ON A FRESNEL IN THE LIGHTING loft in the scene shop.

He didn't look up, though he must have realized I was there. He paid no attention, continued working on the light.

I let him work, glanced around the loft.

The walls were hung with wires and lights, mostly in poor repair. Which of course figured—all those in working condition were presently hanging in the theater.

There was a window high up in the wall with a chair underneath it. The window was open a crack, and I noticed the faint but unmistakable smell of marijuana in the air. I figured Ridley must stand on the chair and try to blow the smoke out the window. That conjured up quite an image—from the looks of it, he'd have to stand on tiptoe, and what getting high like that must feel like I couldn't imagine.

I gave Ridley another few seconds to pretend I wasn't there, then cleared my throat and said, "Ridley?"

Even then it was several moments before he very reluctantly looked up.

"Hi," I said. "I don't think we've been introduced. I'm Stanley Hastings."

The bloodshot eyes staring at me registered zero compre-

211

hension. If he'd heard me you wouldn't have known it. He tilted his head on one side and—as he had when I'd seen him that first night at the theater—once again struck me as the result of years and years of inbreeding.

I felt like waving my hand in front of his face, but I didn't want to piss him off, assuming he was the type of person who *got* pissed off. Freak him out, more than likely. Or whatever phrase his generation would use to refer to that happenstance.

I took a breath. "I'm in the show," I said. "I play Captain Bluntschli. You must know that. You take some of your cues off me. In Act One, you know? When I run around striking matches and you have to bring the lights up?"

Ridley said nothing, turned his attention back to the Fresnel.

"I need to talk to you," I said.

He didn't look up, just mumbled, "Gotta fix the light."

"Of course you do," I said. "That's your job. And you wanna do a good job, don't you?"

Ridley had started to pick up a screwdriver. He stopped, looked back up at me, and this time there was light in his eyes. "You gonna get me fired?" he said.

I looked at him in surprise. "Of course not."

He wasn't convinced. "You got Kirk fired, didn't you?"

"No, I didn't."

"Yes, you did. I was there. I saw."

I shook my head. "Kirk got *himself* fired, Ridley. By doing a bad job. And I didn't fire him. Goobie did."

"You asked him to."

"Let's not quibble. The point is, I don't want to get you fired."

"Did you want to get Kirk fired?"

Shit. Behind Ridley's vacant stare there was some primitive intelligence at work. Some instinctual sense of self-preservation.

"I didn't want to get Kirk fired. I wanted to be prompted by someone competent. It turned out that meant he got fired, but that wasn't what I wanted. I wasn't thinking of Kirk. I was thinking of me."

That was too much for Ridley to follow. I could almost see the thoughts groping to make it through his brain.

He exhaled, said, "Whew," and went back to working on the light.

"I need to talk to you, Ridley," I said. "You wanna work on the light, fine, but pay attention. Do you hear?"

He mumbled, "Yeah."

"Now, look," I said. "I'm not trying to get you fired. This has nothing to do with your job. But Goobie Wheatly got killed, and it's important we figure out why. You can see that, can't you?"

Ridley said nothing, continued working on the light.

"Don't you wanna know who killed him?"

"I didn't do it."

"I didn't say you did. Of course you didn't. You were up in the light booth, waiting for him to give you the light cue on the headset. But someone killed him, and I have to find out who."

"I don't *know* who."

"I know you don't. But I need your help. I need you to answer some questions. Will you do that?"

There was a pause. Then, without looking up, he shrugged.

I took that for a yes. "Fine," I said. "Now look. The dress rehearsal. The night Goobie was killed. I'm not concerned with that now. But the night *before* that. The night *before* the dress rehearsal. Remember when you were at dinner at the diner and they called you up and had you come back because a light fell on the stage?"

Ridley's head jerked somewhat at that, but he didn't look up. "Not my fault," he said.

"I didn't say it was your fault, Ridley. You gotta understand. No one's trying to blame you. I'm just trying to find out why. It's important, so concentrate and try to answer my questions. You remember that?"

"Yeah."

"They called you up and you came back and you found one of the Lekos had fallen and smashed on the stage, right?"

"Yeah."

"And you didn't have one to replace it, did you?"

There was a pause. Then he said, "How do you know that?"

"I was there that night. I saw you working on the stage."

Ridley's head moved slightly. I could see one eye peering up at me. The moment it caught mine it shifted, looked back at the light.

"You were working on the light. Just like you are now. Except this is a Fresnel and that was a Leko. You were working on the Leko, taking pieces of the smashed one and pieces of another old one and putting them together to make a working light. So I figured all the working Lekos were already in the show and you must not have had another one to use. So you were putting one together, see?"

Ridley said nothing, appeared very interested in the plug on the Fresnel.

"You know, I'm wondering if you figured out how that light came to fall?"

"Not my fault," Ridley said sulkily.

"I didn't say it was. So, you replaced the light that fell with the new one you put together?"

There was a pause.

"Ridley?" I prompted.

Another pause and Ridley said, "What?"

"The light you put together. You hung that up in the place of the one that fell?"

Another pause, then he said, "No."

"No? Why not?"

"It wasn't my light."

"What do you mean?"

This time Ridley actually raised his head and looked up at me defiantly. "The light that fell. It wasn't my light. It wasn't from the show."

In spite of myself, I felt a cold chill.

"What's that, Ridley? What did you say?"

He shook his head. "It wasn't my light."

"Then where did it come from?"

"I don't know."

Jesus Christ.

I knelt down on the floor of the loft next to him. It was all I could do to keep from grabbing him by the shoulders and shaking him. Still, I tried to move him by my intensity.

"Ridley," I said. "Think. Concentrate. This light that fell. How do you know it wasn't from the show?"

"It wasn't."

"Yeah, but you *thought* it was. You got another light and you fixed it."

"Yeah, sure. How was I to know?"

"You're saying when you got the light fixed and went in the grid to hang it, all the lights were there?"

"Yeah. All *my* lights were there."

"Then where did this light come from?"

"I don't know."

"You're saying someone took a Leko up in the grid and dropped it on the stage?"

"Yeah," Ridley said. After a pause he added, "But it's not my fault."

I figured I'd given him enough reassurances. So I didn't bother telling him I didn't think it was his fault either.

☆ **33** ☆

CHIEF BOB SHOOK HIS HEAD. "IT DOESN'T MAKE ANY SENSE."

"What do you mean?" I said. "It's perfectly logical."

"And how is that?"

"The light wasn't from the show. The kid puts together a new light, goes to hang it and finds all his lights are there. He's a stupid kid, so he doesn't bother to tell anyone. He's just happy he doesn't have to hang the light and goes off to smoke a joint."

"So?"

"So? So it's perfectly clear. Someone tried to drop a light on my head."

"Why?"

"Because I'm a private detective."

"How would they know that?"

"I have no idea. But Herbie knew. He could have told anyone."

"Why would he?"

"What's the difference? What if he did? The word would get around and people would know. And someone who cared could drop a light on my head."

"Why?"

"I told you why. I'm a private detective."

He shook his head. "Doesn't wash for a lot of reasons."

"Name 'em."

"Who was with you when the light fell?"

"Herbie and Amanda."

"Where were they?"

"Right next to me."

"Onstage?"

"Sure."

"So the light just missed them as well?"

"It missed them. It *just* missed me."

"It was closer to you?"

"Much."

"That's relative and colored by your perception. You almost got hit by a light. How close were Herbie and Amanda standing to you?"

"I don't know. A few feet."

"So while the light was closer to you, it could have been meant for them."

"It's possible, but I don't think so. Why them? They're just theater folk. I'm the private detective."

"*That's* what doesn't make sense," Chief Bob said.

"What doesn't?"

"That part of the theory. That someone tried to drop a light on your head because you're a private detective. That I can't buy. On the other hand, you tell me someone tried to drop a light on Herbie and Amanda, now you're talkin'. See, if they're the targets, either one of them, the whole thing makes sense."

"But I don't?"

"Not at all. They're the head of the theater. Big-time stuff. You'll pardon me, but who gives a damn about you?"

"I'm a private detective."

"Who gives a shit? I'm sorry, but what does it matter? The problem is, this whole thing's the wrong way around."

"What?"

"It's all ass-backwards. If the murder had already happened, fine. Then Herbie brings you in and the murderer says, "Oh, shit, he's bringing in a private detective to get me, I better nail him." But there hasn't been any murder. There's no reason to suspect Herbie's bringing you in for any other purpose but to play the role. See what I mean?"

"Yeah. But . . ."

"But what?"

I frowned. "I don't know. But if the murderer was planning on killing Goobie Wheatly, and the murderer thought Herbie suspected something, and figured that was why Herbie was bringing me in . . ."

I broke off to see Chief Bob shaking his head back and forth and rolling his eyes.

"Oh, come on," he said. "If that's the solution, I'll resign from the force. I mean, double-think? Triple-think? The murderer has to know *in advance* he's killing Goobie Wheatly. Then he has to suspect that Herbie suspects that he's going to kill Goobie Wheatly. Then he has to figure out that because Herbie suspects this, he's going to protect against that eventuality by bringing in a private detective disguised as an actor in the show. You wanna suggest to me any way whatsoever that thought process might have evolved?"

"Not particularly."

"I didn't think so."

"Well, just because *we* don't know what the killer was thinking doesn't mean he couldn't be thinking it."

Chief Bob held up his hand. "Please. I do not wish to get involved in metaphysical speculation. I want facts. Failing that, I want theories grounded somewhat in reality."

"The fact is a light almost fell on my head."

"Which may or may not mean anything."

"Granted. But will you concede the possibility that it does?"

"Of course."

"Then we have that fact. A light falling. And it wasn't a light from the show. That's very interesting."

"Why?"

"Why? It means someone carried a light up there and tried to drop it on us."

"Why?"

I looked at him. "Why does it mean that, or why did someone drop it on us, or—"

"No. Why did someone carry a light up there? There's nothing *but* lights up there. If someone wants to drop a light on your head, why not drop one of those? Why go to the trouble of finding another light and dragging it on up?"

"Maybe he didn't have a wrench."

"Huh?"

"The lights hanging from the grid are bolted onto pipes. That's how they're hung. You can only loosen them with a wrench."

"Oh."

"You didn't know that?"

"My experience in theater has always been from the performing end. I've never worked lights."

"Yeah, well, I have."

"Oh, really? Excellent. No wonder you're so keen on this."

I stopped, looked at him. "My theory that someone tried to drop a light on my head has nothing to do with the fact I once ran lights."

"No, no, of course not. I'm just saying you know the ins and outs. Well, that's interesting. Someone wanting to kill you with a light from up on the grid could only do so if they had a wrench. So they have to go find another light, bring it up there and drop it on your head." Chief Bob frowned, shook his head.

"What's the matter?" I asked.

"The theory. I can't say I like it. I mean, the killer has to go and find another light. They're big, bulky, cumbersome and hard to hide. Assuming the killer isn't Ridley or the tech director, to be seen carrying a light would arouse suspicion."

"Yeah. So?"

"So why would he get a light? Why not a wrench? A small crescent wrench, he could slip it in his pocket, no one would see it, he could climb up on the grid and unbolt the light."

I opened my mouth, closed it again. I felt incredibly frustrated.

"I don't *know* why he didn't do that," I said. "I don't *know* why he got a light instead. But the point is he did."

"Then there must be a reason," Chief Bob said. "No one does things for no reason. If the killer brought a light instead of a wrench, he must have had a reason."

"Suppose he just didn't think of it?"

Chief Bob shrugged. "That's a reason," he said. "It's a *bad* one, but it's a reason. But I'm not accepting it until I see some evidence pointing in that direction. In the meantime, I would suggest that we still look for an explanation of why the killer would have done that."

I kept quiet. As far as I was concerned, Chief Bob was talking in circles and I didn't want to get him started going around again.

He went around anyway.

"We also need an explanation for why this light would be dropped on you. Your being a private detective simply doesn't wash. If this were postcrime, yes. Then that's a theory worth investigating. But the way things stand, with the light falling first, it simply makes no sense. The murder would have to happen first. Before Herbie brought you in."

My eyes widened.

"Yes?" Chief Bob said. "What is it?"

"I just realized why I'm here."

Chief Bob frowned. "You mean because you're a murder suspect?"

I waved it away. "No, no. I don't mean here at the station. I mean *here*."

He frowned again. "I don't understand. What do you mean? Why are you here?"

"Because Walter Penbridge died."

✩ **34** ✩

CHIEF BOB WASN'T CONVINCED.

"You don't understand the problems," he said.

"You don't think this is worth investigating?"

"I didn't say that. I just said you didn't understand the problems."

"Pardon me, Chief, but I don't give a shit. I'm a murder suspect here, I have a theory that can clear me, and come hell or high water it's going to be investigated."

"No need to get testy. I didn't say I wouldn't investigate. I said there were problems. And there are. I'm sorry if you don't like that, but I have my responsibilities as chief of police. And they go beyond this murder investigation. Responsibilities to the people in this town."

"Politics? You're talking politics?"

"Worse than that. I'm talking public relations. Like it or not, I gotta live in this town. I can't go trompin' on everybody's toes."

"This is a murder investigation."

"No. *Goobie Wheatly* is a murder investigation. Walter Penbridge?" He held up his hand, waggled it back and forth.

"I can't believe you're pulling that."

"Pulling what?"

"You can't investigate Walter Penbridge unless it's a murder. But you'll never find out it's a murder unless you investigate it."

"That's hardly fair."

"Fair? Who's talking fair? You won't investigate the one thing in this case that might clear me because it might piss someone off, and you're talking to me about *fair?*"

"If you'd just hold your horses a minute, maybe I can get something done."

"Oh? You're gonna do something?"

Chief Bob ignored that and picked up the phone. "Felix," he said. "You know that actor from the playhouse, dropped dead last week. Name's Walter Penbridge . . . that's right. Listen, look that up for me, willya? Find out what happened with that. Attending physician, disposition of the body. Whatever they got."

Chief Bob hung up the phone, turned back to me.

"You gotta exhume the body," I said.

He made a face. "Let's not go jumping the gun."

"What do you mean, jumping the gun? How else are you gonna find out if it was a suspicious death?"

"All in good time. We find out what the facts are, we know what to do next. Now then, while we're waiting, let's hypothesize. Suppose you're right? Suppose he *was* killed?"

"Then it all fits."

"What all fits?"

"Well, the light falling, for one thing. Just like we were talking about. The murderer kills Penbridge. Then Herbie brings me in, and the murderer thinks that's why."

"Because you're a private detective?"

"Of course."

"Then he must have a lot of faith in your abilities. The murderer, I mean. To think that you could figure this out."

"Thanks a lot."

"Don't take it personally. But since we *can't* figure this out, since we can't even seem to get started, the motive must be somewhat obscure. And if it is, why would a killer fear some investigator stumbling on it?"

"Well, we don't know what was in the killer's mind. Since his motive must be perfectly clear to *him*, he may not realize it wouldn't be perfectly clear to us."

"That's really stretching."

"Give me a break. We're speculating on the unknown here. You ask me to justify why someone would do something when we have no facts to go on."

"I'm glad to hear you say that."

"What?"

"That we can't form theories without facts to go on. I got the impression we were doing exactly that."

I opened my mouth to protest, but Chief Bob held up his hand.

"Anyway, let's go on with this theory. Take it for granted Penbridge was murdered. Can we assume that explains why someone wanted to kill you?"

"I would think so. Wouldn't you?"

He frowned. "I'm not all that happy with it. But, for the sake of argument, say it's true. What does that tell us?"

"Well, for one thing, Herbie and Amanda are in the clear."

"That's obvious. We know they weren't up in the grid dropping lights on their own heads. But what about everybody else?"

I thought a moment. "I was told they were at dinner. The actors, I mean. And we subsequently picked Margie up at a restaurant. I can't vouch for the others, but it's something we could check out. Margie should at least remember who was there. There's only four in the company, plus Margie and Avery Allington. The four in the company were in the show that night. Margie joined me for rehearsal . . ." I broke off, frowned.

"What is it?"

"Avery Allington. It hadn't occurred to me before, because I didn't know. But he's *not* in the regular company, and he wasn't in that night's show. But he didn't come rehearse with me. It was just me and Margie."

"So?"

"Well, that's a little strange. Here I am, fitting into the show on short notice. Since Avery didn't have a performance that night, you'd have thought he could have come along to run our scenes."

Chief Bob considered. "I don't think that's all that strange. The man's a prima donna. Thinks he's hot stuff. A *real* star would be apt to be gracious, show up, put himself out. But a no-talent schmuck *playing* star, it's the other way around. They're too big to go to the rehearsal."

"I'll buy that," I said. "But the point is, he wasn't in the show. So when Herbie said the actors were at dinner, I don't know if he meant him."

"He wasn't in the show, but he would have been at rehearsal that afternoon, wouldn't he?"

"I suppose so."

"Well, it's something we can check. Which is good. It gives us another point of departure: Where was everyone that night during dinner? And this Ridley—you say he came and fixed the light?"

"Right. Herbie asked the girl in the box office to call down to the diner and have him come back. Which she did."

"She reached him there?"

"She must have. 'Cause he came back and fixed the light. I saw him working on it myself."

"But you don't know if he showed up as a result of her phone call. Do you?"

I frowned. "No, I guess not."

"So if Ridley had been in the theater that night and dropped that light himself, and found out people were looking for him to fix it, he could have conveniently showed up and gone to work."

I looked to him. "You're taking this thing seriously?"

He shrugged. "For the purpose of this discussion. If we're going to consider this, there's no point being half-assed about it. The point is, was there anything you observed that night that would eliminate *that* possibility?"

"That Ridley did it?"

"Yeah."

I considered. "No. I don't think there is. But if Ridley did that . . ."

"Yes?"

"Then he killed Walter Penbridge. And why would Ridley want to kill Walter Penbridge?"

"Why would *anyone* want to kill Walter Penbridge? That's another matter which we may or may not get into."

"Depending on local politics?"

Chief Bob frowned. "Not at all. Depending on whether or not it turns out to be relevant. Anyway, that's another thing we need to check out. Whether Ridley was actually at the diner that night. I assume if he was, he was not alone?"

"No, apparently it's an apprentice hangout."

Chief Bob nodded. "That will help."

The phone on his desk rang. He scooped it up. "Yes?" He listened a moment, said, "Thanks, Felix," and hung up the phone. He exhaled, said, "Shit."

"What's the matter?"

"Walter Penbridge."

"Why do I have the feeling I'm not going to like this?"

"Perhaps because I don't."

"What's the problem?"

"The attending physician was Ed Macy. He signed the death certificate."

"So?"

"There's two doctors in town. Ed Macy and Sy. They happen to hate each others's guts."

"Yeah? So what?"

"But they're outwardly very polite to each other. Go out of their way to avoid stepping on each other's toes."

"And?"

"Sy's the medical examiner. A case like this, he's the one would have to make the examination."

"So what?"

"Ed Macy signed the death certificate. Put the cause of death down as heart failure. You're askin' Sy to step in and contradict that determination, you're stirrin' up a hornet's nest."

"Oh, for Christ's sake. Are you telling me it can't be done?"

"No. I'm just telling you before I ask something like that be done, I gotta be pretty sure of my grounds. Sy comes in, cuts up the body and proves he died from other causes—well, there'd be hell to pay, but I can ride out the storm. So can Sy.

"But Sy comes in, takes a shot at it and *can't* prove anything, then I am in deep shit. Cause Ed Macy is going to scream bloody murder, and I won't have a leg to stand on."

"What if he doesn't hear about it?"

"Come on. In a town like this everybody hears everything."

"Well, that's tough," I said. "But you can't just let it go. You've gotta exhume the body."

"Well, that's another thing."

"What?"

"We *can't* exhume the body."

I stared at him. "Why the hell not?"

"To exhume a body, you gotta dig it up."

"Yes, Of course."

"Which we can't do."

I looked at him, gritted my teeth, "And why not?"

"Because it isn't buried yet." Chief Bob smiled. "You can't exhume a body that isn't buried. You can *autopsy* it, but you can't exhume it."

I looked at him in utter exasperation.

Chief Bob held up his hand. "Sorry. Couldn't resist. But that's the fact. This Walter Penbridge is from New York, but he's got no relatives around here. His only living relative is some sister in Oregon no one's been able to contact yet. So no one knows what to do with the body, and it's still on ice at the morgue. Nice for our purposes, if it comes to that."

"What do you mean, if it comes to that?"

"Just what I said. If we decide to go ahead with the autopsy, we're all set."

"Yeah, well, on what do you intend to base your decision?

The way I see it, the facts are all in. You've either gotta do it or not."

"The facts *aren't* all in. I could investigate the possibility first."

"Of someone killing Walter Penbridge?"

"Right."

"That's almost a week ago. You'd be investigating in the dark, because you wouldn't even know how he was killed."

"True."

"And you won't know unless you do that autopsy."

"Yeah, I know."

"So, you gonna do it?"

Chief Bob sighed. He grimaced and picked up the phone. "Felix. See if you can get Sy for me."

He hung up the phone and I said, "Thanks."

"Just doing my job. Can't say I like it, but there you are."

I stood up.

"Where you going?" he said.

"I just got time to go back, get cleaned up, get something to eat before the show."

"Yeah," he said. "Funny, but I'd forgotten about that. But of course the show must go on. Do me a favor, though."

"What's that?"

"Watch out for yourself."

"Because of the light?"

"There's always that. But I was thinking of the other thing."

"Oh? What?"

"I don't know if you considered this yet. But if your theory happens to be right . . ." He shrugged. "Last guy to play your part got himself killed."

☆ 35 ☆

IT WAS NOT A GREAT PERFORMANCE. I SUPPOSE I COULD HAVE guessed that from the seesaw nature of the performances ever since the dress rehearsal—last night was good, so tonight had to be a bust. But it wasn't just that. I found myself sleepwalking through it. I was incredibly distracted and just couldn't get into it.

No, I wasn't looking out for potential saboteurs. Despite Chief Bob's caution, onstage I felt relatively safe. No, what was throwing me off was that right before curtain I called the police station and found out Chief Bob had located Sy, and the medical examiner had already started his autopsy. With that on my mind it was hard to think of anything else. I went through Act One on automatic pilot, barely remembered doing it, got offstage and immediately rushed to the pay phone to call Chief Bob.

To no avail. It was early yet, and he hadn't heard a thing. However, I considered it significant he was hanging around the police station to find out. Though it occurred to me to wonder why Sy couldn't just call him at home. Maybe his home life wasn't happy. Maybe he and his wife were at odds.

Assuming he *had* a wife. It was a question that had never

228

concerned me before, but I speculated on it during the idle stretches of Act Two. I sat in my dressing room, listening to the dulcet tones of Avery Allington wafting down over the speaker system and mulled the whole thing over in my head.

Not that I came up with anything. Not even a halfway decent theory concerning Chief Bob's home life. No, I kept getting hung up on speculating on the damn autopsy result. So much so that halfway through the act I snuck out to the pay phone to call Chief Bob again.

Which answered one of my questions. No, not the biggie about the autopsy. The one about why he didn't go home. He had. I got his voice on the answering machine giving me that number. I called it, got a woman, presumably his wife, who told me he was on his way home. I told her who I was, said I had no number to leave, but to tell him I'd call back.

When I did, ten minutes later, he answered the phone himself.

"What is with you?" he said. "Why aren't you onstage?"

"It's Act Two. I don't come in till the end."

"Isn't it near that now?" he said. "I timed the show, remember? For the murder. As I recall, Act Two comes down long about now."

"Oh, shit," I said.

I slammed down the phone, ran down the hallway and came racing up the stage-right stairs with only a couple of lines to spare. Jesus Christ, that was cutting it close. It wouldn't do to come onstage panting for breath, so I stood there blowing air slowly in and out of my lungs, trying to calm down.

I looked up to see the whole cast standing in the wings watching me. All the men, anyway. The women were out onstage. But the guys were there waiting for their entrances, and they sure were looking at me funny.

I'd just had time to think that when Nellie Knight came offstage to get me. No, I hadn't missed my entrance—her character comes to fetch me in the play.

And suddenly I was onstage. And the actress playing Catherine was grabbing my hand and going into this long monologue about how glad she was to see me but I must leave at once.

I wasn't listening to her. In my mind the phrase kept revolving, "The actor was not on the scene."

What the hell did that mean? If I could solve that, I could solve the whole thing.

And then the moment passed and everyone was rushing out onstage and grabbing my hand, so glad to see me and wouldn't I stay, and I agreed to do it and the act was over.

I got out of there and called Chief Bob again.

He had it!

"I shouldn't be telling you this," he said. "So you don't tell anyone, and you sure didn't get it from me. But Sy just called."

"And?"

"It was cyanide."

☆ **36** ☆

YOU WANNA KNOW WHERE MY HEAD WAS AT DURING ACT Three?

So do I.

It sure wasn't in that show.

I got my lines out and I must have said 'em all right, because occasionally I could hear the audience laughing.

But I really wasn't there.

Penbridge had been killed. Poisoned. Given cyanide. Murder, made to look like a natural death. One clever enough to have fooled the doctor. Granted, if this Ed Macy wasn't the swiftest doctor in the world it would not have surprised me. Even so, the man had been killed, and there had to be a reason why.

I was hard pressed to look for one, never having met Mr. Penbridge. I'd have to start questioning everybody. And I wouldn't know where to start.

Yes, I would. I'd start with Beth. For a lot of reasons.

Hey, give me a break. I mean she's a good source of information. She was the one who tipped me off to the relationship between Walter and Margie-poo. Which was my only concrete lead at the moment.

And which would be an excellent motive for murder.

231

Take a middle-aged man like Herbie. Married to an unattractive woman. A man in the arts, in the position of being the producer/director of a summer theater. A man used to working with beautiful women. A man with a taste for that life.

And then let it happen. Grant him the affair. With a very young and nubile and attractive woman. Add in the fact that he himself has gone middle-aged dumpy and is no longer the sort of man to attract that sort of woman.

But when he does—when he goes middle-aged crazy and chases the impossible dream, and then to his enormous surprise suddenly realizes it—well, you don't trifle with that man. You don't play games with that man. You don't cheat on that man. You don't treat his passion lightly and throw it back in his face.

Because if that were to happen, here's a man could easily snap. Go over the edge. Do something rash, desperate and out of character.

Like kill.

Yeah, that was the problem. The profile fit Herbie all too well. The simplest of all solutions. An age-old scenario, and a very common one. The lover, scorned, kills the other man. Piece of cake.

Only it couldn't have happened.

Herbie was innocent. Bob and I had already established that. Because Herbie and Amanda were standing right next to me when the light fell. No way Herbie was involved in the attempt on my life.

Moreover, it made no sense that he would be. For Christ's sake, he brought me here. He sure didn't bring me here to kill me. And if he were the killer, he didn't bring me here to solve the crime. No, more than likely, he brought me here because twenty years ago I played the fucking part.

Unless . . .

Here I was really on shaky ground. Not that I wasn't on all the rest of it. But here in particular I was really winging it.

Unless my original premise was true. That Herbie really

did bring me in to solve the crime. That he really *did* want a private detective. That one way or another, Herbie suspected foul play in Walter's death and brought me in for protection. Either because he thought he might be accused of the crime or because he thought the killer might really be after him.

I smiled at Margie-poo, who had just told me I had a low, shopkeeping mind, and said, "That's the Swiss national character, dear lady."

Which meant my scene with her was almost over. I couldn't remember having said a word of it. But we were in the right place onstage and she didn't look at all perturbed, so I must have done okay.

Minutes later I was offstage, stumbling blindly back to my dressing room with all these thoughts chasing around in my head. I had a strong urge to call Chief Bob again. I resisted it. No reason to drive the guy crazy. Just because I was driving myself crazy.

I sat in my dressing room, trying to calm down. Onstage, Avery Allington was flirting with Nellie Knight. Which meant I needed to get upstairs because the whole end of the play was coming up again.

Which meant this was somewhere around the time Goobie Wheatly died.

In what way was Goobie Wheatly's death connected with the death of Walter Penbridge? Was one death the result of the other? Or were they two in a series? And, if so, was the series as yet incomplete?

And what would complete it?

Was there an ominous portent contained in that falling light?

I shuddered involuntarily, stood up, headed back to the stage. I climbed the stairs, stood there waiting for my cue.

I couldn't see the stage manager from where I was standing, just as I couldn't see Goobie Wheatly the night he died. It occurred to me to wonder if his replacement was still alive.

I peeked around the corner of the masking flat. Yes, there

he was. Sitting in the chair with the prompt script in his lap, just the way Goobie Wheatly was found.

Only alive.

I wondered if I could tiptoe up behind him and stab him to death. Would he see me? Or hear me? Goobie certainly hadn't. I was tempted to take a few steps just to see if he turned his head.

Except my cue came, and suddenly I was out onstage. And there was Avery asshole Allington challenging me to a duel. For alienating the affections of Margie-poo. Which I hadn't done.

But if Walter Penbridge had played the role, he *had* alienated the affections of Margie-poo. Only not from Avery Allington. From Herbie.

But Herbie had played Sergius. Twenty years ago, to be sure, but he had played the part.

So shuffle the names around, plug in your cast of characters, and there you are. Walter/Bluntschli alienates the affections of Margie-poo/Raina from Herbie/Sergius, and Herbie challenges Walter to a duel.

And kills him.

Good god, it all fit so perfectly it had to be right.

Only it couldn't be.

Because someone tried to drop a light on my head.

With that thought, I involuntarily looked up. The lights hanging from the grid all appeared perfectly solid.

It was only a split second, but when I looked back I saw Avery Allington and Margie-poo looking at me kind of strange. Why not? I had certainly never looked up in the grid in the middle of a scene before. Why would I? The action simply made no sense. What the audience must have thought of it I couldn't imagine.

But I didn't care.

Because in that split second I had had a revelation, and everything was suddenly crystal clear.

☆ 37 ☆

RIDLEY WAS STANDING ON THE CHAIR BLOWING POT SMOKE out the window when I climbed the ladder to the light loft. He must have been doing it out of force of habit—it was eleven o'clock at night, and aside from us there wasn't a single person in the scene shop.

I'd followed him there from the theater after the show. I was hoping the son of a bitch would turn on, and he didn't disappoint me. And doing it in the light loft couldn't have been better. Ditto his standing on the chair.

His back was to me, of course, since he was facing the window, and I crept up on him real quietly, but the floor of the loft creaked when I stepped off the ladder and he wheeled around.

His face for once was animated. It was a caricature of alarm and surprise. His face was flushed and his eyes were bulging out of his head. He had a joint cupped in his hand, trying to hide it. He coughed and exhaled a great cloud of smoke. He blinked, turned back to the window, raised his hand and made a motion which I assumed was flicking away the joint.

"Hey," I said. "No need to start a fire. I'm not a narc."

He winced at the word. Then he half-hopped half-slid

down the chair and wound up sitting on it. He ran his hand over his face, as much to shield it from me as anything else, I would imagine.

"What do you want?" he said.

"Good thinking," I told him. "You're right, Ridley. I want something. If I get it, I won't turn you in for this."

He frowned. "What?"

"Let's take this very slowly, Ridley, and make sure you understand. I just caught you smoking dope. That happens to be a crime. You may not agree with the law, but it happens to be on the books. Which means you're in the wrong. Not just with the law, in terms of the playhouse, too. Goobie would have booted you for drugs, wouldn't he, Ridley?"

Ridley's eyes were wide. "Hey, man," he said. "What are you trying to do?"

"I'm trying to get the truth, Ridley. You wanna come out of this with your ass, you better tell the truth."

Ridley looked as if he were about to cry. "But I don't know anything."

"You're wrong, Ridley. You do. You know a lot. And you know what? You've already lied about it. Got yourself in bad. 'Cause, when a guy lies in a murder investigation, you know what that looks like? It looks like he's guilty."

"I didn't do it."

"Can you prove it?"

His eyes got wide. "I don't *have* to prove it. That's the law. They have to prove I *did*."

"The murder, yes. But there are other things."

He looked at me pleadingly. "Please."

"You don't have to be the fall guy, Ridley. You want to cooperate, you don't have to take the rap."

"The rap? What do you mean, the rap? The rap for what?"

"Where's the light, Ridley?"

The change of subject was too much for him. He frowned, blinked, blinked again. "What?"

"The light, Ridley. Where's the light?"

"What light?"

"What light do you think, Ridley? The Leko. Where's the Leko?"

"What Leko?"

"The one that fell, Ridley. I'm talking about the one that fell."

His eyes shifted and I knew I had him.

"It broke," he said.

"Yeah, it broke, Ridley. But you fixed it, didn't you? I know you did, because I saw you do it. I watched you. You sat there on the stage with the broken Leko. You took another broken Leko and you took the parts out of it and used it to fix the light. You took two Lekos that didn't work and you made them into one that did. Didn't you, Ridley? Isn't that what you said you did?"

"Yeah. So?"

"So where's the light?"

"Huh? I don't know what you mean."

"Yes, you do, Ridley. Don't you remember what you told me? You put the two lights together and you made a new light to replace the one that fell. But when you took it up in the grid to hang it, you discovered all your lights were there. Because the light that fell wasn't your light. Because someone took the light up on the grid and dropped it on the stage. Isn't that right, Ridley?"

"Yeah. That's right."

"So where's the light, Ridley? You didn't have to hang it in the grid because all your lights were there. So where is it? Is it here in the light loft? Is it in the lighting booth back in the theater? Take me to it, Ridley. Wherever it is, I want to see it. Right now."

Ridley said nothing, avoided my eyes.

"Come on, Ridley," I said. "It's show time."

I waited him out, till he had to look back up at me.

"Show me the light."

☆ **38** ☆

"RIDLEY'S A LOUSY ELECTRICIAN."

Herbie blinked. He cocked his head to one side and squinted up at me. "You dragged me away from my table to tell me this?"

Indeed I had. We were in Morley's. I'd gone there straight from my little chat with Ridley in the light loft. I'd found him sitting alone in the corner with Margie-poo, told him we had to talk privately, and unceremoniously dragged him off to one side.

"I'm sorry, Herbie," I said. "But this can't wait."

Herbie looked genuinely puzzled. If I hadn't known what I did, I might have felt sorry for him.

"What can't wait?" he said. "You wanna complain about Ridley?"

"I'm not complaining, Herbie. I'm trying to make a point."

"What point?"

Before I could answer, Amanda came in the front door and bumped right into us.

Herbie's eyes lit up when he saw her. He reached out and grabbed her by the arm.

238

"Did you hear?" he said. "Sold out! Monday night, and we sold out. You should have been there. It was wonderful."

Amanda's smile was patronizing. "Of course we sold out, Herbie. We've had front-page headlines for three days. Someone got killed and people are curious, right? It's nice we sold out, Herbie, but you can't take it as a vindication of your theory of opening on Friday nights."

"We're sold out tomorrow night, too," Herbie said.

She smiled, looked at me, shook her head. "He doesn't listen, does he? Only hears what he wants to hear." She pointed a finger at me. "And you," she said, accusingly, "you didn't turn in your health form."

I almost winced. I hate annoying shit like that. Under any circumstances. Right now, it was almost more than I could bear.

"Right," I said. "I'm sorry. I'll bring it in tomorrow."

"Please," she said. "You're only here two more days. I don't want to have to chase you to New York for this."

I resisted the impulse to ask her what the urgency would be to file a health form for insurance purposes for a job which had already been satisfactorily completed, with the employee suffering no accident or ill health.

"I promise," I said. "First thing tomorrow morning."

"Fine," she said. "Well, I, for one, need a drink."

As she moved off to the bar I grabbed Herbie and said, "Let's get out of here for a minute."

"Why?"

"Before someone else interrupts us."

"Why, Stanley? What's the big deal?"

"Please, Herbie. Just do it. This is hard enough."

He looked at me funny, but he nodded and we went out the front door.

Morley's was set back from the road with a parking lot out front, which was about half filled. To the left of the parking lot was a private house. To the right was a vacant lot.

The vacant lot looked good. I led Herbie over there.

"Now, what's all this about Ridley?" he said.

"It's not about Ridley, Herbie. It's about you."

"Me? What do you mean, me? What are you talking about?"

"I'm talking about the murder, Herbie. Goobie Wheatly's murder."

"Right," Herbie said. "I know you've been working with Chief Bob. You got something?"

"I'm afraid I have."

"Well, don't be so damn gloomy. Let's have it."

"The evidence points to you."

Herbie stared at me. "What?"

"It points to you, Herbie. The evidence indicates that, during Act Three, while you were supposedly sitting in the last row of the theater taking notes on the act, you slipped out through the back door into the lobby, went downstairs through the greenroom, up the stage-right stairs—while all the actors were out onstage, so no one saw you—and stabbed Goobie Wheatly dead."

Herbie was still staring at me with his mouth open.

"What I need you to do, Herbie, is to tell me just exactly what you were doing during Act Three of the dress rehearsal that night. Where you were sitting, what notes you took, who saw you there, anything specific you remember about the show that you could describe that would be an indication that you *had* to have been sitting there that night to have seen it, or any other evidence of any type that you would like to offer to indicate the fact that you are innocent. I'd like you to do that, Herbie," I said. When he didn't respond, I couldn't resist adding, "If it's a problem . . ."

Herbie blinked his eyes. Once, twice. Then he shook his head as if to clear it. "I don't believe this."

"Believe it, Herbie. It's where we've got to. You're my friend, and that's why I'm talkin' to you now. Anyone else, I'd be talkin' to Chief Bob. But you, I gotta bring it to you."

"Bring me what? And what's this about Ridley? I don't understand."

"That was the stumbling block, Herbie. Why you couldn't

have done it. Remember the first night, the light that almost fell on my head?"

"Of course I do. What's that got to do with anything?"

"That was your alibi, Herbie. That put you in the clear. The murderer tried to drop a light on my head—you were standing next to me when it happened, so you couldn't be the murderer."

"Drop a light on your head. Are you kidding me?"

"Not at all. At first I took it at face value. Someone tried to kill me. Why? Because I'm a private detective. They thought I was there to solve the crime. So the murderer tried to kill me. So the murderer couldn't be you.

"Then I twisted it around. The murderer *was* you. And the light was dropped onstage deliberately for the express purpose of convincing me that the murderer *wasn't* you.

"See what I mean?"

"Have you lost your mind?"

"Not at all. I admit that theory doesn't wash. How could you possibly do it? Be standing there and engineer the light to fall. You'd have to have an accomplice. Someone other than Amanda, who was standing there herself. Well, Margie would fill the bill, but she was out dining with the other actors. And I can't see her doing that anyway. I can't see her having the nerve."

Herbie shook his head. "Stanley . . ."

"Yeah, I know. That's crazy. Like I said, it was wrong. The real explanation was much simpler. You gave it to me yourself. Ridley's a lousy electrician. The first thing you said when it happened. And it happens to be true. He *is* a bad electrician, and the light fell because he did a bad job.

"*That's* the secret of the light. No one was trying to kill anyone. The light just *fell*."

I shook my head. "See, I missed it the first time I questioned Ridley. Which was stupid of me. I took his story at face value. Which I shouldn't have. He kept protesting, "It's not my light, it's not my light." Of course that's what he'd say. A punk kid, he doesn't want to take the blame. So he made up this story and, you know, I even helped him do it. Of how when he got a new light put together and went to hang it up he found out he didn't have to hang it because all his lights were there. I take the blame for that—I led him into that lie, and then I let him tell it.

"But what else could he do? He'd painted himself into a corner. If it wasn't his light that fell, then no light needed to be replaced. And he couldn't hang the one he'd just built.

"First time I missed that, stupid me, but the second time I nailed him on it. If Ridley hadn't hung the light, where was it? According to him he'd put it together because there were no working Lekos on hand. Which meant that now there would be one and only one, the one he put together that he couldn't hang. I challenged him to show me a working Leko not in the show.

"Which of course he couldn't do. Because the light that fell *was* his light. And the light he put together is now hanging in its place in the show."

I smiled. "Well, not *really* in its place. See, Ridley's not a quick thinker, or he might have pointed out that when that light fell you were still doing *Zoo Story*—so there was a strike night and the lights were all rehung. But even so, the light plot for *Arms and the Man* would have used every available Leko. And it's all academic, since Ridley confessed. Because he's *not* a quick thinker, it never occurred to him, and when I challenged him with it he caved right in."

I shook my head. "The light falling was an accident, Herbie. It had nothing to do with the murder.

"It doesn't give you an alibi anymore."

"An alibi? An alibi for what? For killing Goobie Wheatly? That doesn't make any sense. That happened the night before."

I put up my hands. "I know, Herbie. I'm saying it badly. The light falling wasn't an alibi. I *thought* it gave you an alibi. It was only when it turned out to be an accident that I realized you didn't have one."

Herbie frowned, put his hand on my arm. He looked concerned. "Stanley," he said. "Are you all right? I know you've been spending a lot of time with Chief Bob. On top of the pressures of doing this part and all . . ."

I shook his hand off. "No, Herbie. Let me finish. The problem isn't just the murder of Goobie Wheatly. The problem is Walter Penbridge."

"Walter *Penbridge?*" Herbie said. "Walter Penbridge died of a heart attack."

"Yeah, but what if he didn't? What if he was murdered too?"

"But he wasn't?"

"Play the game, Herbie. Say he was. And say the evidence points to you."

"What evidence?"

"This is very painful for me, Herbie."

"Yeah, well, I'm not enjoying it a hell of a lot myself. Whatever it is, spit it out and let me get back inside. I just sold out a Monday-night house. My first Monday-night house. I don't care if it's just because my stage manager died, and, no, I didn't kill him just to get a full house, if that's the kind of screwy theory you're playing around with. And Walter Penbridge died of a heart attack, for Christ's sake, and what's any of this got to do with me?

"So, you got a theory, do me a favor. Stop playing this question-and-answer shit you seem so fond of, and give it to me all in one shot. I'm not enjoying this and I'd like to get back in there before last call."

"Fine, Herbie," I said. "Then the facts are these. You and Margie are having an affair. Only she's got roving eyes. She stepped out on you with Walter Penbridge. You found out about it and you killed him."

He blinked. Once. Twice.

"Walter *Penbridge?*" he said.

"That's right."

"Margie and *Walter Penbridge?*"

"Right, Herbie," I said. "I assume that's why you had him in the dressing room with Nellie Knight. You threw him a bone. Tried to tempt him with the nubile Nellie Knight tits. Only Walter wasn't having any. He had his sights set on

Margie. You found out, you were outraged and you killed him."

"Walter *Penbridge?*" Herbie said again.

"That's right, Herbie. I'm sorry to have to say it."

He laughed. A short, braying laugh. Then he frowned, shook his head. Then looked back up at me.

"Stanley," he said. "Walter Penbridge is *gay.*"

I blinked. "What?"

"He's gay. I mean, he *was* gay. I thought everyone knew that."

"I never met him."

"I know. Then how'd you get that idea?"

"Something I heard."

"You heard wrong. The man was gay."

"Are you sure?"

"Absolutely." He shrugged. "I suppose someone could get the wrong impression. He wasn't flaming, campy gay. Or just-out-of-the-closet, talk-about-it-all-the-time gay. But the man was gay, there's no doubt about it."

My world was crashing around me. "But then— Well, he wasn't bisexual, was he?"

"No. The man had no interest in women at all."

"Then he wasn't interested in Margie?"

"Of course not."

"And the reason you put him in the dressing room with Nellie Knight? . . ."

"Because Avery Allington got the star's dressing room, not him."

"No, I mean you put him with Nellie instead of Margie."

"Was just how it worked out. See, the other actors were already in place. Well, three of 'em, anyway. David had the star's dressing room till Avery came. When he had to get out, he moved in with Peter Constantine. Aside from Avery, I had to add Margie and Walter Penbridge for the show. Julie Katz didn't want to share with a man, so I stuck Margie in with her. Nellie Knight, as you know, couldn't give a shit, so I put Walter in with her."

"Isn't there another dressing room on the other side?"

"Yeah. That apprentice boy has it. You know, the one who plays the soldier in Act One."

"Oh, yeah." I rubbed my head. "Jesus Christ."

Herbie looked at me. "Stanley, I don't know what any of this has to do with why Goobie Wheatly got killed. But can I tell you something? Frankly, I don't care. The theater's selling out and saving my life. Everything's going fine. Don't rock the boat. You got two more performances to get through. Tomorrow night's sold out, and the way it's going, Wednesday's gonna sell out too. And the advance sale on *Glass Menagerie* isn't bad either.

"Now, I don't know where you got this idea about Walter Penbridge. He was gay, he died a natural death, and I had nothing to do with it."

Herbie punched me playfully in the arm. "This is an occupational hazard with you, right? You're a private detective, so you think you gotta solve the case. Well, do me a favor, willya? Don't solve it till closing night. I'll tell you why. The way things look, it had to be someone in the cast did it. And if you were to bust 'em . . ."

"What?"

Herbie shrugged. "I don't have an understudy."

☆ 39 ☆

CHIEF BOB LISTENED WITHOUT INTERRUPTING TILL I WAS finished. Then he nodded, jerked his thumb at the hot plate in his office and said, "Want some coffee?"

I took a breath. "Yeah, I want some coffee. I was also hoping for a reaction."

"What do you want, my sympathy? You got it. I would say you made a perfectly sound deduction, and Walter Penbridge turning out to be gay has to be a kick in the teeth."

"You think it's true?"

"Absolutely."

"Oh? Did you know him?"

"Never met the man."

"Then why do you say that?"

"I'd be apt to take Herbie's word for it. But, as it happens, there's corroborating evidence."

"Oh? What's that?"

Chief Bob jerked his thumb. "Autopsy report. Among other things, Walter Penbridge had AIDS."

I frowned. "What?"

"That's right. He had AIDS. That doesn't necessarily mean he was homosexual, of course. But together with

246

Herbie's statement it's a pretty good indication. I'm not saying it doesn't warrant investigation, but I'll bet you a nickel the guy was gay."

"So he wasn't interested in Margie and my theory falls apart."

"I'm afraid so. But don't take it personally. It's all part of the game. If it takes a hundred wrong theories to get to the right one, those hundred wrong ones aren't all bad."

Chief Bob poured two cups of coffee, handed one to me.

"Tell me something, Chief," I said. "Where do you get off talking like that? Like you solved a murder every other day. How often do people get killed in this town?"

He shrugged. "Lately, we've been averaging one a week. But you're right, it's not an everyday occurrence. We certainly have enough crime—robberies, assaults, what have you. And basically, a crime's a crime. Murder's just a little extreme, that's all. Anyway, you're sure you didn't tell Herbie that Walter Penbridge was killed?"

"No. I just said what-if."

"And he didn't tumble?"

"Not at all. He pooh-poohed the idea. Said it was absurd."

"Good."

"How long you gonna withhold the fact he was killed?"

"As long as I can. If the killer doesn't know I'm onto it, it's to my advantage."

"Why do you say as long as you can?"

"Because it's bound to leak out."

"Not through me."

"No, but there's always Sy."

"Won't he be quiet?"

"He says he will. And of course I believe him. But that's a funny situation there. On the one hand, Sy is all crisp, efficient and businesslike. He'll do anything I tell him to help the investigation. His lips are sealed." Chief Bob smiled. "On the other hand, the guy's just bursting at the seams to be able to tell somebody Ed Macy fucked up a death certificate."

"I see."

"Anyway, I think I can count on him to bite the bullet a couple more days. Meanwhile, how'd you like to inspect the scene of the crime?"

I frowned. "The theater?"

"No. Not *that* crime. The Walter Penbridge murder. He was found in his room. Cyanide's pretty fast-acting. We can assume the poisoning took place there."

I frowned. "You haven't done that yet?"

"When would I? The autopsy report came in late last night. I'm trying to keep a low profile here. The guy lived in a house with the other actors. What was I gonna do, go barging in there in the middle of the night and tell 'em to ignore me, that nothing's wrong? Besides, it's been a whole week already. What difference does one more day make? Anyway, you wanna take a run over there?"

"Yeah, I do. Has it occurred to you, Chief, that Walter Penbridge was killed days before I got here?"

"Right," he said. "In order to pave the way for you taking over a role you've secretly coveted for over twenty years."

I looked at him.

He smiled. "Couldn't resist." He gestured to the door. "Shall we?"

I took a breath. It occurred to me, god save me from a police officer with acting aspirations.

I gave him a look, shook my head, and walked out.

☆ 40 ☆

CHIEF BOB PULLED THE POLICE CAR UP IN FRONT OF THE HOUSE.

"What if the actors are here?" I said.

"What if they are?"

"I thought you were keeping this investigation quiet."

"I am, but it doesn't matter."

"Why not?"

"Goobie Wheatly lived here too."

"Oh."

"I've been through his room already, of course. Not that I turned up anything. But no reason why I couldn't check it again. The actors are probably at rehearsal anyway."

"One would hope."

It was a large frame house with a screened-in porch running along the front. We went up on the porch, tried the front door. It opened and we entered a spacious front hall with living rooms off to the left and right.

"So this is how the actors live," I said.

"Oh, you don't live here?"

"Herbie put me in the apprentice house."

Chief Bob grinned. "That's 'cause you're a friend of his. Herbie's a nice guy, but he has a tendency to impose on his friends."

"Oh?"

"Hey, it's nothing malicious and it doesn't make him a murderer. It's just, friends will put up with things other people will piss and moan about. And Herbie tends to choose the path of least resistance."

"Like Margie?" I said.

We were talking real low, but when I said that I hoped to god the actors were all at rehearsal and there was no one there to hear that.

Chief Bob grinned and led the way upstairs. At the top was a hallway with several doors.

"You know which room is which?" I asked.

"Only Goobie Wheatly's. Which is this one here."

Chief Bob turned the knob and pushed the door open. He stepped aside and gave me a look.

"Our next task," he said, "is to check out the other rooms and note their proximity to Goobie Wheatly's."

He said that in an unnecessarily loud voice, then gave me a wink, in case I hadn't realized it was for the benefit of any actor who might be in one of those rooms.

We started in on the rooms. The door to the right was unlocked and looked promising, but the name tag on the suitcase said "Avery Allington."

"I notice *these* rooms have bathrooms," I said, as Chief Bob and I filed out.

"You mean your room doesn't?"

"I've reached a point where I barely miss it."

We tried the door on the left. A bra and panties, rinsed out and hanging in the bathroom, gave a clue that we were on the wrong track.

Third time's the charm. And indeed the next room had an envelope on the night table addressed to Walter Penbridge. That looked promising but turned out to be from Actors Equity, so it was probably unimportant except in establishing that this was Walter's room.

Chief Bob closed the door and we began to search.

It's hard enough to find something you're looking for. But

did you ever search a place where you weren't looking for anything? It sure makes it hard to find it.

I was in the process of not finding anything when I heard Chief Bob whistle.

I looked around and saw him standing in the bathroom.

It occurred to me it was the sign of a rather sick individual to envy a dead man his bathroom.

"What is it?" I said.

Chief Bob held it up. "Take a look at this."

I walked over, saw that what he was holding by the corners with his handkerchief was a white plastic pill bottle.

"See what it says?" Chief Bob asked.

I leaned in and squinted at the bottle. "Retrovir," I said. "What's that?"

"It says it in smaller letters."

I squinted again. "Zidovudine. That doesn't help."

"If I remember correctly, that's the new name for azido-thymidine."

I frowned. "Now why does that sound familiar?"

"It's AZT."

"Oh."

Chief Bob turned the bottle around. On the other side was the druggist's prescription label, made out to Walter Penbridge. "So this is a help. This prescription was filled in New York. This doctor, Dr. Kleinschmidt, will be a New York doctor. I can call him directly, cut through some of the red tape."

Chief Bob whipped out a plastic evidence bag, opened it, dropped the pill bottle in. "This goes right to the lab," he said.

"For fingerprints?"

"For one thing. For another, to check out the capsules. See if they contain cyanide."

I shuddered. "Good lord."

"Well, that's how the man died."

"I know. It's just the idea of it."

"What?"

"Cyanide in an AIDS patient's AZT pills. Just seems inhuman."

"Whereas poisoning his Tylenol capsules would be positively humane," Chief Bob said. "Well, let's get on with it."

We searched the room, failed to turn up anything else significant.

"Want to search Goobie Wheatly's?" I asked as we went out.

Chief Bob shook his head. "No, I've done that already."

"We might turn up something new."

"Such as? No, there's nothing to find. I want to run this over to the lab."

"Where's that?"

"New Haven. It's a bit of a drive. And I don't want to trust it to anybody else."

Chief Bob came out the front door onto the porch and down the steps to his car. I followed somewhat reluctantly. As I climbed in, I couldn't help glancing back at the house.

I knew it was crazy, but it seemed to me there must be something back there that I could find if Chief Bob hadn't happened to be in such a goddamned hurry.

☆ 41 ☆

I WAS HALFWAY THROUGH LUNCH WHEN IT OCCURRED TO ME I hadn't filled out my health form. The one I'd promised Amanda first thing in the morning. Since I was having a rather late lunch, that estimate now seemed a bit optimistic.

Particularly since I hadn't filled the damn thing out yet.

Plus I'd left it back in my room.

As I trudged over to the apprentice house to get it, it occurred to me that the health form must be significant. Not the form itself, but the fact that I'd forgotten it. Because if I hadn't, I wouldn't be going back to the apprentice house now, and in doing so I was probably going to uncover a clue. See something or run into someone. Do something that never would have happened if I'd had the damn form in my pocket like I should have.

However, there was no one in the apprentice house when I got there, and I recovered the health form without incident.

I had to call Alice to fill it out. Thank god she was home.

I hadn't spoken to her since yesterday, so we had a little catching up to do. A whole extra murder.

Alice was predictably shocked but not particularly alarmed. She didn't jump to the conclusion that someone was doing in members of the company and that I would logically be next. Instead, she seemed to treat the whole thing as a logistics problem, and one that she expected me to solve.

I'll say this for Alice. She has infinite faith in my abilities. More so than I have. In my checkered career, it's often been a source of strength for me. To have someone like that rooting for me and urging me on.

Only, in this case, I'd have expected her to be a little more concerned for my safety. Which is silly, of course, because if she had been, it just would have pissed me off and driven me crazy and been one more thing that I had neither the time nor the patience to deal with.

Still, she might have been the *least* bit concerned.

Anyway, Alice provided me with the names and addresses of my various doctors and dentists. Don't get me wrong—it's not like I have a million diseases. But there's the regular dentist, the periodontist and the root-canal man. Then there's the regular doctor, the skin specialist and the sports doctor I went to for acute tendinitis. So getting all the names and addresses was a real bummer. Particularly since I was standing outside at a pay phone when I did it.

I messed up twice—wrote things in the wrong blank and had to cross 'em out and start again. I was working in pen, not pencil. By the time I was finished, my medical form looked like a crazy quilt, but at least I was done.

I hung up the phone and strolled over to the theater.

I came in the back way. I must say I felt pretty proud of myself, figuring that out. Because I'm not that good at direction—yet another not-that-admirable attribute for a private eye. But by taking a left fork long before I reached the turn for the theater, I figured I'd come up on it from the other side.

I figured right. Sure enough, after a few hundred yards I saw the roof of the old barn—the rehearsal hall and scene shop—across the field to the right.

I cut through the meadow and walked by the scene shop. The girls were still painting flats on the lawn. Beth was there in another bikini—she seemed to have an endless supply of them. Among other things. At first I was pleased to see her.

Till I noticed Avery Allington. The son of a bitch was hitting on her again, and this time he was actually helping her paint the flat. He was smiling and laughing and coming on to her, and she was smiling and laughing and talking right back at him. So much so that she didn't even see me.

Which really pissed me off.

Don't get me wrong. I'm a married man, I had no designs on the girl myself. It's like I was a noncom, nothing I could do.

But still.

These things can break your heart all the same.

I felt like going up to her and shaking her. No, Beth. Not with *him*. Please. My god. Don't be so stupid. I really couldn't bear it. Anything but him.

I felt like doing something. I had to tell myself, hey, it's all right. The schmuck can't do anything in broad daylight. Not on her working time, with a dozen other people around.

I tore myself away and walked on down to the theater. Amanda was sitting on the steps out front. She stood up when she saw me.

"There you are," she said. The way she said it gave the impression she'd been sitting there waiting for me since early that morning. "Do you have the form?"

I pulled it out of my pocket. "Yes, I do."

"Filled out?"

"Absolutely," I said, handing it to her.

She took the form, looked it over. "That's a relief," she said. She smiled. "I hate to be a bitch about it, but you have no idea the paperwork that goes into a summer theater."

"It must be awful," I said.

She turned the form over, frowned. "What's this?" She exhaled, said, "Oh dear."

I could feel my heart sinking. "What's the matter?"

She pointed to my list of doctors. "This is a mess. What's all this here?"

"Oh. I started writing in the wrong blank. I had to cross it out and start again."

"Well, I can't even read it. What's this say?"

I looked. "Montclaire. Dr. Montclaire."

She shook her head. "I can't read it. I wouldn't know unless you told me."

"Oh, come on. That's Montclaire, see?"

"I'm sorry. You'll have to do it over."

I looked at her. "You gotta be kidding."

She shook her head again. "It's not legible. Just copy it over. I'll give you another form."

I exhaled. "Oh, for god's sake."

"Hey," she said. "Sit down, do it right now. Take you five minutes. Get it over with. I know it's a big pain in the ass, but come on, whaddya say?"

I think I mentioned my problems in dealing with high-powered women like Amanda Feinstein. Anyway, one thing she said made sense—it sure would be nice to get it over with.

"All right," I said.

"Fine," she said. "Come on. I'll get you a form."

I followed her inside and into the box office.

Rita, the box-office manager, was on the phone taking reservations. *"Arms and the Man* is sold out," she said. "We still got tickets for *Glass Menagerie.*"

"The whole show's sold out?" I said.

Amanda nodded. "Yup. And the first two nights of *Menagerie* too. But don't be like Herbie and take all the credit. Yes, it's a good show, but we know why it's selling out."

"Right," I said. I couldn't help wondering how fast tickets would be selling if they knew there were *two* murders.

Rita, still on the phone, said, "No, the matinee's sold out too."

"Matinee?" I said. "What matinee?"

"Tomorrow's matinee," Amanda said. "It sold out too."

"We got a matinee tomorrow?"

"Of course we do. Didn't you know that?"

I shook my head. "Nobody tells me anything."

Amanda smiled. "Oh, it can't be as bad as all that. Well, there's a matinee, two-thirty. It's sold out, so be sure to be there. Now, then. Let's get that form."

I followed her through a door at the end of the box office into what proved to be a small inner office. Just room for a desk and a couple of file cabinets.

"Sit down," she said, handing me back my form. "You can do it right here."

She pulled open a drawer of one of the file cabinets, riffled through the files and pulled out a manila folder which proved to be filled with medical forms. She flipped to the back of the folder, selected a blank form and handed it to me.

I sat down and picked up a pen.

Rita called from the next room, "Amanda, you got a call on two."

There was a phone on the desk, and line two was blinking.

"I'll get out of your way," I said, and started to get up.

She stopped me. "No, no. Sit. Fill out the form. I'll take it in the box office."

"Are you sure?"

"Really. It's no trouble."

She smiled and slipped out into the other room.

I sat at the desk, feeling very much like a kid kept after school to copy over his sloppy homework assignment. I sighed, started to fill out the form.

Which is when I noticed Amanda had left the manila folder on the edge of the desk. It was lying open, and half on and half off the desk, where I had a good chance of knocking it over.

So I moved it.

When I did, I noticed that as well as blank forms it contained forms that had been filled out.

The form on top said, "Walter Penbridge." That made sense. When he died, they naturally checked the file to see if they had his form.

I glanced at the door of the box office. It was half closed, and I could barely see Amanda or Rita at all. But I could hear Amanda busily engaged, talking on the phone.

What the hell. I picked up Walter Penbridge's medical form, turned it over.

Surely Mr. Penbridge had had many problems, but filling in the right blanks was not one of them. His penmanship was also excellent, and I had no problem reading the names of his doctors. Aside from his general practitioner, he had listed the name of Dr. Kleinschmidt as specialist.

I wondered if Chief Bob had reached Dr. Kleinschmidt on the phone. If so, I wondered what the doctor could have possibly told him. Yes, the man had AIDS. Yes, I prescribed AZT. No, I did not put cyanide in it.

I wondered how Chief Bob was making out at the lab. And whether he'd stick around for the results, or drive back and wait for them to phone.

I wondered if I should write down Kleinschmidt's number in case Chief Bob hadn't got it. I realized that was ridiculous—the address was Manhattan, as he had supposed, and the doctor would not have an unlisted phone.

I glanced at the door to the box office again. Amanda Feinstein was still talking.

Well, what the hell. I wasn't sure what I was looking for, but I flipped through the other health forms.

The first few were not particularly rewarding. I learned the name of Margie-poo's gynecologist. I wondered what tales that man could tell, if such men ever talked shop.

I chided myself for the thought, flipped another form.

And stopped dead.

Son of a bitch.

A familiar name.

Coincidence?

Maybe.

But what-if?

Good god.

What-if?

I heard Amanda hanging up the phone, so I quickly flipped the folder shut and went back to my form.

But I must confess, I was so preoccupied with what I'd just seen that I wrote in the wrong blanks again, and wound up having to tear it up and start over.

☆ 42 ☆

I CAME OUT THE FRONT DOOR OF THE THEATER AS IF IN A DAZE.

What the hell did I do now?

First off, I should call Chief Bob. I tried, but he wasn't in.

So now what? Try to call him in New Haven at the lab? Not the swiftest of all possible moves when keeping a low profile. And I didn't even know what he meant by *the lab*. To find out I'd have to call the station and ask Felix. Which might or might not be cool—had Chief Bob even told Felix where he was going?

So I was really at a loss. The thing was, I had information I needed to check out, but how? I could call myself, say *I* was Chief Bob, but it occurred to me I could never bluff it through. And even a phone call from the real Chief Bob might not suffice. A doctor's not going to give out information about a patient over the phone.

No, I needed an ally in New York. Someone to make the approach for me.

Sergeant MacAullif would have been good, if I could have counted on him to do it. But there was no way. I'd need hard evidence to sway him. All I had at most was a theory.

Richard Rosenberg would have loved to come up with

some legal way to force the doctor to divulge the information, but even if it worked, that would take time, and I didn't *have* time.

On the other hand, one of Richard's clients was a thief named Leroy Stanhope Williams who could have broken into the office for me, no sweat. Only not during office hours. And it occurred to me that though an accomplished art thief, Leroy would probably have scruples about breaking into a doctor's office.

No, the only way for me to pull it off would be to go back to New York, make an appointment with the doctor and during the examination distract him somehow and rifle his files. Which would have been a hell of a long shot even if I'd *had* a car and it hadn't been too late to do it today.

Jesus Christ.

I walked around downtown a long time just trying to calm down and figure out what the fuck to do. I can't say I really accomplished either. What I really did was kill time, hang around and continue making fruitless calls to the police station. I'm not sure how many calls I made, but the intervals between 'em must have been getting shorter and shorter, because I noticed Felix getting progressively more pissed. It was a relief when he finally put the answering machine on and went home. Though the first time I got it I must admit it occurred to me how bizarre it was to be living in a town where you could call the police and get an answering machine, even though the message did give a number where a policeman could immediately be reached.

I began making wider circles in my walks, getting farther away from the center of town. On one of these I walked right by the actors' house. Actually, on *two* of them I did, but the first time I walked by it without even seeing it. That's because I'd only been there once, and that time had been in the car with Chief Bob. So the first time by it didn't even register.

The second time it only did because Nellie Knight came out the front door.

"Going to dinner?" she said.

Good god, was it really that late?

"No," I said. "Just taking a walk."

Which was a silly thing to say. As if I wasn't going to have dinner before the show.

But I wasn't. I couldn't have eaten a thing. And seeing the actors' house and Nellie Knight had given me an idea. All the actors would be going out to dinner. Or at least going to the theater. Maybe I could do the job from this end.

But not just yet.

I waited till Nellie Knight set out, then walked in the opposite direction. I had to get away. Had to think.

Had to call Chief Bob.

He wasn't in yet, of course. Not that it mattered, now that I had a plan of my own.

I hung out, kept walking around.

Only now I was careful not to walk by the actors' house. I just kept strolling around, trying to keep calm and occasionally calling Chief Bob.

I got him at seven-ten.

That was a surprise. I kept calling in, to see if the answering-machine message would change, rerouting calls to him, when he picked up the phone himself.

"What happened?" I said. "Did you get it?"

"Yeah, I got it. Are you where you can talk?"

"I'm at the pay phone downtown."

"Come on in."

"There isn't time. I got a show tonight. What's the score?"

"There's no fingerprints or anything else helpful. Which is too damn bad."

"Oh?"

"Yeah. The top three pills were laced with cyanide."

"Son of a bitch."

"Yeah. We got our means, not that it helps us much."

"It may."

"Oh?"

"I got a new theory on the case."

"What is it?"

"I gotta check it out first."

"Tell me now."

"There isn't time. I gotta do the show."

"Then how you gonna check it out?"

"I'll call you later. Fill you in."

"Damn it, tell me now."

"Sorry, Chief. Gotta go," I said, and hung up the phone.

I looked at my watch. Fifteen minutes till half hour. It was gonna be close. Assuming I could do it at all.

I wondered if Chief Bob would hop in his car and come screeching out to find me. It wouldn't be hard. He was only blocks away. Not that I was standing there waiting for him. I was hotfooting it down the road.

To the actors' house.

I got there at seven-twenty. There was no way they were still there. Not ten minutes till half hour.

I went up on the porch and in the front door. The place seemed deserted. I hesitated just a moment, then went up the front steps. I stopped at the top of the steps and looked around. Damn it, which door was it?

It was at that moment that it dawned on me that I was doing just what every nitwit in every detective story ever written always did. I had arrived at the solution to the crime, *but I hadn't told anyone*. Instead, I had gone to investigate myself. Told Chief Bob I'd check it out and call him later. Implied that I had cracked the case.

And it occurred to me, what if it happened that in life's rich pageant I was not the hero, the leading man, the solver of the crime, but merely that mainstay of mystery fiction, the supporting character who gets killed before he can divulge what he knows?

A phone rang and I jumped a mile.

Jesus Christ, that was loud!

I looked down and there it was, right there in the hallway on a little end table. As I looked, it rang again.

And a door down the hall opened.

I was scared to death. Good god, what did I do now?

There was a door right behind me. I didn't care where it went. I jerked it open, slipped inside.

The good news was there was no one in the room I'd just entered.

The bad news was it was a broom closet.

And the lights were out and there were mop buckets on the floor. It was all I could do to keep from stepping in one. I teetered on one foot, held my balance.

The door was still open a crack. I leaned forward, peered out.

And down the hall came our stage manager.

So. He lived here too. But what the hell was he doing here now? He was gonna miss half hour.

He strode down the hall, picked up the phone and said, "Hello, Joe Warden here."

I had to keep from laughing. It suddenly struck me funny that, after all this time, this would be how I would finally learn his name.

I wondered if I'd learn anything else.

Not likely. Joe said, "I can't talk now, it's almost half hour," and hung up the phone.

He went tripping down the stairs and out the door.

Of course. The guy had a car—he'd picked me up in it the day I'd been late. It would take him two minutes to drive to the playhouse and he'd make half hour easy.

But I wouldn't. Because now I could be sure everyone was gone.

I opened the broom closet, stepped out.

All right, enough fucking around. It was that door, wasn't it? I walked to it, jerked it open. Yes, that was right. Of course, no one was there.

I slipped inside, began my search.

☆ 43 ☆

WHERE THE HELL WERE YOU?" JOE WARDEN SAID.

I had a wild impulse to say, "Back in the actors' house, learning your name." I stifled it, said, "Sorry, I got hung up. Don't worry, I'll be ready."

He shook his head. "You're real late," he said.

"I know," I said. "I'm sorry."

I couldn't blame Joe for bawling me out. For one thing, it was the second time I'd missed half hour. For another thing, while he stood in my dressing room doing it, he had a marvelous view of Nellie Knight's tits.

I also couldn't blame him because I'd found what I was looking for. If I hadn't, I might have missed curtain. Because I was really determined by that time. But, as I said before, it's a lot easier to find something when you know what you're looking for. So I'd found it just in time.

Though not in time to call Chief Bob. If I'd done that, I *would* have missed curtain. As it was, it was going to be close. At least I had a five-minute grace period before my entrance.

Act One went reasonably well, considering where my head was at. As soon as the act broke I went to the pay

265

phone, called Chief Bob and got a recording telling me to call him at home.

Only I'd just used my last quarter. Also, I didn't have a pencil to write down his phone number. Talk about frustrating.

I went back to the dressing room, got a dollar out of my pants. Then I had to wait till intermission was over so I could go to the lobby and ask lovely Rita, box-office maid, for four quarters. A pen and paper were not readily available, but armed with the quarters, a paper towel and an eyebrow pencil, I finally got the job done and reached Chief Bob.

Who seemed not at all surprised to find out I was still alive. Somehow I thought he would be. But the man was perfectly calm.

"What's up," he said.

"I got the dope. We gotta talk."

"What you got?"

"Not on the phone. I'll meet you after the show."

"Okay. Come by the house."

He gave me the address and directions, which were a mess in eyebrow pencil, but somehow I got it down.

It was on my way back to the dressing room that I realized that once again I had tempted fate by stalling off giving him the solution. Plus, my costume had no convenient pocket, so I had to put the directions to Chief Bob's house in my pants, where anyone could come into the dressing room while I was onstage and find them, and find out what I was up to.

I worried about that for the rest of the show, and even after the final curtain came down. In fact, if the truth be known, I was looking over my shoulder the whole time as I attempted to follow the smeared directions to Chief Bob's.

As well as going over my theory and trying to form a plan.

As far as my theory went, I figured it was basically sound. It was the plan I was having trouble with. As far as the plan went, my basic problem was that I didn't really *have* a plan. At least, not one that made any sense.

I knew what I'd like to do. If it were possible, what I would have liked would have been to do it like Dustin Hoffman in *Tootsie*—nail the killer onstage in performance in front of everybody. God, what a scene that would be.

I knew that was outrageous, off the wall and would never work, and that there was a big difference between movies and real life, but given my druthers, that would have been my plan.

Especially since I had no *other* working plan.

Anyway, with all that rattling around in my head, it's a wonder I even *found* Chief Bob's house.

But I did. After all, he lived in a house only a few blocks from the police station. That figured—in this town, *everything* was a few blocks from everything else.

Chief Bob met me at the door and introduced me to a plump but attractive-looking woman with a pleasant smile.

"Allow me to present my wife, Deborah," Chief Bob said. "Dear, this is Stanley Hastings."

"Oh," she said pleasantly. "The murderer."

She and Chief Bob looked at each other and laughed, and I realized they'd rehearsed it.

Deborah excused herself to make coffee and Chief Bob sat me down in the living room and we went over the case.

I must say, I had serious misgivings.

In the first place, the byplay with his wife drove home the point that in this instance I was not dealing with the majesty and solemnity of a big-city police force.

But that was the least of my worries. As I began talking, I realized that while my theory made perfect sense to me, the minute I tried to verbalize it, it sounded like absolute gibberish. I really was taking a button and sewing a vest on it. I had no concrete evidence. I had one fact, which didn't necessarily have to mean anything, and which certainly didn't *prove* anything. The rest was all conjecture.

And as for my plan, well, the plan I finally came up with was worse than my theory. Because, even if it worked perfectly, even if it came off without a hitch, there was no reason it would necessarily trap the killer. If the murderer simply said, "That's very interesting, go ahead and prove it," Chief Bob and I would be up shit creek without a paddle. And while I was a douche-bag, ambulance-chasing private detective who could be expected to pull a foolish stunt like that, Chief Bob, upholder of the law, pillar of the community and public official, could not.

So before I even got halfway through laying out my plan, I just knew Chief Bob was going to hate it.

I was wrong.

He loved it.

☆ 44 ☆

EVEN THOUGH I HAD TOLD CHIEF BOB MY THEORY, I WAS still on guard for potential saboteurs on my way back to the apprentice house. It occurred to me that having Chief Bob know just what it was that had gotten me killed would be small consolation to me in the event I actually happened to turn up dead.

And how would the killer know whether I told Chief Bob or not? Assuming the killer knew I knew anything. Or perhaps I should say *suspected* anything. Or perhaps I shouldn't say anything, I should just keep my eyes open.

Believe me, I did. As I said, it was not too long ago that I got shot meddling around in something that was really none of my business. Just like the Goobie Wheatly affair. I had been brought here to play a part, for Christ's sake. That was the job. Anything else was extracurricular.

I became aware of the lights of a car following me.

Son of a bitch.

I told myself I had to be imagining it. I mean, come on, who would be following me in a car? With intent to kill. It just didn't compute.

But sure enough, the headlights were creeping along about half a block behind.

I considered turning right at the next corner to see if the lights turned. I considered stopping and doubling back to see who was in the car.

I also considered screaming and running like hell.

I did none of the above. It took considerable effort, but I continued walking along at an even pace as if I hadn't noticed anything was wrong.

And the lights kept coming.

That was the bad news. The good news was, they didn't seem to be getting any closer.

I walked another block, turned onto the street of the apprentice house. And, oh, the towering feeling, knowing I'm on the street where I live.

I quickened my pace, reached the front of the apprentice house. As I turned in at the walk, the car following me pulled up and drove on by.

It was Chief Bob.

He hadn't offered to drive me home. No surprise there, since like everything else, it was only a few blocks. But he'd followed me to make sure. Either to see that I got home safe or to see if anyone was taking an interest in me.

Which told me one thing: Chief Bob was taking what I'd told him seriously.

I went inside and up to my room.

The place was quiet. That figured. It was after one in the morning, and the apprentices needed their sleep—tomorrow was strike night.

I went in my room and switched on the light.

And discovered I didn't have a bathroom.

Yeah, I knew I didn't have one. Even so, it always came as a shock.

I went back out and plodded down the hall. The door next to mine was open and the light was on. So someone *was* still up. Beth. But where was she at this time of night?

Then I noticed the bathroom door was closed.

Oh, great. Beth was in the john. And she was a nice girl and all that, but at this time of night I was damned if I wanted to stand in the hall for god knows how long while she took off her makeup or whatever.

Plus I really had to go to the bathroom.

So there I was, standing there in the hallway, teetering back and forth from one foot to the other and thinking about the fickleness of fate. I mean, five minutes ago I'd been concerned about getting killed. Now my biggest worry was peeing in my pants.

I'd just had that thought when the bathroom door banged open and Ridley came out.

Ridley?

That didn't compute.

"Ridley," I said.

He was as surprised to see me as I was to see him. He blinked at me. "Yeah, what?"

"Where's Beth?"

I felt like a fool when I said it, but I couldn't help myself.

It didn't help when he looked at me kind of funny. "She went out."

"Where?"

He shrugged. "I don't know. She went out with that guy."

"What guy?"

"That actor. What's-his-name. The one on TV."

"Avery Allington?"

"Yeah, him."

Son of a bitch!

I turned and ran down the stairs.

☆ 45 ☆

THEY WERE SITTING AT A TABLE AT MORLEY'S. THANK GOD. IF the son of a bitch had got her up to his room at the actor's house, I don't know what I would have done. But I checked out Morley's on the way and they were there.

I strode up to the table, said, "Hi, Avery. Hi, Beth."

Avery looked put out to see me, but Beth gave me a smile.

Then I said what any red-blooded hero would have said under the circumstances.

"Excuse me, I have to go to the bathroom."

I went in the men's room and emerged a minute later feeling much better. First off, I had taken care of business. Second off, they were still there. If Avery had spirited her away while I was busy in the men's room, I never would have forgiven myself. But no, they were sitting there with their drinks.

I walked over to their table, pulled up a chair and sat down.

Avery Allington gave me the most incredulous look, like he couldn't quite believe I'd actually done that.

"Excuse me," he said. "Beth and I were having a private conversation. Do you mind?"

"Not at all," I said. "Say, that was some show tonight."

Avery stared at me in exasperation. I understood his predicament. How do you deal with some boorish clod who's willfully misunderstanding you? There I was, sitting there, smiling affably like a fool and not taking the hint. And if he lost his cool and got pissed off about it, started treating me in the manner I so richly deserved, he'd look like a schmuck in front of the girl he was trying so hard to impress.

So what the hell could he do?

The way I saw it, he had only one option—accept the challenge and take me on in mortal conversation.

Surely that shouldn't be too big a risk for a big TV star like him.

As if to cement the idea, I said, "Matinee tomorrow, you know."

He gave Beth a look, as if inviting her to share his contemptuous amusement at this pitiful creature bearing yesterday's news.

"Of course I know," he said.

"Yeah, well, *I* didn't," I said. "I just found out this morning. That's the problem with being a fill-in. Everyone forgets you weren't there the whole time and assumes you know everything. I didn't know about the first matinee either."

"Really?" Avery said. He raised his eyebrows. "I'd have thought when you found out about that one, you'd have asked if there were any others."

I smiled ruefully. "You're absolutely right. Unfortunately, when I found out about the first matinee I was in the diner eating a cheeseburger and it was already past half hour. Joe was less than thrilled when he snaked me out of there, and our conversation wasn't particularly chatty."

"You missed half hour?" Beth said.

I turned to her, smiled. "You didn't hear about that? It was pretty embarrassing. I almost got back too late to hear them laugh at Margie in her nightgown."

"*That* I heard about," Beth said.

"Wasn't that something?" I said. I jerked my thumb at Avery. "And the other thing about matinees is, he winds up signing autographs for camp kids. It's funny, huh? Kids can't even read yet, asking for his autograph."

"I didn't see them asking you for yours," Avery said.

Score one for the good guys. I'd goaded him into it, and he'd said it.

He knew it was a mistake the minute the words were out of his mouth, but it was too late. Beth looked at him, and the look was not kind. He'd just lost considerable ground.

Avery flushed somewhat, and I could feel the anger in him. Still, he kept control, knowing somehow that if he exploded now it was over.

But I wasn't about to let him off the hook.

"That's right," I said. "No one does. Of course, you couldn't expect them to. I haven't acted anywhere in years. I'm not an actor anymore, I'm a private detective. I just came out of retirement to bail Herbie out of a tight spot." I smiled modestly, looked at him. "So if my performance doesn't measure up to yours, I still have the satisfaction of knowing, if it weren't for me, you wouldn't have the chance to perform."

Avery blinked again. What could he say to that? Tell me I was absolutely right, my performance sucked? Say, yes, his performance was much better than mine?

I'd say it was a fairly good indication of how flustered I'd got him by that point, that it took him a few seconds to fall into what ordinarily would have been his natural response— condescending faint praise.

"I appreciate it," Avery said. "And you certainly do the job. I think only professionals would be able to tell that you were filling in."

"That reviewer certainly couldn't," I said. "He reviewed me as Walter Penbridge."

Avery frowned. "What?"

"The guy who reviewed the show for the paper. He didn't even know there'd been an acting change. He had Walter Penbridge playing Captain Bluntschli." I shrugged. "Of course, the man didn't know anything about theater."

I smiled up at Avery. What can you say to that, schmuck?

Avery raised his eyebrows. "Oh? Were you mentioned in that review?"

Strike two, Avery. Almost as bad as the autograph bit. Belittle a little guy. None too heroic. Sink in the fair damsel's eyes.

Beth shifted position uncomfortably. She picked up her drink, took a sip. I noticed she was drinking a martini instead of her usual beer. It probably wasn't her first. I wondered how many the son of a bitch had plied her with.

"So," I said. "The matinee tomorrow. Final performance tomorrow night. Then it's back to New York for both of us. Got a job lined up, Avery? Another show?"

"I have several offers. My agent's sorting them out."

I nodded. "Unemployed, huh? That's a bitch. You have enough weeks to qualify for unemployment insurance?"

His eyes blazed, but he hesitated a moment. I knew why. The bastard obviously collected.

Not that he was about to say so here. "I'll have a job," he said. "If worst comes to worst, I'll do a few weeks on a soap." He shrugged. "Slumming, I know, but if times are tight, what the hell."

"If a soap opera's slumming," I said, "what do you call summer stock?"

Avery glanced at Beth. He wasn't about to say anything that was going to offend her, since she was spending the summer here. On the other hand, the real answer, that it was a place for a nobody like him to be a star, wasn't exactly what he wanted to say either.

He took a breath, cleared his throat. "Summer stock," he said, "is a chance for an actor to practice his craft, without the pressures and constraints of movies and television. It's an opportunity to try things out, to expand oneself, to—"

I'm afraid I didn't get to hear the end of that particular pompous speech, because at that point I reached across the table for a potato chip and managed to knock Avery Allington's glass of Scotch squarely into his lap.

Avery sprang to his feet.

"Shit! You clumsy schmuck!"

Strike three, Avery. Yer outta there.

He was indeed. The Scotch was a direct hit. It looked like he'd peed in his pants, and he had to retreat to the men's room for paper towels to wipe it off.

Time for my move.

I can't remember the last time I tried to pick up a girl in a bar, but it must have been at least twenty years ago. And I'd be willing to bet you it didn't work.

This time it had to.

Going for me was the fact Avery Allington was an asshole, and she knew it. Plus, I'd managed to hammer that point home.

Going for me was the fact that, in this show at least, he was a bad actor and I was a good one. And she had recognized that fact from the start.

Going for me was the fact that I was a nice guy and he was a prick. Though that didn't always work with women— often the reverse was true.

Going against me was the fact that, like it or not, Avery Allington *was* a TV actor, minor light though he might be. And I wasn't any kind of actor.

Though I *was* a private detective. Which had elevated me in Beth's eyes. Ironically enough, almost as unfairly as being a TV star might have elevated Avery Allington.

Well, come on, schmuck, time's a wastin'.

I took a breath, looked over at Beth.

On the debit side, put down the fact Avery Allington was probably only in his late twenties, while I was old enough to be her father.

Never mind.

Time to make my move.

I leaned in, looked her right in the eyes.

"Hey," I said. "Whaddya say you and me get the hell out of here?"

She did!

☆ 46 ☆

ALICE SHOWED UP RIGHT AFTER THE MATINEE.

I greeted her with mixed emotions. I was glad to see her on the one hand, and didn't have time for her on the other. Plus I was all keyed up from the events of the past twenty-four hours.

Not to mention the show I'd just done. You wouldn't have believed the way the matinee played. If Avery Allington had been hostile before, today he was out of sight. When he challenged me to a duel in Act Three, I could see it was all the poor man could do to keep from drawing his sword and running me through on the spot.

No problem for me, playing the calm, cool, efficient Captain Bluntschli. The wilder he got, the cooler I got. And the funnier it became, and the more I had the audience eating out of my hand. Even the matinee audience, once again consisting of the very old and the very young, this time found themselves getting a kick out of me.

Boy, Avery, when things go bad they just go bad, don't they?

Twit.

Anyway, I got offstage from the matinee and went downstairs to my dressing room to discover a half-naked Nellie Knight and a fully clothed Alice. Not an ideal combination.

"You were right," Alice said, after Nellie Knight finished dressing and finally went out the door.

"About what?"

"Your roommate has nice tits."

"Uh huh."

Alice looked at me. "Is that all you have to say?"

"Sorry, Alice. I'm a little distracted."

"I can see why."

"That's not it."

"Oh? What then?"

I looked at her and thought, where to begin. I hadn't had a chance to call her last night, so she didn't know I'd cracked the case.

Among other things.

"I have a lot to tell you," I said. "But right now I've got to see Mary Anne."

Alice frowned. "Mary Anne? Who's Mary Anne?"

"The costume mistress. I gotta catch her before she leaves for dinner."

"Stanley—"

I held up my hand. "One moment. Be right back."

I ran out of the dressing room, hurried through the greenroom to the costume shop. It wasn't until I walked in that I realized I was holding my pants and running around in my underwear. Not particularly unusual for summer stock, but what must Alice think? Particularly after Nellie Knight.

Mary Anne was just gathering up her purse.

"Hi," I said. "Glad I caught you."

She looked at me holding my pants, frowned. "What's the matter? Did you rip your trousers?"

"No, no. Nothing like that."

"Lose a button?"

"No."

"You don't need me to sew them then?"

"Actually, I do."

She frowned, then cocked her head and smiled. "I don't understand. What do you want me to do?"

"First off, I want you to be quiet."

She frowned again. "I beg your pardon?"

"I mean, don't tell anyone about this. It's kind of a secret."

"What is? What do you want?"

"I want you to sew a pocket in my pants."

☆ 47 ☆

IT WAS THE BEST SHOW YET.

Sometimes you get your wish. Alice had seen a bad show, and I really wanted her to see a good one. She got it and then some.

First off, it was standing-room only. Literally. With the show sold out and people still clamoring for tickets, Herbie, after caucusing with the fire inspector and other local powers that be, had begun selling standing room, and damned if people weren't buying it. Which was beyond me. I wouldn't pay good money to stand up and see a show, no matter how many people had been killed in it.

Which, by the way, as far as the public was concerned, was still one. Much as it might have tortured him, Sy, the medical examiner, was sitting tight on the rather juicy tidbit that Walter Penbridge had been murdered too, and that Ed Macy had blown the death certificate.

Even without that information, two hours after it went on sale, standing room also sold out.

Fortunately, Alice had a seat. That's because one of my few fringe benefits as an actor was getting two complimentary tickets to the shows. Of course, like everything else in this production, nobody told me about it, and I wouldn't have even known I had them if Herbie hadn't asked me for them back after the show started selling out. In fact, I'd paid for Alice's ticket the first time she'd seen the show. But when Herbie asked, being from out of town and having no one I wanted to invite, I had cheerfully relinquished all my complimentary tickets except one for the final performance, which I held on to just in case Alice managed to get up for the last night. Alice had, and so there she sat, center orchestra about halfway back, a prime location from which to see the show in this standing-room-only crowd.

And what a show it was. Act One played like gang busters. I knew it was going to be good before I even got onstage. The women even got laughs in their simple, expository scene of locking the windows, which didn't usually happen. When Margie-poo blew out the candle, hopped into bed, and I came climbing through the balcony window with my gun drawn, you could feel the electricity in the air. There was an expectant hush from the huge crowd, waiting for something to happen.

They ate it up when I held Raina at gunpoint. They liked it even better when I grabbed her robe and put the gun down, saying the robe was an even better weapon, I'd keep it so she made sure no one came in and saw her without it. And then, when the soldiers bang on the door, and I relent and give her back her robe, and she relents and hides me from them, I could tell the audience was with me all the way.

Tonight I paid attention while the young Russian officer searched the room. He was, of course, Beth's would-be suitor, the young apprentice whose name I naturally couldn't remember. He was young, handsome, dashing and very earnest in the performance of his three-line role.

Then he was gone and Margie-poo and I were into the scene and it was great. Really great. As good as I felt on opening night, this felt even better. Act One finished to a thunderous ovation.

Tonight even Act Two went well. Or as well as it could have, given the handicap of Avery Allington's performance.

Though, to give the devil his due, tonight even his part seemed to play. Or maybe it was just that the audience was so into it. But by the time I made my entrance at the end of the act, I had no doubt this was the show to end all shows.

Act Three.

The last act.

The final act.

Zero hour.

Oh, boy.

I could feel the adrenaline surging as the curtain went up. *This is it.*

The beginning of the act, no problem, everything plays fine and before you know it the other actors are offstage and it's just me and Margie-poo. No letdown there. Margie had been getting better throughout the run, and tonight the scene was just aces. It was almost a disappointment when Nellie Knight appeared onstage to bring me the letter that led to my exit.

Almost, but not quite.

Because this was the time it happened. Not exactly now, I mean between now and the end of the show. But this was the time Goobie Wheatly died. And the last time I would ever be going over that ground.

The moment I got offstage I went to the stage-right stairs, sat on the top step and began reading my script, which I'd left there just before the start of the show. I was sitting with my back to the stage, just as I had the night of the dress rehearsal. It was an exercise I'd performed many times since, re-creating the scene of the crime, so I knew exactly what would happen next.

Margie-poo and Nellie played their scene onstage. Then Margie exited and went past me, down the stairs to her dressing room.

Onstage, Nellie played the scene with Peter Constantine/Nicola, who had entered from down left.

Moments later, Avery Allington came up the stairs. He passed me and took up his position for his entrance. I turned and watched him while he disappeared from sight behind the masking flat. Then once again I turned my back on the stage as if I'd been absorbed in my script.

From there I heard Avery Allington enter, Peter Constantine exit, and then Avery's scene, coming on to Nellie Knight.

And then it was over and I was onstage again.

And all at once the whole thing seemed as if it were a dream.

Because there was Avery challenging me to a duel. And there I was, making my usual cool responses. And there was the audience, roaring with laughter and eating it up.

Yet at the same time I knew this wasn't all that was going on. I had so much other stuff in my head.

And then Margie made her entrance and the three of us had at it, Bluntschli getting the best of it from all points of view, particularly with the audience. And Avery Allington/Major Sergius Saranoff getting the worst.

And then Nellie Knight is discovered listening at the keyhole and we go at it *four* ways, gradually sorting the relationships out.

And then Major Petkoff enters wanting to know about the picture of Raina inscribed "to her Chocolate Cream Soldier" he found in the pocket of his coat. Which leads to a sorting out of the relationships all over again, including the revelation that Sergius Saranoff is now infatuated with Louka.

Major Petkoff, quite confused, says that this is impossible, since Louka is engaged to Nicola.

Peter Constantine, in his one halfway decent scene, says she is not engaged to him, they gave that information out only for her protection, and he bows and exits.

Downstage left.

The opposite side from which Goobie Wheatly was killed.

But the audience isn't aware of that—they're roaring at every revelation.

And then the woman playing Catherine, whose name I *still* hadn't learned, enters from upstage right—the side from which Goobie Wheatly *was* killed—only to find Nellie Knight in the arms of Avery Allington.

"What does this mean?" she demands.

Whereupon Major Petkoff, in one of the most marvelous understatements in the history of the English theater, replies, "Well, my dear, it appears that Sergius is going to marry Louka instead of Raina." When she is about to break out indignantly at him, he adds, "Don't blame me. I've nothing to do with it."

The lines that come next are ones that I know well. Catherine exclaims, "Marry Louka! Sergius, you are bound by your word to us." Whereupon he folds his arms, striking his classic pose, and announces, "Nothing binds me."

Not tonight.

Before Catherine could say, "Marry Louka!" I stepped in.

"Excuse me, madam," I said. "Let me set the record straight. Major Sergius Saranoff is not going to marry Louka either. In fact, he is not going to marry anyone. I'm afraid I simply can't allow it."

All eyes onstage turned to me in utter astonishment. The audience had no way of knowing this wasn't in the script, but the actors sure did.

The actress playing Catherine *appeared* to be looking at me, but her eyes were actually darting around wildly, imparting the message, "I'm totally lost, I have no idea what's going on." This was not entirely new to me. In the course of my career I had been onstage before with actors who had said the wrong line, missed a cue, forgotten a prop, or in some way or another screwed themselves up so royally that they had no idea what to do next. "You're on your own," was what that look said. "Please do something because *I* can't."

I was fully prepared to carry on myself, but at that moment the actor playing Major Petkoff, with all the coolness of a seasoned pro, picked up the cue and fed me a line.

"Why, may I ask, is that?" he said. "Why should Major Sergius Saranoff not be allowed to wed?"

"Because he's HIV positive," I said.

I reached into the pocket that Mary Anne had sewn into

my pants and pulled out the white plastic bottle I'd pilfered from his room just before the show.

"I have the proof right here. A prescription for AZT pills made out in his name. I'm sorry to say it, but I'm afraid there's no mistake. The man has AIDS."

There came a rumbling from the audience. They may not all have known exactly what was going on, but the majority of them sure as hell knew George Bernard Shaw never wrote about AIDS.

And even without the anachronism, they would have known something was wrong. Because Avery Allington looked like he'd just been slugged in the solar plexus. I've heard the expressions before—his face drained of color, his face went white as a sheet—but this was the first time I'd actually seen it.

He opened his mouth as if to speak, but nothing came out. Which was just as well. I was fully prepared to carry the ball.

"Now," I said, spreading my arms. "That in itself would not be a bar to his marriage." I turned and pointed. "But he was ashamed of having the virus. Thought it carried a stigma. To cover it up, he murdered two people. And that is why I cannot allow this match."

I turned and gestured toward the wings. "Officer," I said.

And onto the stage strode Chief Bob, giving his finest cameo performance ever. He was dressed in the Russian officer's uniform from Act One. It had been made to fit the taller, thinner apprentice, so on Chief Bob it was a little long in the sleeves and snug in the waist, but in my eyes he looked quite splendid indeed.

Yeah, it was *Tootsie* time after all. As the standing-room-only crowd watched, Chief Bob strode across the stage straight up to Avery Allington.

"Major Sergius Saranoff," he said, "alias Avery Allington, I have a warrant for your arrest for the murder of Walter Penbridge and the murder of Gilbert N. Wheatly. You have the right to remain silent. Should you give up the

right to remain silent, anything you say may be taken down
and—"

It was, to the best of my knowledge, the first time in the
history of law enforcement a Miranda warning was ever
drowned out by a standing ovation.

☆ 48 ☆

IT DIDN'T GET THE PRESS COVERAGE IT DESERVED BECAUSE the reporter for the *Daily Sentinel* hadn't been at the show. He'd asked to come, but Herbie wouldn't give him a ticket. With the seats selling out, Herbie wasn't about to give one away for free. A poor business decision, in the light of what happened, but I couldn't really blame him. After all, he didn't know anything special was going to happen during the show. Still, it was kind of a shame.

But that's not to say the event didn't get covered. It did, and not just by the *Sentinel*. It also made the *New York Post* and the *Daily News*.

Only thing was, it was just like the review all over again. You wouldn't have known I had anything to do with it. Me or Chief Bob. It was all, "TV star Avery Allington." Oh sure, there was mention of the fact that a police officer had appeared onstage to arrest him in full view of the audience. But it was all from Avery's point of view.

Naturally.

But despite the sensationalism of the headlines, it should be noted that at this time absolutely nothing had been proven. You wouldn't believe how many times the word *alleged* appeared in the articles.

Because Avery hadn't confessed as yet, and we certainly had no proof. We could prove he was an AIDS patient, but that was it. We couldn't prove anything about the murders.

Because I certainly hadn't solved the case in the classic way. I hadn't, for instance, figured out where Avery could have obtained the cyanide and then sprung it on him in the classic manner—"Aha! You didn't think we knew your Uncle Bart was a noted toxicologist and you would have had access to his laboratory, etc. etc." Or I hadn't manufactured some witness who saw him sneaking into the prop room on the day of the dress rehearsal to pocket the knife. Or someone who saw him tampering with Walter's AZT. Or some witness to Goobie's supposed blackmail attempt.

I'd done none of that.

No, I'd merely stumbled on a health form indicating that Avery Allington and Walter Penbridge had both seen the same doctor, who happened to be a specialist in the treatment of AIDS. Then searched Avery's room and found his prescription.

But the rest of it—that he killed Walter Penbridge because Walter knew he had AIDS and could not be trusted to keep it quiet, that he killed Goobie Wheatly, either for the same reason or for knowing he'd killed Walter Penbridge— that was pure conjecture.

But I knew in my heart it was true.

It all fit too well.

Avery Allington had the star's dressing room. Right across the hall from the prop room. You come out of the star's dressing room and, bang—it's right there in front of your eyes. If you're walking down the hallway, the door is off to the side—you'd only see it if you turned your head. But coming out of the star's dressing room you can't miss it—you see right through the chicken-wire door, and right in front of you is a shelf labeled *Zoo Story,* on which there sits this large switchblade knife.

Because I'm sure Goobie put it there with the other props after Jack, the prop apprentice, returned it to him. I'm sure it was there that night, and Avery Allington picked it up. Not necessarily during Act Three—he could have got it any time during the dress. But he killed him during Act Three, and the reason he did, the son of a bitch, was he knew that then I would be the one to find the body. Because I would exit stage right, leaving everybody else onstage. Elevating me to the position of prime suspect that was rightfully his.

Yeah, Avery could have killed him just fine. And I know he did, right in the middle of Act Three. He told Chief Bob he came up the stage-right stairs and saw me sitting at the top, studying my lines. Well, he probably did. Then he walked by me and took up his position at the entrance door.

Masked by a masking flat. So there would be no way I could see him if he'd walked downstage, come up behind Goobie Wheatly as he sat in the folding chair holding the prompt script and plunged the knife into his heart. He was there, downstage, instead of in the doorway where he should have been.

The actor was not on the scene.

Yeah, it's a totally meaningless phrase, but there you are.

The actor was not on the scene.

But he *was* on the scene moments later. He was onstage, coming on to Nellie Knight.

The more I think back on it, that was really the key to the whole thing.

I remember what Chief Bob said, that it probably *wasn't* one of the actors, because how could anybody kill someone and then go onstage and act without it showing? Without anyone realizing something had happened?

Well, of all the actors in the show, Avery Allington was the only one who could have done that. Because his performance was so overblown and out of proportion anyway, you wouldn't notice him acting unnatural. Because his whole performance was unnatural.

As far as I was concerned, that was convincing. He and only he could have committed the crime.

But aside from that, there was no actual proof against him.

Not that that really mattered. To me, or to Avery Allington. As far as Avery was concerned, it was all over. It was the revelation that he had AIDS that was the crushing blow, not the revelation that he was a murderer. To him, that was almost incidental. In fact, his image as a macho leading man could have withstood the insinuation that he was a murderer.

But not that he had AIDS. Not in his own eyes. Not in his own image.

No, I rather thought Avery would confess. Eventually. Once he got around to it. Because, given the revelation, it was the only thing left for him to do. He couldn't fight anymore. But he could confess. Confession is good for the soul. Maybe it would be good for his.

Not that I care.

You may think me heartless for ruining a man's reputation by revealing publicly that he had AIDS. Considering, I mean, the fact that I had no proof he was a murderer. But I have to tell you, that doesn't bother me one bit. If he had just shut up and gone quietly about his business, it would have been a different matter. But the son of a bitch was so concerned with his image as a macho TV-star stud, that he was willing to seduce and infect a poor young girl like Beth.

And probably would have, if I hadn't intervened. Boy, she must have really thought I was an old fogy when I finally got her back to the apprentice house that night and sent her off to bed. I certainly hope the next night she realized why. Realized that old fart had been like a TV star himself, rushing in and rescuing the damsel in distress.

Well, even if she didn't, Alice understood and that's all that matters.

Plus, she got to see the show. Not the whole show, but most of it. And she'd seen the ending at the second night's less-than-wonderful performance. Thank god that wasn't the only performance she saw. That I don't have to go through the rest of my life knowing I was better than she thought. Knowing she would never know it. That no one would ever tell her.

Certainly not reviewer Harvey Frank of the Daily Sentinel.

I still have his review, though. I pasted it into our photo album, just so I wouldn't lose it. Even though I wasn't really mentioned in it. Even though it listed Walter Penbridge instead.

Pretty neat irony there—that Herbie wouldn't manage to get the programs changed, or even an insert printed up, listing me as playing the part, and that as a result the reviewer would name, instead of me, the actor whose murder I had solved.

Yeah, small irony there.

But the bigger one, I should think, would have to be that, after a twenty-year layoff, after getting The Call, after fulfilling every actor's dream of stepping into a leading role at the last moment, after coming back on two days' notice and playing the part without a script, so well in fact that no announcement of an actor substitution had to be made, after playing to the audience and hearing them respond—though admittedly George Bernard Shaw deserved the credit as much as me—well, after all that, it had to be somewhat ironic that the only tangible evidence of my performance, my one souvenir, would turn out to be Avery Allington's rave review.